Glass Slipper Press

Beyond the Darkness

By

Lilly Gayle

The Darkness Series, Book Three

"Ms. Gayle weaves a delightful tale that keeps you entertained and wanting to turn those pages to find out what happens next."~ Romancing the Book Reviews

Cover Art by AGW Visual Alchemy using AI generated images: https://agwvisual.myportfolio.com/

Published in the United States of America

Digital ISBN: 978-1-7323904-6-1

Print ISBN: 978-1-7323904-7-8

Dedication:

For Jennifer and Lauren~
Your love and support are everything.

Prologue

Eight Years Ago

Axle Travers stepped off the elevator into the lobby, a quiet smile tugging at his lips. Night security at Lifeblood of America wasn't glamorous, but it was stable. Safe. A far cry from construction sites and the darker paths he'd once considered—like selling drugs for Enrique. His shift was split between hourly patrols and manning the front desk with Grant Simmons, while Richard Baxter kept watch over the security feeds. Axle preferred the patrols. They gave him time to think. To breathe. To marvel at how far he'd come from the chaos he'd lived in with his mother.

He owed it all to the man Shannon swore had never wanted him—because he was "only half Black."

Shannon was his mother in name only. After the divorce, she vanished with a trucker named Harry, dragging Axle across state lines like luggage. They spent a year on the road, living out of motels and truck stops, until Harry got tired of Shannon's volatility and dumped them in Richmond. From there, it was a blur of strangers' couches and broken promises. Shannon chased men like they were lifelines, but they always frayed. Just before Axle's freshman year, she met Jefferson Cross—a white man with a felony drug charge hanging over his head. When Jefferson fled to Asheville to hide in the mountains, Shannon followed, dragging Axle with her.

For three years, Axle tasted normalcy. School. Football. Friends. A life. Then, one morning during senior year, Shannon yanked him out of class to chase Jefferson back to Richmond. Six months later, Jefferson overdosed in a motel bathroom. Axle dropped out of school, got his GED, and took a construction job. Someone had to keep the lights on. Someone had to feed Shannon when she couldn't even lift her head.

Then came the arrest—prostitution and possession. Axle didn't cry. He didn't rage. He just waited. And a few days later, a private investigator named Doug Brinkley showed up with a truth that cracked something open in him: his father had never stopped searching. He'd even moved to Asheville, hoping Axle might return.

That same afternoon, Axle packed his duffel and boarded a bus. His father—a corporate attorney—welcomed him with open arms. No questions. No judgment. Just love. Brit Travers' biggest client was Lifeblood of America, a blood and tissue bank owned by Vincent Maxwell and Gerard Delaroche. Both men had a rare genetic disorder that made sunlight lethal, but that hadn't stopped them from building an empire. They hired Axle as a security guard. His stepmother didn't flinch when he moved in. His kid brother treated him like a hero. And Olivia Huntly—the cheerleader he'd dated in high school—was back in his life.

For the first time, since his parents' divorce, Axle felt like he belonged.

Grant looked up as Axle approached the reception desk. "You took long enough."

"Hey, it's three floors and two parking lots," Axle said, keeping his voice even. Grant wasn't usually so irritable.

Grant stood and came around the desk. "Yeah, sorry, bro. Didn't mean to snap. I just got the call—Emmy's in labor. I gotta jet."

Axle's face lit up. "It's about time. Congrats." He bumped Grant's fist. "So what are you waiting for? Go!"

Grant fumbled with his keys, nearly tripping over his own feet. "Tell Richard."

"Got it. Now move," Axle said, tugging the keychain from his belt. "I'll lock up behind you, bro."

He watched Grant sprint across the asphalt, then made one last circuit of the lobby before heading back to reception. At the security office, he swiped his badge. The lock blinked yellow. He punched in his code and placed his palm on the scanner. The door clicked open.

Inside, flickering monitors cast ghostly shadows across the walls. Richard glanced up from his crossword each time a screen shifted. When Axle entered, he looked over his shoulder. "Grant gone?"

"How'd you know?"

Richard nodded toward the monitors. "Saw him get the call. Got twitchy when you weren't back. Missed him leaving, though."

Axle shrugged and pulled up a chair. "Can't catch everything. Too many angles. Anything happen while I was out?"

Richard glanced away from the screens. "Not much. Dr. Harper didn't come in. Just Tina Gallagher and she's been in the lab since she arrived."

Axle leaned forward, watching the feed outside the lab door. No cameras inside. "You ever wonder what they do in there all night? I mean, what can they do at night that can't be done during the day?"

"Never thought about it," Richard said.

"You're not curious?"

Richard turned. "It's a blood and tissue bank. I figure they type blood and dissect organs and shit. Probably could do it during the day, but Harper's married to Maxwell, and Gallagher's dating Delaroche. Since both guys avoid sunlight, I guess the women work nights to match their schedules."

"I know they've got some weird skin condition," Axle said, "but my dad never said what it is. Why not just wear a hat or use sunblock?"

Richard lowered his voice. "Because they're actually vampires."

Axle snorted. "Come on, man. What's the real deal?"

"XP. Xeroderma pigmentosum. I'd never heard of it before working here. It's a rare genetic disorder—sunlight's deadly. So yeah, they're pretty much vampires—minus the blood-drinking. Harper's sister had it too. That's how she met Maxwell."

"Huh." Axle frowned. "Support group?"

"Yeah. VA—Vampires Anonymous."

Axle smirked. "Funny. Not."

"I try," Richard said, glancing back at the monitors. "Hey, since Grant's gone, you'll need to take his patrol before escorting Dr. Gallagher to her car. I'll keep an eye on the lobby and answer the phone if it rings."

Axle checked his smartwatch—a gift from his dad. There'd been a lot of gifts lately. "Shit. I better hustle," he said, rising. "Ms. Gallagher likes to leave before sunrise."

"Watch out for vampires," Richard called as Axle headed out.

Axle laughed—but the joke curdled forty minutes later when he found Richard's body stuffed in a janitor's closet two doors down from Ms. Gallagher's lab. Richard lay on his back, a gaping wound in his neck.

There wasn't a single drop of blood on the floor.

Chapter 1

Present Day

Haley Connors turned into the frozen food aisle—and froze. There he was. No cart. No pretense. Just Josh Patterson, standing dead center like he'd been waiting.

Her pulse spiked. Her heart jammed in her throat. She couldn't speak, couldn't swallow. Her fingers clenched the plastic cart handle, white-knuckled. Turn around? Walk past him and pretend he was a stranger?

Her knees knocked as she pushed forward on unsteady legs. Their eyes locked. Her heart stuttered. She dropped her chin, turned away, and reached for the nearest freezer door with a trembling hand. Cold air blasted her face. Her breath hitched.

"Hello, Haley," Josh said, his Southern drawl slow and syrupy—molasses on a cold morning.

The sound of his voice—so familiar, so wrong—ripped through her like a blade. Her stomach clenched. Her skin prickled. She slammed the freezer door shut.

"Stay away from me. I have a restraining order, and you're violating it." Her hand darted to her purse in the cart's seat, fingers brushing her phone. Her thumb hovered over the emergency dial.

Josh smiled. Slow. Easy. Everything about him was deliberate. Calculated. Six months ago, she might've called him sexy. Now, he made her skin crawl.

"I'm just getting groceries," he said. "Same as you. Since Helene, this is the closest store unless I want to drive to Asheville."

Whisper Falls had taken a beating from Hurricane Helene. Torrential rains had flooded rivers across Western North Carolina and Tennessee, destroying homes and infrastructure. Mudslides followed, cutting off power, transportation, and communication for weeks—months in some places.

In the worst-hit towns—Black Mountain, Hot Springs, Bat Cave, Lake Lure, Chimney Rock—road closures and damage still plagued residents almost two years later. Whisper Falls had been luckier. Only two deaths. Most businesses had reopened, including the town's lone grocery store.

"Then I'll go to Asheville," she snapped. Her voice cracked. She grabbed her purse and turned, abandoning her half-filled cart.

Josh's hand shot out, clamping around her wrist. "No. I'll leave," he said softly. But his steel-gray eyes were hard. So was his grip.

Haley shivered. Her breath came in short, shallow bursts. Her vision tunneled. She yanked her arm free. "Don't touch me!" Shoppers turned to stare.

"I'm sorry, darling. Didn't mean to upset you." Another smile—less smooth this time. More threat than charm.

She backed away, legs trembling. Her body screamed for escape, but her mind was stuck—flashing through memories she'd buried: hang-up calls from an unknown number, the feeling of being watched, the nights she'd slept with a knife under her pillow.

She brushed past him, ignoring the curious glances. Her feet moved faster. Josh followed two steps behind.

"I never shop on Fridays," he said casually. "Too crowded." He kept pace, shadowing her.

She walked faster, pulse pounding in her ears. He didn't fall back.

"Funny we both chose today," he continued, relentless. "Must be fate. We were meant to run into each other. Let's not waste it. Let's settle this misunderstanding between us. Okay?"

Sweat beaded her brow. Her breath came in ragged gasps. Her chest tightened. She was almost at the door. Just a few more feet.

The automatic doors slid open. Josh stopped on the black rubber mat in the breezeway.

"We belong together, Haley. Remember that."

She bolted. Ran to her car. Fumbled the keys. Hands shaking. Heart thundering.

She didn't look back.

#

A week after the grocery store incident, Josh showed up at the urgent care clinic in Whisper Falls where Haley worked. He claimed he'd been in a wreck, but there wasn't a scratch on him—and still, no arrest.

With Whisper Falls' police department wiped out by Helene and no plans to rebuild, the Buncombe County Sheriff's Department sent Deputy Matt Harden to investigate. After taking Haley's statement, he told her she and Josh just needed to talk.

No surprise there. Harden was one of Josh's poker buddies.

The next day, Haley left work early and drove to the sheriff's office in Asheville to speak with Deputy Gordon Sikes. They'd graduated high school together, but that familiarity did nothing to ease her nerves. Sitting across from him, she twisted her purse strap around her fingers.

"Josh Patterson is still stalking me."

"I know it's frustrating," Gordon said, "but stalking's hard to prove. Without evidence, I can't arrest him."

Haley exhaled sharply. She was sick of hearing that Josh hadn't broken any laws. This time, he had.

"When I signed the restraining order, I was told it worked like a protective order. But Josh keeps showing up. That's illegal. I want him arrested."

Gordon leaned forward, elbows on the desk. "I reviewed the report. According to the deputy, Josh didn't follow you. He was in an accident near the clinic and hurt his wrist. That's a legal reason to seek medical treatment."

"He knows where I work, and he caused that accident."

"He got a ticket for rear-ending the other car," Gordon said. "As far as the law's concerned, that's his only crime."

"But he knows I work there," she repeated, her voice cracking.

"It doesn't matter," Gordon said. "Thanks to Helene, there aren't many clinics left. It was either yours or a thirty-minute drive to Asheville with an injured wrist."

"There wasn't anything wrong with his wrist." Not that she'd seen it. Dr. Belcher had sent her to the break room to keep Josh away. "From what I heard, it wasn't even swollen."

Gordon sighed. "Officially, I'm supposed to tell you to go to the magistrate's office and request a criminal warrant."

Her heart sank. "And what good will that do?"

"If he's found guilty, he could get up to 150 days in jail."

"Great. Just enough time to piss him off." Even if Josh were arrested, he'd be out in forty-eight hours on bail. Then his lawyer would drag things out, and if convicted, he'd serve a measly sentence. It hardly seemed worth it.

"You could file a civil contempt order, but I don't think you have a case."

Haley closed her eyes, fighting tears. The restraining order only lasted a year. It barred Josh from physically following her or sending threats—but he didn't follow. He just appeared. At the Food Mart. At work. At the gas station. Always in public. Never threatening. He lived in the county, his shop was in Asheville, but he only stalked her in Whisper Falls or just outside the city limits. That made it the sheriff's problem. And now Gordon was telling her it wasn't a problem they could prove.

She twisted her purse strap tighter, cutting off circulation in her fingers. "He's never hit me or threatened me, but I feel threatened."

"I know," Gordon said gently. "But until he commits a crime, there's nothing I can do. Showing up at the Food Mart isn't illegal."

"So what am I supposed to do?" Her voice rose. "Wait for him to put a knife to my throat?"

Gordon ran a hand through his short, dark hair and leaned back. "I hope it never comes to that. But we need proof—something concrete."

Haley rolled her eyes. "He's too smart to leave proof. Too smart to put anything in writing."

"We're doing all we can," Gordon said. "I'm sorry, but if he's still stalking you, we haven't been able to catch him."

Haley's blood boiled. "'If'?"

Gordon raised a hand, forestalling her argument. "As far as the law's concerned, he's just running into you in public."

Impotent fury clawed at her throat. "He's never going to stop. Is he?" Tears stung the backs of her eyes. Since Helene, crimes like stalking weren't a priority. Resources were stretched too thin. She bit her lip and blinked hard.

Gordon shifted. "I can't do much as a deputy. But I can give you advice—hire a private investigator. Get the proof we can't. Then we can act."

Haley snorted. "Who? I don't know any PIs. And I probably couldn't afford one if I did."

"It won't be that bad," Gordon said, reaching into his desk drawer. He handed her a business card. "Call Axle. He got his PI license a few years back. Lost the office during Helene, but he's back downtown. Does work for some government agency nobody's heard of, so you'll need an appointment."

Her heart thudded. Axle? It couldn't be the same Axle Travers from high school. But how common was that name?

"Axle?" she asked, throat tight.

"Yeah. Axle Travers," Gordon confirmed. "Played varsity football sophomore and junior year. Shy, biracial guy with weird-colored eyes. Lived with his mom and that redneck drug dealer in the mountains. They moved a few weeks into senior year."

"Oh. That Axle." Shame burned her cheeks. She'd had a secret crush on him back then, but had kept it to herself. Not because he was half Black—but because everyone judged him by his mother and her boyfriend. And to be honest, some kids had been racist, and she hadn't had the guts to break the unspoken racial barrier.

Maybe her gutless nature was what attracted Josh. But she was done being a doormat. She glanced at the card in her hand. Axle's card. "Is he any good?"

Gordon's brows lowered. "I wouldn't have recommended him if he wasn't. People judged him for his mom and that piece of shit Jefferson Cross, but Axle's solid. He was a hero during Helene's cleanup. Located bodies. Saved lives. And he's a damn good detective."

Haley swallowed. "He was a good guy in high school. I just haven't seen him since that second week of senior year."

"I'm surprised you haven't run into him. He's been back awhile. His dad and stepmom moved from Durham to Asheville not long after Axle left town. No one—not even his dad—knew where they'd gone. Then, about eight years ago, Axle came back. Stayed with them. Worked security at Lifeblood of America...until the abduction and double homicide."

Haley's breath caught. She'd heard the story—or at least the rumor, but there'd been so little coverage of the double murder and kidnapping, even when it was still an active investigation.

"Axle was the security guard abducted by that doctor doing illegal cloning experiments," Gordon said. "It was huge news back in 2018."

Local news, maybe. But Haley had been living in Florida then. "That was before my divorce, but Dad and my cousin, Geoff, told me about it. Then Mom got sick, and I moved back to help Dad. I heard they found Axle alive, but after that... I didn't keep up. Between Mom's appointments, her death, and then the hurricane, everything else faded."

Her mother's diagnosis had come just after her divorce. The day she got the call, she packed up what was left of her life and drove home. For two years, she ferried her mom to Asheville for treatments while her dad kept working. Then came the funeral, the paperwork, the quiet grief. Her brother Joe had wanted to help, but he lived in San Antonio with his wife and son.

Despite the prognosis, her mother had fought hard. After the funeral, Haley bought her first home—hers alone. Then on September 27th, 2024, it washed away while she was at work. Her father's house and most of the farm had survived, so she moved back in. Six months ago, she'd moved out again, renting a freshly renovated apartment near the clinic and away from the river.

She'd tried to learn more about Axle's abduction then, but after the FBI and two Asheville detectives rescued him and shut down Dr. Weldon's operation, the story vanished. Maybe it was buried for national security reasons—Weldon had been a former Army doctor. Still, research assistant, Tina Gallagher, and a guard named Richard Baxter had been murdered, and Axle had been taken hostage. It should've been front-page news. Six years later, it was eclipsed by hurricane coverage. Now, she couldn't even find it mentioned online.

"I was sorry to hear about your mom," Gordon said gently. "And your house."

Haley nodded. "Thanks. I was sorry about your grandmother. I wish I could've helped with the search."

"You did more than enough," he said. "Helping Dr. Belcher at the Mobile Disaster Hospital? That was huge. And at least we found Granny's body. Last I heard, five people were still missing in North Carolina."

A lump rose in Haley's throat. So many had been injured. So many had lost everything. She'd spent countless days beside Dr. Belcher in what felt like a MASH unit. Then she'd helped clean up his office in Whisper Falls. Her town had changed—open fields where forests once stood, abandoned buildings where businesses had been, but it was still home.

Pisgah National Forest had taken a beating, but the landscape around Whisper Falls—the waterfall that gave the town its name—was healing. Soon, it would bear few visible reminders of Helene's wrath. But the

Flowering Bridge on Lure Lake was gone, and residents in Bat Cave were still navigating packed gravel roads barely wide enough for the commercial trucks hauling in supplies.

She and Gordon sat in silence, each lost in thought. Then she cleared her throat. "So... you think I need a PI?"

Gordon sighed. "I don't think it would hurt."

She glanced down again at the business card in her hand. "How's Axle doing since... everything?" Between the abduction, losing his business in the hurricane, and helping recover bodies, he had to carry scars. Who wouldn't?

"All things considered, he's doing okay," Gordon said, his voice dipping low. "But what happened at Lifeblood shook a lot of people. Vincent Maxwell sold the company and moved to Amsterdam with his wife, Dr. Harper. Amber Buckley—one of the detectives—got involved with Gerard Delaroche, Maxwell's partner. They moved to Austria with her dad. He's some rich guy who owns a ski resort."

Haley blinked. That was a lot of movement. A lot of escape.

"Reid Sheridan, Detective Buckley's partner, helped Axle get his PI license before taking a job with that national security agency I mentioned earlier. He's in Colorado now. Axle's the only one who stayed in Asheville."

Gordon paused, then added, "He'll talk about the hurricane if you ask. But Lifeblood? Not ever."

Haley nodded slowly. "Can you blame him? I'm sure it was traumatic. He probably has PTSD."

She stared at the card again, her thumb brushing the embossed lettering. Would Axle even take her case? After the way she'd acted in high school—he had every reason to hang up the moment she called.

Her stomach twisted. Maybe she didn't deserve his help. But she needed it anyway. Josh wasn't going to stop. And no one else was going to protect her.

Chapter 2

Haley's hand trembled as she pressed the button to raise the top on her 1970 Pontiac LeMans convertible. Would Axle remember her? She was thinner now, her ginger hair toned down from its old orange hue—but he'd always been out of her league. He probably hadn't thought about her once since high school.

Blowing out a nervous breath, she pulled down the mirrored visor and ran her fingers through her hair to coax the layers into something wind-tousled rather than hurricane-ravaged. Then she freshened her makeup—like that would help—and got out of the car.

As she crossed the parking lot, she glanced over her shoulder, looking for Josh. He owned Patterson Restoration and Auto Body. With access to dozens of vehicles, he could easily claim he was test-driving a customer's car. That's how he'd rear-end someone on purpose—no insurance claims, no paper trail. He fixed the damage himself. It was one of the ways he stayed invisible. He could follow her in any car, and she wouldn't know until he was standing in front of her.

A shiver rippled through her. She quickened her pace, nearly tripping over the curb as she reached the sidewalk. Straightening, she checked to see if anyone had witnessed her near collision with the trashcan—especially Josh.

The lot was mostly empty, the cars unoccupied. For now, she felt safe. But that feeling wouldn't last. Josh hadn't followed her to the strip mall where Axle's business was located, but he could be waiting for her at home. Too many places to park near her apartment . Too many unknowns. That constant dread—the not knowing when or where he'd show up—was what finally pushed her to call Axle's office. She'd booked the appointment through his secretary, hoping he had a partner. The last thing she needed with her nerves already frayed, was to come face-to-face with Axle Travers after all these years.

Was he still the tall, dark, and brooding jock of her teenage fantasies? Still carrying that defensive chip on his shoulder—or had it grown into a full-sized boulder? She knew little about what had happened to him eight years ago, but clearly, he'd survived. Thrived, even. If this was the right address, his business sat in a strip mall located in a high-dollar district where there was little remaining evidence of Helene's previous destruction.

Nestled between a lawyer's office and a jewelry store, stood a discreet glass door stenciled with the suite number Gordon had given her. Without the card, she'd never have guessed what kind of business operated behind door 202. Even if Josh had followed her, he wouldn't know she was seeing a PI—unless he walked in or Googled the address.

The thought was of little comfort.

Taking a deep breath for courage, Haley pushed open the door and stepped inside Travers' Investigations. A blast of icy air slapped her cheeks. She shivered, removed her sunglasses, and slipped them into her purse.

"May I help you, honey?" A young voice asked.

Haley looked up. The entrance was as nondescript as the door, but instead of the sleek receptionist she'd imagined, she found someone's grandmother. Someone's cold grandmother. The thin, dark-skinned woman wore a heavy pink sweater as if it were mid-January instead of a month before the official start of summer. Then again, the office was freezing.

Haley rubbed her arms beneath the sleeves of her ivory blouse. She should've worn the herringbone blazer that matched her fawn-colored slacks, but in a vintage convertible with no AC, she'd have melted. Shivering from more than just the chill in the room, she stepped forward, hoping her smile masked her nerves.

"Hi. I'm Haley Connors. I have an appointment."

The tiny, bird-like woman smiled, and her teeth gleamed so big and bright in her dark face they had to be dentures. "Have a seat, Ms. Connors," she said in her disconcertingly young voice. "Mr. Travers will be with you shortly."

Haley sank into a chair. If she had to face Axle again, did it have to be under such embarrassing circumstances? She was a stalking victim, for God's sake. How pathetic was that?

To distract herself, she pulled out her phone and scrolled through social media. She'd searched for Axle countless times, but he had no personal profile—just a business listing with no photo. She definitely remembered him from high school, but maybe he wouldn't remember her or the fool she'd made of herself at her brother's graduation party. Axle had been drunk, and it was a long time ago.

If only Joe and Geoff hadn't needed a designated driver that night.

Her brother, Joe, was a year older than Geoff and her, but her brother and cousin were best friends, and the entire football team and all the cheerleaders had been invited to Shane Danvers' graduation party. They were all under aged, but Shane's older brother had scored a keg. Joe only invited Haley because he and Geoff needed a designated driver.

She'd felt like such a loser, hovering near the pool house, hoping for a moment with Axle. Then she overheard Shane call him the "N" word, and Axle got up in his face. She thought they'd come to blows, but Shane quickly backed down, claiming it was a joke. Only Axle didn't think it was funny. Neither did Haley. After calling Shane a racist jerk she tried to talk to Axle, but he brushed her off and headed for the keg.

He got so drunk that night Geoff asked her to take them home early and pick up Joe later. That's when she saw the rundown place Axle called home. A few months later, he and his mom left town with Jefferson Cross, and she never saw him again.

"Ms. Connors?"

Haley jumped. Then looked up—and froze when she saw Axle for the first time in fifteen years. His eyes weren't a weird color as Gordon had described them. They were two amber-brown jewels set in a caramel face, and a trim goatee framed full lips, any woman—and some men—would die to kiss.

His hair was buzzed short now, the wild curls and high fade gone, and he was no longer lean and lanky. He was as tall as she remembered, but he'd bulked up. Considerably. His shoulders were wide, his chest deep, and his designer suit was tailored to perfection.

Her breath caught, and she nearly dropped her phone. "Yes?" The word was more of a squeak than an actual reply. Flushing, she rose to her feet, and her heart did a familiar flip-flop she hadn't felt in years.

Axle stepped closer and held out his hand. "Hi. I'm Axle Travers."

His smooth baritone sent a jolt straight to her solar plexus. His fingers curled around hers, and a long-buried, helpless desire surged through her.

Great. Ab-so-freaking-lutely great. Once again she was crushing on Axle, and he didn't even remember her.

"Hello Axle."

He frowned and released her hand. "Have we met? You look familiar."

God, she hoped not. The last time he saw her, she was forty pounds heavier and painfully shy. She lifted her chin. "We went to high school together. You were friends with my cousin, Geoff Pratt."

"Haley?" Axle's eyes raked over her, and heat crawled up her neck to settle in her cheeks—and much lower. "Wow. Haley Pratt," he said with an appreciative smile. "I barely recognize you. You've grown up."

Her outward appearance wasn't the only thing that had changed since high school. She forced a smile. "It's Connors now, not Pratt. I got married." A familiar mix of shame and disappointment flooded her. "Or at least I was married. Ben and I are divorced."

Just one more thing to add to her list of accomplishments. Item number one: stalking victim. Item two: motherless divorcee and all around failure at relationships.

Axle lowered his brows, and the smile slipped from his face. "Is your ex-husband stalking you?"

"No. I—"

"Let's finish this in my office." He abruptly turned. "Follow me," he tossed over his shoulder as he crossed the waiting room to a door that opened into an interior hallway.

Axle motioned her through, and Haley stepped around him into a carpeted corridor. After closing the door behind them, Axle cupped her elbow and prodded her down the hall.

"I'm sorry," he said as he propelled her forward. "I should have waited until we got to my office before asking questions about the case, but you caught me off guard." He stopped in front of a closed door on the left and smiled down into her eyes. "I wasn't expecting to know my next client."

He didn't know her. He had never known her. And she had never known him. Not really. She tugged her elbow free and stepped away from him—away from his large, imposing body. He opened the door and dropped his hand to the small of her back, nudging her inside.

A shiver pulsed through her. Josh had manhandled her like this too, and just as sweetly. Josh was so attentive, so solicitous—so damn controlling and manipulative.

She stiffened but Axle didn't seem to notice. He stepped around her and into the room, stopping beside one of two gray office chairs facing his desk. "Please, have a seat," he said.

Haley clutched her purse, holding onto the strap like a lifeline as she lowered her hips. "How did seeing me again catch you off guard? It's not like we were good friends or anything." It was a bitchy thing to say, but she was off balance. Defensive.

Axle tensed, his shoulders stiffening as he walked around the desk to sit down. "No, we weren't exactly friends," he said with a smile as false as his secretary's teeth, "but seeing you again brought back uncomfortable memories. One of the last times I saw you, I was pretty wasted. And as I recall, I threw up down the side of your car."

Great. He remembered that night, but did he remember Shane's insult and her clumsy attempts to comfort him—attempts her cousin laughing said looked more like a bear mauling a salmon? He probably hadn't thought twice about that kiss. He didn't even remember the last time he'd seen her outside of school wasn't the night he'd gotten drunk. It was a couple of weeks later–in the River Arts District in Asheville. They'd spent an entire afternoon together drinking lattes outside of a trendy coffee shop the summer before senior year–the summer before he moved. Sadly, that coffee shop no longer existed. Helene's flood waters destroyed the entire block, and the owners of SoHo Coffee had moved back to New York.

Haley twisted her purse strap around her fingers and forced a smile. "Yeah, Joe and Geoff were pretty pissed about that. As soon as Dad saw the car, he knew y'all had been drinking, and he called Uncle Roy." Haley smiled a genuine smile as she recalled the trouble her brother and cousin had gotten into. "Aunt Jean and Uncle Roy cut off Geoff's allowance. He actually had to get a job that summer."

Axle smiled too. A more relaxed smile. A smile that warmed Haley's skin.

"Come to think of it," he said, "I do remember Geoff being pissed at me for about a week after that."

"He and Joe should have washed the car before Dad saw it," she said, grinning.

Axle held her gaze, and Haley couldn't help noticing the darker brown radiating from his pupils like a starburst. She loved the contrast—black hair, caramel skin, light eyes.

"You know, I went to your house a few days later to apologize for being a jerk," he said softly. "You weren't home, but Joe told me to stop by later."

Haley lowered her eyes. "Hmm. Joe never mentioned it, and I don't recall you stopping by that summer."

Liar. She remembered waiting for Axle to call or come by—waiting for him to acknowledge the mind-blowing kiss they'd shared that night. Even after Joe told him what time she'd be home, Axle never came back, and Joe called her chicken shit for not calling Axle to thank him for stopping by. Maybe she would have if Geoff hadn't set her straight. He'd told her Axle was seeing one of the cheerleaders and not to make such a big deal over one drunken kiss. Then he'd jokingly said that kiss was probably why Axle had thrown up.

Haley had known he was joking, but that didn't stop her from having doubts before she met Ben. Then again, if Ben had thought she was such a good kisser he wouldn't have screwed one of her bridesmaids a week before the wedding.

"I would've stopped by again after you got home that night, but Shannon got wasted after Jefferson slapped the shit out of her, and I had to take care of her." Axle's eyes darkened, and his fingers curled into a fist.

Haley couldn't help but notice he'd called his mother by her first name. "I'm sorry," she said, and instantly regretted it. Axle had never wanted anyone's pity.

"Don't be. It was a long time ago. Now, let's get down to business."

Uncurling his fingers, Axle leaned forward and plucked a pen from the fancy desk set in front of him. Haley followed his movements, noticing the way his jacket pulled tautly across his broad shoulders. When a picture sitting at an angle on the corner of his desk caught her eye, she strained her neck, trying to see around the edge of the frame.

It was a photograph of a small child—a blue-eyed, blond-haired little girl about three years old. The child didn't look mixed. Then again, Axle was half white with light skin, and genetic traits were often unpredictable.

Axle glanced up and noticed her staring. "My daughter," he said as he turned the frame toward her.

She glanced at Axle and then at the child's picture, forcing down the silly lump that rose in her throat because he had a child and she didn't. "She's beautiful."

"She looks like her mother." Axle smiled but it was hard and cold and didn't invite further comment. Then his face relaxed and the frost left his eyes. "Olivia and I got married six years ago. It lasted three. I'm also divorced."

"I'm sorry. I'm sure divorce is much harder when a child is involved." Geoff had never mentioned that Axle got married. Then again, Geoff had lost touch with Axle a long time ago.

"It's definitely complicated." His expression darkened, and Haley could almost feel a chill in the air.

"But at least you have your daughter. Ben didn't want children." She snorted. "Come to think of it, I don't think he really wanted a wife either."

Axle tapped his pen on a yellow legal pad and sighed, "I don't usually do business like this. Normally, I try to keep things on a more professional level."

"I understand." He obviously didn't want to know anything about her unless it was related to the case, and that hurt. She took a deep breath and swallowed. Now that they'd gotten the pleasantries out of the way, she'd have to tell him about Josh and try to convince him she wasn't a paranoid drama queen.

Axle nodded. "Okay, so tell me what brings you to Travers Investigations?"

She tensed. "I don't know where to start."

"Just relax," he said with a smile meant to put clients at ease. But Haley didn't like that his smile made her feel all warm and fuzzy inside.

"I'm not here to judge," he added softly. "I'm here to help. So why don't we start with a name. Do you know who's stalking you?"

"Josh Patterson." She took a deep breath and tried relaxing her stiff shoulders. Tension radiated down her spine with a throbbing ache. "We went out a couple of times, but when I tried to break it off, he wouldn't take no for an answer."

"Did he threaten you?"

"No but..." She twisted and untwisted her purse strap around her fingers. "Look, he never directly threatened me, but his behavior is threatening. He calls me his soul mate and says we're destined to be together until death."

And it was the death part Haley found the most threatening. She shivered, twisting the strap tighter. The ends of her fingers throbbed. She untwisted the strap and set the purse on the floor by her chair.

Axle inhaled slowly, nodding his head as if in sympathy—as if he were about to tell her that he understood but could do nothing for her. Her stomach knotted. She twisted her fingers together in her lap.

"North Carolina's stalking law has a specific intent requirement that's limited to aggravated or serious stalking," he said, "and so far, yours sounds like a case of simple stalking."

"There's nothing simple about it." She wanted to surge to her feet and march gracefully out the door, but her trembling legs would probably crumble and send her crashing to the floor instead.

"There never is," Axle said with a reassuring smile, "but before I can assess the danger, I need to know everything. So, why don't you start from the beginning?"

Haley sighed and nearly melted with relief.

Chapter 3

Axle studied Haley as she bit her lower lip and dropped her gaze. Damn, she looked good. She'd been cute in high school, sure—but back then, he'd kept his distance. Geoff's cousin. Off-limits. Besides, he'd been a jock trying to fit in, pretending his mom wasn't an addict shacked up with Buncombe County's most notorious drug dealer. Now, his problems were bigger. And far more dangerous.

He rolled the pen between his thumb and index finger and met Haley's chocolate colored eyes. They were still just as guileless as he remembered. "How did you and Josh meet?"

She shifted uncomfortably. "At Patterson's Body Shop. He does body work and restorations, and I have a classic car that needed restoring after Helene."

"You still have the convertible—the '70 muscle car you and Joe shared?" The one he'd puked on? That car had been legendary in high school. Half the football team had wanted a ride. Just not with brainy Haley Pratt. Maybe that was for the best. Half those guys had been horny pricks.

Haley smiled. "Sure do." Then her mouth flattened. "Joe drives an electric car now and didn't want it. My ex wanted to sell it. So, Dad held onto it until after my divorce. When I moved home after Mom got sick, he signed the title over to me. I drove it to work the day of the hurricane. Otherwise, I'd have lost it with the house and the Toyota."

"I'm sorry about your house. I lost my business, but I was able to rebuild. My place in Broader Valley only took minimal damage," Axle said, watching her body language, resisting the urge to read her thoughts—a skill he'd acquired thanks to Dr. Weldon, the scientist who'd kidnapped him.

"And I'm sorry about your business. And what happened when you came back to Asheville." She briefly met his gaze and then looked away again. "Losing two co-workers like that... and then being kidnapped by the man who killed them? I can't imagine. I'm just glad you're okay now."

Axle grunted. She had no idea. No one did—except Reid Sheridan, his silent partner, and a strange mix of mortals and benevolent vampires who'd helped pull him out of Weldon's hell. "It was a long time ago. Now, back to your car—and Josh."

Haley sighed. "It had been raining for days before the hurricane hit. The Toyota was low on gas, so I took the Pontiac. By eight that morning, flooding had already started. I stayed at the clinic overnight, helping Dr. Belcher and the staff secure equipment and supplies. By the next day, there was two feet of water inside the clinic—and water up to the dashboard of the Pontiac."

Axle nodded. His Asheville office had been swept away. Fortunately, he'd backed up task force and client files on a secure server he could access from home.

"About six months ago, a mechanic checked the engine, wiring and critical components. They were fine, but the body was banged up—trees, debris—and the interior was ruined. Josh came highly recommended, so I took it to Patterson's. During the restoration process, we had lunch a few times. Then he asked me out." She flushed, eyes sliding away.

Nerves? Guilt? Embarrassment? Maybe all three. Axle made a note and nodded. "So, how long were you involved with Mr. Patterson?"

Haley's chin snapped up. "We weren't involved. It was lunch a few times and three official dates. That's it."

"But, you do have a restraining order." Maybelline had noted that when she scheduled Haley's appointment. His step-grandmother wrote everything down. It helped her manage her memory loss. She was surprisingly good at her job, and Axle appreciated her forgetfulness. If she ever mentioned something wild, people chalked it up to dementia. It was a win-win. He loved Maybelline more than he'd ever loved either of his biological grandmothers.

Haley nodded. "Josh voluntarily signed it, but when he showed up at my job, the deputy didn't arrest him."

"Did you have the order with you?" Without it in hand, enforcement was tricky.

"Yes," Haley said. Then she described two more incidents that occurred after the judge signed the order.

Patterson wasn't stupid. He'd signed the order without protest. That meant the judge validated it without a finding of fact. No official record of violence, harassment, or stalking. On paper, Josh Patterson looked clean. Maybe he was. Axle didn't know Haley anymore. "Tell me about your relationship with Josh." His pen hovered over the yellow legal pad.

Haley's brows drew together, two sharp lines forming between her eyes. "It wasn't a relationship," she snapped. "It was three dates."

So, she did have a temper. In high school, she'd been too shy, too polite—except that one night after graduation. She'd ripped into Shane Danvers for calling him the "N" word. Axle had been too angry to do much, afraid of confirming the stereotype people already believed. He hadn't trusted his temper then. He still didn't. But now, the stakes were higher.

"Sorry," he said with a soft smile. "Let me rephrase. Tell me about the dates—and what led you to file the restraining order."

Her face flushed, and her eyes flicked to her purse as if tempted to grab it—maybe to twist the strap again. Instead, her fingers found the hem of her blouse, rubbing the edge like a rosary. Axle bit back a smile. Haley had changed since high school, but she still fidgeted when she was nervous.

He watched her inhale, the slow rise and fall of her chest. She'd filled out since high school, her figure more defined now.

Damn Travers. What the hell is wrong with you? Haley's a client.

He snapped his gaze back to her face. She was blushing, chewing her bottom lip—a soft, unstudied gesture that made it all the more alluring.

Heat crept up his neck. Was Maybelline messing with the thermostat again?

Haley released her lip and knotted her fingers. "On our first date, Josh took me to dinner. He was a gentleman—opened doors, pulled out my chair. And he didn't even try to kiss me goodnight."

Axle shifted in his seat, forcing his thoughts back to her words, not her face. *Stick to business, Travers.*

He nodded, channeling his best Dr. Phil. "So you felt safe going on a second date."

"He seemed like a nice guy, and I enjoyed his company. Not a single red flag. I don't know how I got it so wrong." She flushed, lifting one shoulder in a half shrug. "Things were fine on the second date, even if he seemed a little fast. But by the third, I felt smothered. He hovered. Like he didn't want anyone else near me. So when he asked me out for the next Sunday, I told him we should slow things down."

"Smart move. Early signs of toxicity can be subtle." She might not have seen red flags, but she'd trusted her gut. "How did he take it?"

"He seemed hurt. So I told him I was going to my uncle's house for a painting party. All the repairs from Helene had been completed, and to save money, the family decided to host a pig picking and asked friends and neighbors to help paint—kind of like an old fashioned barn raising." She sighed, shaking her head like she was acknowledging a mistake. "I thought he understood. But then he showed up at Uncle Roy and Aunt Jean's house—as if I'd invited him. He even brought drop cloths and paint sprayers from his shop," she added with a touch of humility.

Axle's brows drew together. Was Patterson just a nice guy trying to help? A pushy suitor who couldn't take a hint? Or did he have a personality disorder that impaired his judgment?

"How did you handle it?" If Patterson had psychological issues, Haley's actions might've unintentionally triggered the stalking. Not that he'd say that aloud. Like most women in her position, Haley probably already blamed herself.

She ducked her chin, a wisp of cinnamon-colored hair falling over her left eye. "I didn't. It was a nice gesture, and I didn't want to seem ungrateful," she said, tucking the strand behind her ear. Then she looked up, locking those wide, innocent eyes with his. "So I didn't say anything until it was time to leave."

Her eyes tugged at something cold and dormant in his chest. He ignored the heat rising in his blood and focused on her mouth—wide, lush, pouting.

Look somewhere else Travers. He dropped his gaze to her chest. *Not there, dumbass.*

He shifted his hips and glanced down at the legal pad on his desk, forcing his focus back to the case. Haley was a client. He shouldn't need the reminder. "Did anything happen—or did he do anything—that made you feel uncomfortable or afraid?"

"No. Josh was great, actually. A big help. When we were alone, he even apologized for showing up uninvited." Her eyes clouded with confusion. Axle didn't need to read minds to see she was second-guessing herself. But if Josh wanted a relationship, Haley's response didn't matter. Neither did her feelings. Most stalkers lacked insight. They fixated on what they wanted—nothing else.

Patterson wasn't some delusional stranger imagining intimacy where none existed. They'd dated. Haley hadn't ghosted him or told him to get lost—she'd asked for space. Most men would've respected that. Some didn't. Some were oblivious to nuance. Or maybe Patterson was just a tone-deaf mofo. Or worse.

If he was a narcissist, rejection wouldn't sit well. If he had borderline personality disorder, he likely had a history of volatile relationships and would see Haley's boundaries as a challenge. It got more complicated if Patterson believed Haley was the only woman he could ever love. That kind of emotional fixation could drive him to control her—and the relationship. He'd told her they belonged together. Or maybe he was just your garden-variety sociopath: charming, manipulative, and dangerous as hell.

"How did you respond to the apology?" Axle asked. A sociopath fed off fear and distress—it reinforced their behavior.

She shrugged. "My whole family was there—Dad, Joe, Amy, my nephew, Joey. Geoff, his sister, Brenda, and her family. Geoff even brought a date–some Italian girl named Gina or Genovia–something like that. A bunch of neighbors came too. Everything was going so well, I didn't say anything. Geoff and Joe seemed to like Josh, so I kept my mouth shut and tried to enjoy myself. Pretty stupid, huh?" She shrugged again, her face coloring. Again.

Was it a redhead thing? Or a Haley thing?

"No. But it might've been a little misleading," he said. Her eyes widened, and the pulse in her neck jumped. He softened his tone. "It may not have mattered how you responded. A harsher reaction could've triggered something worse—violence, escalation." And if Patterson was more than a stalker, Haley could be in real danger.

"It definitely escalated," she said, averting her gaze.

Axle nodded, letting silence settle. Reid always said a good investigator kept an open mind until all the facts were in. Reid Sheridan—mentor, silent partner—had never steered him wrong. If Patterson wasn't what he seemed... "What time did Josh show up? Before or after sunset?"

Haley's brow furrowed. "Before. Painting took most of the day. Aunt Jean made pies, catered the sides. Uncle Roy started the pig around six that morning. We finished painting around four, and everyone gathered outside in paint-spattered clothes around five to eat. Why?"

He shrugged. No way he was telling her the real reason for the question. "Just gathering facts. What happened after the pig picking?"

"At the end of the night, Josh walked me to my car. I thanked him for helping but reminded him we weren't a couple. Not that it mattered. He insisted on following me home. Even tried to come inside."

"Is that when you broke it off?"

"There was nothing to break off," she snapped, eyes flashing. "It wasn't like we were going steady."

Axle raised his brows. Shy little Haley Pratt—correction, Haley Connors—had grown some serious backbone since high school. Back then, she never argued. Never stood up for herself when kids called her Ginger, Chubs, Nerd, or Red. But she'd stood up for him. Not just to Shane Danvers, He remembered her defending him to her brother and Geoff after he'd puked down the side of her car.

He exhaled to keep from smiling. "It's possible Patterson imagined a relationship that didn't exist—and got upset when you ended it."

Haley let out a soft, audible breath that tugged at something deep in Axle's gut. "He said he loved me," she said with a shrug. "I guess that confirms your theory."

Did it? Some men tossed the L-word around like confetti. Just because Haley said it wasn't a relationship didn't mean they hadn't slept together. Then again, the Haley he remembered wouldn't have. But that Haley was a teenager. Not a woman.

He frowned. "Were you intimate with Mr. Patterson?"

Her cheeks flushed. "We didn't have sex. And we weren't in a relationship. What part of three dates don't you understand?" she snapped. "Maybe the rest of the world screws around without emotional attachments, but I don't do casual sex."

"I had to ask," he said, more relieved than he should've been. "Intimacy increases the risk of violence. It can change the dynamic."

"We were never *that* intimate," she said again, calmer now. Then her flush deepened. "Let's just say we never needed a condom and leave it at that. Okay?"

Axle smiled despite himself. "Okay. But if Patterson sees himself as an estranged lover, he may still be angry. And if he has a criminal record or owns a gun, the risk goes up."

Haley shook her head. "No record. Gordon said he doesn't have a gun permit either."

Which didn't mean squat. Any yahoo could buy a rifle and ammo. In North Carolina, inherited guns didn't need to be registered. Patterson could own a handgun passed down from his father, uncle, grandfather—no paperwork required.

"Okay. So, besides knowing where you live and work, what other personal info does he have?"

"He knows everything." Her voice rose, teetering on hysteria. "He has all my contact info—work, cell, my brother's and dad's numbers. Even my email addresses. When he restored my car, I paid with checks and a credit card. Axle, he has my bank account, debit card, and credit card numbers."

Hearing her say his name did strange things to his insides. It shouldn't. But it did. Damn. He wasn't in high school anymore, and he wasn't some confused kid. After the abduction and rescue, his life had flipped upside down. Then Olivia told him she was pregnant—and the baby was his–which had only complicated his life more. Hell, it was still complicated, and Haley wasn't the sweet virgin he remembered. She was a thirty-three-year-old divorcee with a serious problem, and she needed his help–his professional help.

"You did the right thing getting the restraining order," he said. "But from what you've told me, Patterson's keeping a low enough profile to stay off the legal radar."

"But he's still stalking me." Her voice cracked, and Axle's heart clenched. He'd never gotten used to that helpless feeling when a woman was openly afraid. But he couldn't let emotion cloud his judgment. Growing up with his junkie mother had taught him to guard his heart. Since the abduction, his heart was the least of his worries.

"Has he harmed you or damaged your property?"

She shook her head. "I think that's why the police don't take me seriously. He's never done anything. He just keeps showing up in public places, saying we belong together. Telling me he won't give up until I agree to see him again."

"There's no requirement for physical harm in stalking statutes. But there has to be reasonable fear from repeated, unwanted contact. You've told him to stop. He hasn't. That's a violation."

"But Gordon said there's no proof he's following me. He's only showing up in public places. He hasn't come to my house—or my family's—since the pig picking."

Just because Patterson hadn't knocked didn't mean he hadn't been there. It only meant Haley hadn't seen him. If he was just infatuated, the restraining order should've been enough. But if he was still stalking her—and using high-tech methods—the authorities might never catch him.

"Any idea how he's keeping tabs on you?" Axle scribbled a note to request Haley's case file from Gordon Sikes.

Haley shook her head. "I think he's switching vehicles. He's got access to a ton of cars through his body shop, and he told the cops it was just a coincidence we ended up at the same place. But he shows up everywhere I go, and not just in Whisper Falls. And I didn't mention this before, but—I never told him where Uncle Roy lives."

Axle shrugged. "Small towns make it easy. He could've found your uncle's address with a quick internet search." He kept his tone neutral, resisting the urge to jump to conclusions. These days, anyone could track someone online. And if Patterson had even basic tech skills, he might be stalking Haley digitally as well as in person. Axle tucked that thought away and added, "It's still possible these run-ins are random. Maybe he's just using them to rattle you."

"Two or three 'random' run-ins a week?" she said, snorting. "I don't freaking think so."

So much for shy little Haley Pratt. She'd grown teeth. "Neither do I," Axle said.

"What can I do to end this—for good?"

Axle leaned back in his chair, a confident smile tugging at his mouth. "Hire me."

Chapter 4

Axle was going to take her case. After the interview in his office, she'd written a check to retain his services, and he'd given her some useful safety tips. Gordon had already recommended changing her email address and phone number and blocking Josh's number. But Axle went further—vary her schedule, switch up where she did business, and start a stalking log. If things escalated, documentation could make or break her case in criminal court.

Axle hoped Josh would back off once he realized she was serious about the restraining order. Haley wasn't convinced.

Before heading home, she stopped at Hadley's Country Store. The original store had been a local landmark since the 1920's, but a mudslide after Helene had wiped it off the map. Now it was a prefabbed building with all the charm of a shipping container and carried little more than canned goods and dry staples. But she hadn't shopped since abandoning her cart at the Food Mart, and she couldn't risk running into Josh again.

She kept her head down inside, grabbed a few essentials, and hurried out.

At her car, she held the cart steady with one hand and slid the key into the trunk with the other. Her vintage LeMans didn't have keyless entry or automatic locks—just cold steel and stubborn mechanics. As she pulled the key free, her purse slipped from her shoulder. She reached for it, lost her grip on the cart—and watched it roll backward.

It bumped into someone. A hand caught it before it hit the truck parked beside her.

"Thanks," she said automatically, turning.

Steel-gray eyes. That smile. Her heart slammed against her ribs. "Josh."

Her knees nearly gave out. How? How had he found her? She hadn't been in the store long. She hadn't seen a vehicle behind her on the winding road from Asheville. The curves were tight, the shoulders narrow. She would've noticed a tail.

"You're welcome, Haley," he said, voice smooth as silk. His smile was warm. Familiar. Possessive.

Terrifying.

She backed away from the cart—away from him. Her hand dove into her purse, fingers fumbling for her phone. "I'm calling the police. You're violating the restraining again, and this time, I can prove it."

"Can you?" His brows lifted. "I'm just buying groceries, and this store isn't on your list."

Her thumb hovered over the screen. "But you're talking to me."

"No. I stopped your cart from hitting my truck. You thanked me." He gestured to the vehicle beside hers.

His truck. Not a rental. Not a coincidence.

She hadn't seen it when she pulled in. She was sure of it. Axle's advice had made her feel safe—until now.

"You parked beside me," she said, voice shaking. "You knew this was my car."

Josh's smile widened. "You parked beside me, darling. I was here first."

He was lying, but she couldn't prove it. Hadley's didn't have security cameras.

Keeping her eyes on him, she backed toward the driver's door, opened it, and slid behind the wheel. Her hands moved on autopilot—key in ignition, ragtop up, windows cranked. Her breath came fast and shallow. Her skin prickled with sweat.

She slammed the door and locked it. The click felt useless. She shifted into reverse and glanced at the rearview mirror. The trunk blocked her view. She couldn't back up without knowing what was behind her.

Josh stepped into frame, lifting a grocery bag from the cart. Then he disappeared behind the car.

"Why are you shopping here?" he called, voice muffled through the glass. "Why not get your groceries while you were in Asheville?"

Her stomach dropped. How did he know she'd been in Asheville? She hadn't told anyone. He hadn't followed her to Axle's office. She would've seen him. Wouldn't she?

She wanted to floor it. Just go. But a car was parked in front of her, and Josh was behind her car now, holding the second bag. No way out. Not unless she ran him over.

The thought flashed through her mind like lightning, and she was tempted to follow through.

"Get away from my car!" she shouted, voice cracking.

Josh didn't flinch. He loaded the second bag. Then the third. Slowly. Methodically. Drawing it out.

Her blood pounded in her ears. "I said move!"

She gunned the engine. The V8 roared, loud enough to turn heads. Still, he didn't move.

Sweat pooled under her arms. The vents blew hot air from the engine inside the car. She cracked the window for air. Her skin burned. Her nerves frayed. "Move, or I'll back over you!"

Josh finally closed the trunk. The car shuddered. Haley flinched. Then Josh strolled to her window, calm as ever, leaving the cart behind her bumper.

"Why did you go to Asheville today?" he asked, voice low and intimate through the glass.

She eased the car back. The bumper nudged the cart. It rolled into his truck. He didn't stop it.

"You're not seeing someone behind my back, are you?" His smile vanished. His eyes darkened.

Haley twisted, arm over the seat, and kept backing. Josh leapt aside at the last instant. He stayed rooted, watching, as she shot through the stop sign and onto the road.

Her grip locked on the wheel. Breath came in ragged bursts. Sweat slicked her palms. The car didn't have air conditioning. The hot, dead air stifled her, but she didn't dare release the wheel to crack the window.

Her pulse hammered in her ears. No truck behind her. Still, the blind curves of High Mountain Road hid everything. He could be back there—or headed to her apartment to await her arrival. She couldn't go home. It was no longer safe.

It was after four, but Axle's office didn't close until five. He could still be there.

She pushed the speed limit, tires squealing, the LeMans rocking through the turns. When she hit the highway, she didn't slow down.

Traffic was thick leaving Asheville, but she was heading in, and there was no sign of Josh's truck. She didn't care. She kept going. If a cop pulled her over, fine. At least she'd be safe.

She turned onto Amherst Drive, slowed with traffic, and pulled into the strip mall. Axle was locking his office door.

She threw the car into park, killed the engine, and bolted.

"Axle!" she cried, voice raw.

He turned, startled. "Haley?"

She reached the sidewalk and collapsed into him. He caught her, arms wrapping around her as she shook.

"What is it?" he asked, voice low and steady.

She couldn't answer. Couldn't breathe. But in his arms, the panic began to ebb. She trembled against him and melted.

#

Axle held Haley to his chest, her fear vibrating through him like a struck chord.

"He's still following me," she whispered, her body trembling against his.

Axle stiffened, scanning the empty parking lot. "He's not here, Haley. It's just us."

She lifted her chin, meeting his gaze. He let go. Comforting clients was part of the job. Hugging them—and feeling something—wasn't.

Stepping away from him, she wrapped her arms around her waist and took a step back. Her eyes were damp and glistening, but she wasn't crying. Not yet, anyway. Then she inhaled through her nose, exhaled through pale lips—lips he shouldn't be noticing, not now.

"Josh is following me," she said, voice unsteady. "I took your advice. I avoided Whisper Falls and Asheville. I went to a tiny market in the mountains. Off-grid. When I came out, he was there. Waiting. I didn't see him until I unlocked the trunk. My cart rolled back and nearly hit a truck. His truck. Then he was there, catching it like some damn hero."

Coincidence? Maybe. But Axle didn't buy it. Patterson had been warned. Sure, maybe he shopped there too. But the odds? Slim. Even if it was chance, showing up like that—cornering her—was a power play.

Axle stared into her frightened eyes, resisting the impulse to touch her. Oh yeah. The bastard had definitely scared her. He could feel it. "Did he threaten you?"

She shook her head, eyes downcast.

Axle exhaled, slow and shaky. "Okay. Good." For a minute, he'd actually been afraid. Now, how damn professional was that? "Did you call 911?"

Her chin snapped up, eyes blazing—not with tears, but heat. He almost smiled. She had fire.

"No. What would I have told the cops if they'd shown up before Josh left? That I ran into him at a grocery store not on my list and that when my cart rolled into him, he stopped it from hitting his truck and then loaded my groceries like a gentleman? You think that would explain the fear crawling under my skin?"

Axle pinched the bridge of his nose. She had a point. If it was a coincidence, calling the cops would make her look paranoid. *Boy who cried wolf. Girl. Woman. Whatever.*

He dropped his hand. "Did you speak to him?"

"I told him to stay away from me and threatened to call 911. He claimed he was getting groceries and that he was there first. He wasn't. I would have noticed his truck and gone elsewhere."

Axle sighed, raking a hand over his freshly buzzed scalp. In his tailored suit, he looked like a cop—or a soldier. Not the street kid with a junkie mom. He was a professional. Time to act like it.

"Next time, walk away," he said, voice clipped. "Call 911. Make a report. Build a paper trail. And don't talk to him. I don't even want him hearing your voice on your outgoing voicemail. And keep a record of any messages he leaves so we can build on the evidence we already have."

"But..."

He raised a hand, cutting her off. "I know you've blocked him and changed your number. That won't stop him. Every time he hears your voice, his attachment grows—or his satisfaction. Either way, fear gives him power. Don't let him see it. Don't let him hear it. If a stalker is ignored a thousand times, and on the thousand and first you respond, he learns persistence pays."

"And just how am I going to call 911 without him hearing my voice?" she snapped, and Axle smiled.

"The cops don't expect you to stay with your stalker until they arrive. So leave and then call. They'll tell you what to do next. Then call me."

"I'm sorry," she whispered, as though he wasn't being a hard-ass and she'd actually done something wrong. "I just want him to leave me the hell alone and nothing seems to work."

"I know." He wanted to reach for her and pull her into his arms again, but she was a client–nothing more. He glanced around the parking lot. "Is it possible he followed you here?" If so, Axle would make damn sure he never followed her again.

She hugged herself and shook her head. "I don't think so. He was still standing in the parking lot when I pulled out, and I didn't notice him following me, but I didn't see him follow me to Hadley's either, so..."

"So, he probably didn't."

"It doesn't matter," she said, visibly fighting tears. "I've filed a restraining order and called the cops on him twice, but it doesn't seem to matter."

"Look, I'll call Gordon and let him know what happened. In the meantime, why don't you head home and get some rest. Gordon can come by your house or interview you on the phone. Then you can stop by my office Monday after work and we can follow up. That'll give me a couple of days to look into Josh's past."

Haley blew out a frustrated breath. "I don't see what good knowing his past will do. I'm worried about now."

"Past behavior predicts future behavior," Axle said. "If there's a history of violence, we need to know." There was always a potential, and he'd rather not trust Haley's safety to chance.

She squeezed her eyes shut for a second and released a quivering breath. "He doesn't have a history of violence," she said, meeting his gaze. "According to Gordon, Josh was born and raised in Butner, North Carolina and has never been arrested. He's never even gotten a traffic ticket until he rear-ended that car."

Axle snorted. He didn't have a record either. Didn't mean he hadn't broken the law. Selling pot for Enrique. Illegal street races in Richmond. The years before he reunited with his father—those were wild. He'd never been accepted by racist pricks like Shane Danvers or Olivia's father, but he'd made friends. Raised hell. He and Geoff Pratt had gotten away with plenty. Nothing serious. But definitely stuff a Black street kid or redneck trash wouldn't have gotten away with. They were never caught—at least not by the cops. So yeah, Patterson could've gotten away with a hell of a lot more than underage drinking and smoking dope.

"Did Josh ever mention an ex-wife or girlfriend." Some stalkers liked to paint themselves as a victim in any failed relationship to gain sympathy. Others were a bit more secretive.

Haley frowned. "Now that you mention it, no. Even after I told him about my ex."

If Josh wasn't seeking sympathy, he was hiding something. "Most men mention an ex at some point in a relationship."

"Three dates. Not a relationship," Haley said, jaw tight.

"And a cookout," he countered with a smile.

"And a cookout nobody invited him to." Her lips stretched, and the tension in her face and shoulders eased, reminding Axle of just how pretty she was.

Get a grip, bro.

Axle smiled back, then stepped away, reestablishing boundaries. "Feeling better?"

She nodded, and the smile slipped from her eyes. "Better–not safer."

"That's a start." Then, instead of walking her to her car, he touched her. His palm pressed to the small of her back—too intimate for a client.

Haley stiffened, cheeks flushing. He dropped his hand, pretending he hadn't just crossed a line.

"You know," he said, forcing a smile, "my SUV's got a dent in the bumper I've been meaning to fix. I think I'll take it to Patterson's Body Shop Monday. See if Josh can give me an estimate."

Haley nodded as Axle walked her—without touching her—to her car.

"I'll see what I can learn from his employees," he said. "If I find anything useful, I'll update you Monday evening."

"What if something happens over the weekend? Do I call you or just the cops?"

"If you're in imminent danger, call 911. Otherwise, call me." He didn't usually work weekends—unless it was for Reid Sheridan and the BBTF—but he'd make an exception for Haley.

"I might go to my dad's tomorrow. So, I should be okay." She shrugged. "Since all this started, I kind of hate being alone."

"Do you have a pet?" He remembered the corgi she had with Joe in high school.

She smiled, but it didn't reach her eyes. "I have a cat. Bootsie. But he's not much company. My apartment came with a doggie door, so he comes and goes as he pleases." She shrugged again, but her eyes flickered with worry. "I haven't seen him since yesterday evening."

"Does he disappear like that often?" Axle asked cautiously. He didn't want to alarm her, but missing or dead pets could be an ominous sign. If Patterson was responsible, it could be a prelude to violence.

"Yes, but he's usually home for breakfast. I was home most of today and didn't see him." She frowned. "He probably came back after I left."

"You're probably right. But if he's still missing in the morning, call me. Okay?" He tried to sound casual, but Haley wasn't stupid. She saw the concern.

Her eyes widened. Her cheeks lost color. "You think Josh took Bootsie. Or killed him. Don't you?"

"Not necessarily." Damn. He wanted her alert, not afraid.

"Fine. I won't jump to conclusions," she said, steadying herself. "But I'm looking for Bootsie as soon as I get home. If I can't find him, I'm calling you—no matter how late. So don't turn off your phone."

He'd given her his business card earlier, but it only had his work number—and he shut that phone off at night. From his sport coat, he pulled another card and scribbled his personal cell on the back. "This is my personal number. Call me if you can't find the cat." Or if you need comfort. Or someone to talk to. Or—

Stick to business, Travers.

She took the card. Their fingers brushed. Heat shot up his arm—an electric spark, a chemical burn. He jerked his hand back and stuffed it into his pocket. "You call me. Anytime."

"Okay."

She turned toward her car, patting her left hip, then her right. Leaning forward, she peered through the window. Her breath hitched. "Oh damn," she whispered. "I locked my keys and purse in the car."

Chapter 5

Haley peered through the driver's side window. Her purse sat on the passenger seat. Keys dangled from the ignition. Both doors were locked. Her stomach knotted. If Axle hadn't been there she couldn't even call for help because her phone was in her purse.

Axle leaned over her shoulder. His breath fanned the side of her neck, warming her chilled skin. His hand rested lightly on her shoulder. "It's okay. We'll figure something out. It's an old car. Back in the day, people used to keep hide-a-keys in magnetic boxes under the fender. Maybe your dad stashed one?"

She shook her head, throat too tight to speak. Normally, a man standing this close would make her tense. But right now, all she wanted was to lean back and feel his body against hers.

"Do you have a spare key?" he asked, giving her shoulder a gentle squeeze before stepping back.

"My dad does. At his house. I could call, but he's probably out on the farm. He only keeps the cell on him because I insist — in case of an accident." She smiled faintly. "He's not as young as he used to be."

Axle's fingers brushed her shoulder again — a fleeting touch that sent a shiver down her spine. Her muscles clenched. So did her thighs. A frustrated sigh escaped. She was locked out of her car and having a hormonal flashback.

She wasn't a teenager anymore. And she hadn't seen Axle in years. He shouldn't still have this effect on her.

"I won't leave you out here alone," he said, smiling. Her heart thumped. That toothpaste-commercial smile. Why did he have to look like that?

"Okay. So now what?" Would he unlock his office? Or were they just going to stand here, awkward and exposed? Not that she minded the view. Axle looked good. Real good.

She glanced into his intense brown eyes, then quickly looked away. *How awkward is this?*

With a sigh, she leaned against the front fender, not caring about the red dust coating the glossy white paint—a souvenir from last Sunday's drive to her dad's. The highway had washed out during Helene, cutting her off for weeks. The road was cleared now, but still unpaved.

Axle frowned. "Don't you have a spare at your place?"

"Well yeah, but there's no one there to bring it to me." Her smile wobbled. Axle was too close. Her body too reactive. "I wouldn't mind sitting in your office — air conditioning sounds amazing." Memorial Day was a week away, but the blacktop in the parking lot was baking her feet through her strappy sandals.

Axle flashed those dimples. Her gut knotted. Heat bloomed in her belly. Or maybe it was just steam rising from the pavement.

"We don't have to wait here," he said. "Why don't I take you to dinner? Then we'll swing by your place for the spare key and look for Bootsie if he isn't home yet."

"But..." Would he add the cost of the meal to her bill? Did she assume they'd each pay their fair share? Or should she ask who was paying?

Even before they were married Ben had always paid—even while cheating. That credit card bill from a restaurant she'd never been to, dated a week before the wedding, should've been her first clue. But he'd been so smooth and charming...until he got caught. Josh had been different. Polite. No flirting. They split the bill until he asked her out. That's why she'd said yes. And look how that turned out. Obviously, she was a bad judge of character.

"I don't know," she said, hesitating.

Axle smiled again. "Hey, we both have to eat. I'll even put it on my expense account."

Haley exhaled, shoulders sagging. It was like he'd read her mind. "Well, if you're sure."

"I'll drive, obviously," he added, flashing another killer smile

Haley stilled. The last time she'd been in a car with Axle, he'd puked out the window. She'd given him a bottle of water and a mint, and when she got to his house, she'd helped him out of the car. In the course of his thanking her for the mint and apologizing for his actions, she'd somehow wound up pressed against the hood of her car with his tongue in her mouth and his hands down her pants. And she'd had her hands...

Oh God. She could still remember the feel of him in her hand—long, smooth, and hard. Even after all these years, the memory lingered. If Geoff hadn't woken up in the backseat, she would've lost her virginity on the hood of the very car she was now leaning against. She jerked away from the bumper as if it had shocked her.

"If it'll make you feel better, we'll even talk about the case so I can write it off on my taxes," Axle said. "Seriously. What better way to discuss it than over dinner?"

Could she spend an evening with Axle and not fantasize about what might have been? She blew out a breath she hoped sounded frustrated rather than nervous. "Okay, fine."

"Good," he said with a nod. He turned and led her across the parking lot to a big, black SUV. As he opened the door and she climbed in, he looked down into her eyes and added, "I just need to stop by the house for a minute to let the dog out."

#

Tiny paws scrabbled across hardwood as Axle opened the door and stepped into the front hall of a sleek two-story home in an upscale neighborhood. Haley followed, her mouth dropping open as big, strong Axle Travers dropped to one knee and spoke to a butterscotch fur ball like he was addressing a toddler.

"Hey girl," he cooed, stroking the dog's curly head. "Do you need to go out?"

The poodle practically danced in place, yipping and licking Axle's chin—until it noticed Haley in the doorway. Then it bared its tiny teeth, snarling and barking like Haley couldn't just drop-kick it across the room and be done with it.

"It's okay, Princess," Axle said gently, smoothing the dog's fur. "Haley's with me."

A stab of delight pierced her chest. Then she reminded herself he was talking to a dog–not his jock buddies from high school. She was so not that needy girl anymore, and she most definitely was not "with" Axle.

"Cute dog," she said, keeping her voice carefully neutral. The dog yipped again and wagged its fluffy tail. It was cute, though Haley had always been more of a cat person. Trixie, the corgi she and Joe had years ago, was the exception. This little dog was smaller than Trixie or Bootsie. No way it could sniff her crotch or blow doggie snot in her face like Geoff's obnoxious Rottweiler. She hated that damn dog—and the feeling was probably mutual.

Axle stood but kept his attention on the poodle. "Yeah. She's a real sweetie," he said with paternal pride.

A man who loved children and small animals was such a turn-on. Ben hadn't cared for either. And who the hell knew if Josh liked kids? Everything she'd thought she knew about him had been a facade—bait to reel her in and take control.

"What's her name?" she asked, and her voice squeaked.

Axle actually blushed. "Princess Paw Paw."

Haley laughed. She couldn't help herself. "You're joking. You, former varsity quarterback for Asheville High named your dog Princess Paw Paw?"

His flush deepened. "Yeah. She was a puppy when I got her, and that's what Bonnie named her," he said with a sheepish, little-boy smile that sent a stab of longing straight to Haley's heart. The man was adorable. And God help her, she still wanted him.

She looked down at the dog. "I take it your ex wouldn't let Bonnie keep her after the divorce."

Axle grunted in the affirmative and turned away without comment. "Make yourself at home in the living room," he said, gesturing to the right. "I need to let the dog out."

He turned left and walked through the dining room. Princess Paw Paw trotted after him.

"Well, alrighty then," Haley muttered as she stepped into the next room.

The living room was tastefully decorated in dark woods and leather, but the walls were bare. So were the tables. No pictures. No artwork. From what she'd glimpsed of the dining room, it was the same—expensive furniture, a florist shop arrangement, and nothing personal.

It was obvious no woman had played a hand in decorating his home. But what about family photographs? Where were the pictures of his daughter?

Granted, Ben had only let her display family photos in their bedroom, but even then, the walls hadn't been bare. Before he brought her home to the brick executive mansion on a deep-water canal outside Tampa, an interior designer had filled the rooms with framed prints and oil paintings.

Ben had never wanted her to add personal touches. When she suggested they buy something together, the arguments started. Haley had wanted to build a home. Ben had wanted a trophy wife to decorate the one he already had. Her "home" had looked staged from day one—just like her marriage. While she tried to make it work, he was busy sleeping with a co-worker of hers who'd been a bridesmaid in their wedding. And of course, he was cheating on her too—with a secretary at his law firm.

She didn't know who Axle was sleeping with—if anyone—but his house looked like a showroom. After growing up in that junky shack with his mom and her boyfriend, maybe he craved order. The house wasn't empty, but it was so impersonal it felt staged—like Ben's, minus the expensive art. Other than the small dog, there wasn't a single sign that anyone had ever lived here with him. Not even his own child.

"Ready to go?" he asked, reappearing in the doorway. The yippy dog was nowhere in sight.

"Where's the dog?" She wanted to ask about his daughter, but it wasn't her place. Axle wasn't someone she'd known for a long time. He was someone she'd known a long time ago.

"She's enjoying her dinner," he said. "So we need to sneak out before she notices I'm gone."

#

Axle glanced at Haley as he pulled out of the driveway. She sat beside him, fingers twisting in her lap like she was trying to wring out her nerves. He couldn't blame her. The last time they'd been in a car together, he'd puked out the window before practically mauling her on the hood. If Geoff hadn't woken up and she hadn't pulled away, he might never have ended up with Olivia that summer. Then again, if he hadn't dated Olivia, he wouldn't have become a father. Short-lived as it was, being Bonnie's dad had been the best damn thing that ever happened to him.

He cast another glance at Haley. Was she thinking about that night too? About the conversation after Shane's racist remark? She'd praised him then—talked about his moral compass and kind heart like she actually knew him. If she'd met his mother, she'd have known better. Shannon had done her best to drag him down with her. If he hadn't discovered his father was still searching for him, he probably would've ended up in jail beside her—or worse.

Shannon had always told him he wasn't any better than her or the parade of losers she brought home. She'd stuck with Jefferson Cross the longest. Jefferson never laid a hand on Axle, but he slapped Shannon around—just not in front of Axle. Maybe to keep up appearances. More likely, self-preservation. By ninth grade, Axle was built like a grown man. Leaner than he was now, but still bigger than Jefferson.

Not that Jefferson could've known Axle wouldn't beat the crap out of him if he saw him hit Shannon. Axle had never wanted to prove her right. He'd wanted to be the man Haley thought he was. But he wasn't. His clumsy apology the night of her brother's graduation had ended with her sprawled across the hood of her car and his hands down her pants. It was a miracle she'd ever spoken to him again—let alone hired him. If she knew the truth about him now, she'd probably jump out of his SUV and run like hell.

"How hungry are you?" he asked suddenly, cutting through the silence.

Haley turned toward him, then dropped her gaze to her lap. "Hungry enough. Anywhere you stop is fine."

Axle smiled to himself, remembering her appetite. She used to put away food like a linebacker, and maybe that's why she'd carried a little extra weight in high school. It hadn't made her any less beautiful. His mother had always been skeletal—choosing heroin over meals. Maybe that's why he liked a woman with some meat on her bones. Haley was thinner now, but she still had hips thick as honey—and probably just as sweet.

Stop looking at her damn curves.

He refocused on the road, tightening his grip on the wheel. "Maybe Bootsie will come home while we're out and save us the trouble of looking. I'm sure he's fine." He hoped Patterson hadn't taken the cat—or worse.

"I'm sure you're right," she said, though her voice lacked conviction. She worried her bottom lip.

"For now, don't worry. Let's enjoy dinner and talk about your case." He wanted to take her somewhere nice. Somewhere she could relax. Somewhere he could get to know her better.

Damn it, Travers. It's not a date. Stick to business.

He stared straight ahead, refusing to look at her again. There was no reason to rekindle anything with Haley. Hadn't he learned his lesson with Olivia?

"So, where do you want to eat?" he asked, voice gruff. He was trying to reestablish boundaries. Haley was a client. Not a friend. Definitely not a date.

"Wherever you want is fine," she said, a little defensive. Or maybe he was just feeling guilty for sounding cold. "I'm not that hard to please."

"Right," he muttered. Olivia had been impossible to please. So had his mother. Shannon hadn't demanded gifts or attention, but nothing he did was ever good enough. In her eyes, he was just another piece of trash.

He glanced at Haley. As far as he could tell, she was nothing like Olivia. Granted, he'd been thinking of Haley as the girl he'd known in high school–the girl who never made demands or stood up for herself–the girl he'd never had the guts to ask out for fear of liking her more than he should.

Olivia had gone out with him, but she'd never told her parents. The only reason she'd finally confessed to dating a Black man after he returned to Asheville was because she'd gotten pregnant and had named Axle as the father. The wedding had been rushed, the ceremony small—nothing like the lavish affair she'd dreamed of. Her snobbish parents hadn't wanted a bastard grandchild, but they'd wanted even less to admit their high-society white daughter was marrying a biracial man raised by a junkie. Even if his father was a prominent lawyer. Especially because that lawyer was Black—and his mother was in prison.

If he'd dated Haley back then, would she have kept it a secret too? Geoff and Joe would've known, but what about her parents? Would his background have bothered her? Would it bother her now? It didn't matter. He had too many secrets and too many responsibilities to get involved with anyone, much less Haley Pratt–correction–Haley Connors.

He stole another glance. Haley stared straight ahead, fingers still knotted in her lap. If her purse hadn't been locked in her car, she'd be mangling the strap. Then she turned and met his gaze. He looked away fast.

"Is Barclay's okay with you?" he asked.

"No," she said, and he jerked his head toward her. Mischief sparkled in her brown eyes.

"I may not be hard to please," she added, folding her arms, "but I'm not in the mood for seafood. I'd prefer steak. Something I can stab without getting arrested."

Axle laughed, and Haley smiled.

"Homesteaders it is," he said. And despite every internal warning, it was starting to feel a hell of a lot like a date.

Chapter 6

Haley took another sip of wine and met Axle's gaze. They were talking about Josh, but there was no urgency. No panic. For the first time in weeks, she felt relaxed around a man who wasn't family. Comfortable—like she was venting about an ex with someone who might become more than a friend. The thought made her choke.

She coughed, set the glass aside, and tapped her chest with a lightly balled fist. Axle's eyes flicked to her hand, then away. Had he just checked out her breasts?

Heat crawled up her neck and bloomed in her cheeks.

"He's average," she said, answering Axle's question.

He nodded. "Do you have a picture?"

She scrolled through her phone and found one her brother had taken at her uncle's painting party—Josh smiling, her expression flat. She held up the screen. "Average height. Average build. Dark hair, blue eyes. Okay, maybe not so average. Josh is a good-looking guy. Just like my husband was. But neither of them were who I thought they were."

"People seldom are." Axle dropped his gaze and took another bite of steak.

Haley mirrored him, cutting another piece.

Ben was fit, blonde, and radiated the confidence of a successful lawyer. Josh had dark hair and a country-boy charm that was easy to like. Both men were polished, likable—at first. But neither was who they pretended to be. Ben had never scared her the way Josh did, but both were controlling. Ben treated her like an accessory. Josh treated her like property.

The difference? Ben let her go the moment he realized she didn't want his house, his money, or his art collection. She'd walked away with little more than her dignity. Josh had looked her in the eye and said he'd never let her go.

How did Axle view women now, after what had to have been a messy divorce? She didn't think he was dating. Was he choosy—or just bitter?

She watched him chew, his jaw flexing. There was nothing boyish about him now. He still had that quiet charm from high school, but something had changed. It wasn't just the broader shoulders. There was a darkness to him—a mystique. Slightly dangerous. And yet, she wasn't afraid. Which didn't make sense. She was terrified of Josh and his secrets.

Unsettled, Haley dropped her gaze and finished her salad before turning back to her steak. Raw nerves made her ravenous.

She swallowed and looked up. "What is it about me that attracts controlling men like Ben and Josh?"

Axle wiped his mouth and lowered his napkin. "Don't blame yourself. You're kind-hearted and avoid confrontation. Men like Josh and your ex see that as weakness."

"Do you?" She winced. Why did it matter what Axle thought?

She wasn't weak. She'd walked away from a wealthy husband, an executive mansion, and more designer labels than any woman needed. She'd sold the jewelry—including the wedding band—and bought a house with her own money. Sure, a hurricane took it, and with barely any equity, but she'd landed in a nice apartment, damn it, and it was hers.

She had a job. She paid her bills. She stood on her own, and she wasn't weak. Just a lousy judge of character.

Axle smiled. "No, Haley. I saw you stand up to Shane Danvers. You may avoid conflict, but you don't back down when it counts. And I've done my homework since taking your case. You didn't walk away with anything you hadn't brought into your marriage. You're doing just fine."

"Except I clearly have terrible taste in men."

His gaze locked with hers. "Maybe you're just too honest to expect deception. But when you see it, you try to get out. You're not naive—you just don't trust your instincts. I bet your gut warned you about Ben and Josh, and you didn't listen. Instead, you gave them the benefit of the doubt because you're genuine, and you expect the same from others."

Her cheeks flushed, her chest warmed. "Thanks for that. I just feel like such a loser, hiring a private detective to fix my mess. I must've done something wrong."

"No. You did most everything right," He smiled again. "But Josh doesn't play by the same rules you do, and he's not afraid to break the law. He most likely has some form of personality disorder, and he's definitely a narcissist."

"Or a psychopath." Her return smile trembled.

Axle reached across the small, round table and touched her hand. "I don't think he's a psychopath. He most likely has borderline personality disorder with narcissistic tendencies. He doesn't see anything wrong with his behavior if it gets him what he wants, and he obviously wants you."

"But what happens if he doesn't get what he wants?"

Axle squeezed her hand. "I won't let anything happen to you."

His words calmed her and excited her at the same time. His touch made her as breathless as if she'd just run a mile. The moment he moved his hand from hers, she picked up her fork and pushed another bite of steak into her mouth.

"What do you know of Josh's personal life," he asked as if the intimate contact hadn't affected him in the least.

She swallowed her steak and washed it down with another sip of wine. He'd touched her hand. He hadn't kissed her. She'd hired Axle to do a job, and that's all he was doing. His job. She needed to keep that in mind or he'd break her heart again.

"I know where he lives and that he grew up in Butner, and I know he played football in high school." She didn't really know much more than that. In the months she'd known him, he'd said very little about himself, but he'd found out almost everything about her.

How could I have been so stupid?

"He never said much about himself, and I never asked. He was such a good listener that I just talked." And talked and talked. "I can't believe I went out with someone I knew so little about."

"Don't beat yourself up," Axle said. "Some guys just don't talk much about themselves. Doesn't mean they're stalkers or serial killers."

No. It didn't. Some guys just kept secrets. Like Axle. He had a daughter he'd barely mentioned. He didn't talk much about himself either. Same as in high school—except for that one night outside the coffee shop. Back then, he still believed his father had abandoned him. He'd been ashamed of his drug-addicted mother and the way they lived. He'd had a rough start, but he'd pulled himself out of the gutter and had made a name for himself. So even if he kept quiet, she still knew more about him than she ever did about Josh.

Haley exhaled and forced her shoulders to relax. "You don't say much about yourself these days, but I assume you're not a stalker or a serial killer." She met his heavy-lidded brown eyes. "Unless they're handing out PI licenses to just anybody now."

Axle flinched, and the walls went up. "No. They don't," he said with a tight smile. Then, lowering his gaze, he added, "I'm not that secretive. I'm just trying to keep this meeting professional."

Haley's appetite vanished. How had she managed to insult his career and sound like a flirt in the same breath? She was talking like they were on a date, and he was clearly trying to set boundaries. She reached for the linen napkin beside her plate, curling her fingers around it in a tight fist.

"Professional. Yeah. Sure. I know. This is business, and I shouldn't treat it like a da—a social occasion." And maybe she shouldn't open her mouth again either.

Axle reached across the table and touched her fist. His warm palm pressed against the back of her cold hand, pressing gently until she relaxed her fingers. Her eyes snapped up to meet his. If he didn't stop touching her hand, she'd never get over her foolish crush.

"This is more than just business," he said, voice low and husky, sending heat curling through her belly. "We're old friends. There's nothing wrong with getting reacquainted."

Did seeing her again make him as uncomfortable as it made her? He'd gone from smooth and confident to nervous and unsure without missing a beat. Or was he just dusting off those old boyish charms—the ones that had drawn her to him in high school?

Haley pulled her hand away and picked up her fork, shoving a bite of potato into her mouth to buy time. Axle had broken her heart once before. He might've dated Olivia that summer, but the week after he'd come by her house to apologize for getting drunk, he'd seemed genuinely interested. They'd spent the whole afternoon talking and laughing. He never mentioned that mind-blowing kiss, and he didn't mention Olivia either. She'd been smitten—and hopeful. He'd promised to call or stop by. He never did. Two months later, he left town with his mother and Jefferson Cross, taking her heart with him.

Was she strong enough to risk getting close to him again?

Oh, hell no. She was already dodging a stalker. She didn't need to get personal with Axle.

Swallowing hard, she raised her chin. "Were we ever really that well acquainted?"

Axle's lips twitched. "Well, the last time I saw you, I think I told you more about myself than you ever wanted to know."

He'd been unusually talkative that day in Asheville. He hadn't brought up the kiss, but he'd opened up about his mother and the man she lived with. He'd even apologized for living like "trash," as he'd put it.

A smile tugged at Haley's lips as she recalled the two of them outside that art deco coffee shop, sipping lattes like college students. The shop—and most of the River Arts District—had been leveled during Hurricane Helene, but the memory lingered, untouched.

Her smile deepened. "You were rather talkative, but I didn't mind listening." Back then, she would've listened to him recite the alphabet. "I think you even said something about wanting to be a cop."

Axle snorted. "And my mom and Jefferson reminded me that street kids who sold pot didn't become cops."

"Well, Olivia had faith in you. So did I." That kiss the night her brother graduated, and the afternoon they'd spent sipping lattes and watching the sun dip behind the mountains—those were the only moments that had ever truly mattered between them. So why did she still ache for what could have been?

Axle grunted. "Back in high school, Olivia never even told her parents we were dating. When I came back to Asheville—after learning my dad hadn't abandoned me but had moved here because it was my last known location—she wanted to pick up where we'd left off. I thought she'd changed. But she still kept me a secret—until she was six months pregnant and starting to show."

A flicker of hope sparked in Haley's chest. She quickly squashed it. Axle wasn't interested in her, and she had no business diving into another relationship when Josh was still a problem. "But you two got married soon after, right?"

"Yeah, well, she was pregnant," he said, raising a brow. "We'd only been dating six months, but I was ready to settle down, play house, and be a normal family. I'd never had that—not since my parents split and my mom kidnapped me. Olivia went into labor two months later, and that's when I started to suspect she'd already been pregnant before we got back together. Then Bonnie was born—blond hair, blue eyes. Olivia confessed. She'd been dating Chris Cramer before he deployed to Afghanistan. Found out she was pregnant the same week I moved in with my dad. She didn't want to raise a baby alone if Chris got killed, and she didn't want her dad to know she'd gotten knocked up out of wedlock. So she said I was the father."

Poor Axle. Family had never come easy to him. Maybe that explained why he hadn't mentioned having a child. Bonnie wasn't his, and he no longer claimed her.

A frisson of anger heated her blood and her words. "Is that why you didn't mention having a daughter?"

He arched a brow, voice edged. "No. Bonnie will always be my daughter. But the moment Chris came home, Olivia left me. Once they got married, she wanted me gone. Said I confused Bonnie, kept her from bonding with Chris. She wouldn't even let Bonnie keep the dog. I might be her legal father, but a blood test proved Chris is her biological dad."

Haley's heart thudded against her ribs. She couldn't tell if his anger was aimed at her or Olivia, but something darker simmered beneath his expression. "I'm sorry I assumed. I should've known you'd never walk away from a child, no matter whose blood she carried."

His face softened, but shadows still lingered behind his smile. "Trust me, Bonnie's better off with Chris." The darkness ebbed, replaced by something quieter. Sadder. "But I'll always cherish the three years I got to be her dad."

Pity tugged at Haley's heart. She saw the love in his eyes, felt the weight of his heartbreak. For one brief moment, Axle Travers was an open book. And then he wasn't. The subdued anger returned, hovering just beneath the surface.

Oh yeah, Axle Travers had secrets, but he wasn't sharing them with anyone, least of all her.

When the waitress came to clear their plates, Axle declined a second beer and asked for the check. After a tense silence, Haley said, "You may not have become a cop, but you're an investigator. So you did follow your dream, in a way."

"I guess," he said with a faint smile. "I did manage to get a BS in Criminal

Justice and put it to good use."

Haley shrugged. "A BS degree is no small accomplishment."

"Especially considering my upbringing." His gaze locked onto hers across the candlelit table. "But you could've been a doctor. What made you change your mind about med school? You had the grades. The brains."

His words warmed her. He remembered.

"Time and money," she said. "I wanted to start my life, not spend a decade in school." She'd wanted marriage. A family. She still did. But that dream felt farther away than ever. And her biological clock was ticking.

Tick-tock.

"And don't forget," she added, swallowing the ache in her gut, "my dad's a farmer. He couldn't afford med school." She'd never wanted him to sell off the last of the family land just so she could chase a dream.

Axle leaned in. "Your dad didn't lose the farm after the hurricane, did he?"

The Pratt farm had been in the family for over a century. Uncle Roy had subdivided his portion years ago. He still had the house and ten acres, but he'd stopped farming—a blessing, really. More than a year after the Swannanoa River flooded Western North Carolina, the fields along its banks were still buried under sand and silt, and debris formed small mountains where crops used to grow.

"Uncle Roy sold most of his riverfront land years ago, so he only lost a few outbuildings and had some damage to the house. Dad's land sits farther from the river and was spared the worst. He lost forty percent of his timber, but he managed to plant tomatoes and cucumbers by spring. I know he won't be able to farm much longer, but that land is Joe's inheritance—and Joey's legacy. Even if Joe stays in Texas, maybe Joey will want to come home and farm someday."

"The world definitely needs more farmers. And nursing's not a bad career," he said. "But I guess neither of us turned out the way we thought we would back in high school."

And somehow, Haley didn't think he was talking about careers.

Chapter 7

Haley's appetite was as hearty as ever. When the waitress cleared their plates, all that remained on hers was a hollowed-out baked potato nestled in crumpled foil. Axle had matched her bite for bite.

"You know," he said, drawing Haley's attention as they waited for the check, "after I found out my dad was still looking for me, I left my mom and followed your advice."

"My advice?" Her eyes widened. "I don't remember giving you any advice. We talked a little the night Joe graduated, but mostly... well, mostly we didn't."

Color rose in her cheeks. She remembered that night as vividly as he did—and was just as reluctant to revisit it.

"I don't mean that night," he said, clearing his throat. "I'm talking about the afternoon we ran into each other outside that coffee shop. I don't recall everything I said about wanting to go into law enforcement to make up for my mom's mess, but I remember you telling me to be true to my dreams. You said I should get a degree in something useful—so I'd have a career, not just a job."

"I said that?"

"Yeah," he smiled. "You said that, and I listened. I'd always wanted to be a cop, but after moving to Richmond, I quit school to take care of mom. She constantly played the victim card, and believe it or not, she even played the race card."

"Isn't that your card?" Haley asked with a tentative smile, then flushed, as if she'd crossed a line.

"I've never played that card," Axle said with a snort. "But yeah, it was pretty shitty of her. She claimed she was discriminated against for being a white woman with a Black kid. Maybe she was. But the real reason she couldn't keep a job? She was a junkie."

Haley lowered her gaze. He couldn't see her hands, but he'd bet she was twisting her fingers beneath the table. "I'm sorry."

"Don't be. Like Kelly Clarkson says, what doesn't kill you makes you stronger." And damn if he wasn't stronger–stronger than any human had a right to be, and that scared him. What if he couldn't control the power Dr. Weldon had embedded in his DNA? Power was seductive. Corrupting. And with his past, he didn't trust himself not to abuse it.

Oblivious to his spiraling thoughts, Haley said, "I thought you were a classic rock and Motown man."

He smiled, pushing the darkness aside. "I have eclectic taste."

When the waitress returned with the check, Axle laid down some bills and stood. Haley rose before he could pull out her chair. He'd wanted to be the gentleman she'd once believed him to be, but maybe she didn't need that anymore. Despite everything Josh Patterson was putting her through, she seemed fiercely independent.

He placed a hand at the small of her back as they walked out. She didn't flinch, so he left it there as they crossed the parking lot. The silence between them wasn't uncomfortable, but Haley was deep in thought. Axle felt her sympathy before she spoke.

She glanced up at him with kind eyes and a hesitant smile. "You didn't have it easy. And I'm sure getting kidnapped and finding your co-workers murdered didn't help. I know you don't want to talk about it, but I think your accomplishments are impressive. I'm sure your parents are proud."

"I doubt Shannon—my mom—is," he said, shaking his head. "I was her excuse and her meal ticket. But yeah, Dad is. So's LaDonna."

"Your stepmom?" she asked as he reached for the door handle. The automatic lock disengaged at his touch.

"Yeah. She's more of a mother than mine ever was. Not that she warmed up to me right away. After Dad and I reunited and he asked me to move in, she made me take weekly drug tests for a couple of months."

Haley slid into the seat and met his gaze. "Did you pass?" she asked with a teasing smile.

"Mostly." He winked. "But I was kind of a pothead back then." He shut the door and walked around the vehicle. Haley was still smiling when he slid behind the wheel.

The ride to Haley's apartment was quiet, but not tense. The complex consisted of four clusters of five two-story units. Haley lived in an end unit—its front porch smaller than the middle ones, but it boasted a wraparound deck and a side door. All units had fenced backyards, five feet high. Dog-proof, maybe. But a cat could easily leap it.

As Haley unlocked the front door, she glanced over her shoulder. "The doggy door's in the kitchen. I know I should keep Bootsie inside, but he was a stray who showed up on my deck one day. I fed him once, left the doggy door open, and we kind of adopted each other. He still comes and goes, but he's fixed, vaccinated, and usually waiting on the side deck rail when I get home."

"You're usually home earlier than this," Axle said gently. "He probably got tired of waiting. I bet he's inside, curled up by his food bowl." But he didn't believe that. He suspected Josh had taken the cat—and he just hoped the animal was still alive.

Haley opened the door, but Axle stepped in front of her just in case Josh had harmed the animal and shoved its carcass back inside through the doggy door. The house had an open floor plan and nothing seemed amiss in the great room, but the doggy door was in the kitchen.

"Bootsie," Haley called, her voice trembling. "Here, kitty, kitty." Silence met them as they stepped into the kitchen. The food bowl was full. The cat was gone.

"He's not here," she whispered, voice cracking.

Axle touched her shoulder, feeling her tremble. "Let's not jump to conclusions. We'll check the closets, under the beds. Then we'll look outside. It's not totally dark out, and the parking lot is well lit."

But Bootsie was nowhere—inside or out. Haley's panic was rising. "He's never stayed gone all day and night. Not since I took him in. He's always waiting when I get home. Even if he goes out, he's back before sunrise, but I haven't seen him since yesterday."

"I don't think Patterson would hurt him," Axle said, trying to keep her calm. "But I do think he took him. He needs a legal excuse to contact you—and he will. The moment he does, you let me know."

"And what do I do in the meantime?" Her eyes shimmered with tears. Axle pretended they didn't gut him, but damn, she was breaking his heart.

"Grab your spare key. Let's go get your car."

They rode in silence back to Asheville. At his office, Axle took her keys—but instead of unlocking the car, he popped the hood. "Josh keeps showing up wherever you are, even when you're not home. The only way he could track you that closely is with GPS devices—on both cars."

Haley's eyes widened. Her face paled. "But he only had access to the convertible. He's never worked on my hybrid."

"He could've planted a tracker while the Pontiac was in his shop. Then waited for you to drive it. Once you left, it would've been easy to go to your apartment and tag your other car," Axle said, raising the hood and locking it in place.

Haley stepped closer. "Wouldn't that take time? What if someone saw him and called the police? Would he risk it?" She sounded hopeful. Axle wasn't.

"It only takes seconds to slap on a magnetic tracker. And people don't pay much attention to their neighbors anymore."

"He's never going to leave me alone, is he?" Her voice caught.

Axle's heart clenched. "We'll catch him."

Using his phone's flashlight, Axle leaned in and found a magnetic GPS mini tracker hidden behind the motor. It allowed real-time tracking with only a six-second delay.

He showed it to Haley. "Josh didn't have to follow you. As long as this had a signal, he knew your location within a few yards. If the signal dropped, it would alert him the moment you came back into range."

Haley reached for the device, her hand trembling. Then she let it fall to her side. "Wouldn't it need recharging, like a phone?"

Axle flipped it over, checking the serial number and battery specs. "Yes, but this one lasts about two weeks. Patterson wouldn't recharge it—he'd just replace it. I'm sure he has more than one."

Her face crumpled. "He knows I went to your office today. Even if there's no sign on the door, he's probably looked up the address. He knows I saw a PI."

"It doesn't matter. He knows you reported him to the police. It won't surprise him."

"I guess," she murmured, biting her lip again.

Axle tried to ignore the unconscious gesture that tugged at him. "Depending on his carrier, he might not have a good signal in the mountains, but—"

"But Asheville has good service," she said, cutting him off. "So does Whisper Falls."

He nodded. "Doesn't matter. He knows about the restraining order. He knows he's violated it. He just doesn't think he'll get caught—or that you can prove it." He placed a hand on her shoulder. "Let's get your car back to your place. I'll follow and check the hybrid for a tracker."

Haley slid behind the wheel. "Stay close," she said, fear in her eyes.

"I'll be right on your tail."

He followed her back to the apartment complex. Once the convertible was parked, he got out of his car and met her beside a blue hybrid.

"I disabled the tracking device between here and Asheville. With any luck, Josh will think the battery died. When he comes to replace it, he'll assume it fell off and that's why he lost the signal."

She nodded. "Okay, but what will you do with it?"

"I'll give it to Gordon. Don't drive the convertible again. Leave it here so Josh doesn't suspect anything. From now on, drive this one," he said, tapping the hybrid's hood.

"Ok," she whispered. "But what if he has a tracker on this one too?"

"He probably does. But unlike the convertible, newer cars have interior hood latches. He couldn't access it unless the car was unlocked." Axle circled the vehicle, feeling along the wheel wells. He found the second tracker behind the right rear quarter panel—same make and model.

Haley's face crumpled. "He knows every place I've been since he planted those damn things."

Axle tamped down the protective instinct her vulnerability stirred. She was his client. That was all. He placed a hand on her shoulder. "I know I told you to drive the hybrid, but maybe you should stay close to home. Take a week or two off."

"That won't be a problem. Dr. Belcher already gave me next week off and the following Monday for Memorial Day. But what about that tracker?" she asked, nodding to the one he'd just removed. "Won't Josh know it's gone too?"

"Maybe not." Smiling, Axle walked to a neighbor's sedan—same color as Haley's hybrid—and tucked the tracker under its wheel well. Then he turned and winked. "With any luck, he'll follow the wrong car for a few days."

"And then what?" she asked, eyes wide.

Axle's heart clenched. "Let me worry about that," he said, walking her to her door. "You just stay put. Keep the doors and windows locked."

He wanted to stay—to make sure she was safe. Instead, he said goodnight and got the hell out of Dodge.

Chapter 8

Patterson wasn't working when Axle rolled his SUV in on Monday for an estimate. The scraped indentation on the rear bumper wasn't catastrophic, but he knew enough about cars to recognize it would cost a small fortune to fix.

"If you've got time to wait, I can get you an estimate," said a young man with a scraggly beard, taking Axle's keys. His pale blue shirt bore the name Lou, stitched in red. "But you'll need to make an appointment next week to get it fixed. We're slammed right now."

"Will Patterson do the actual body work?" Axle asked.

"Nah." Lou scratched at his jaw, revealing a patchwork of adult acne—or maybe a rash—beneath the beard. "Josh sticks to the older cars. Me, Hugh, and Dewey handle the newer stuff."

Axle twitched. Dewey, Hugh, and Lou? They sounded like cartoon ducks.

Suppressing a laugh, he headed inside and sank onto a battered black vinyl couch. He should've gotten the bumper fixed years ago. Then again, he'd done far worse to Chris Cramer's car the night he tore out of Olivia's driveway. He still wasn't sure if he'd hit it on purpose or if he'd just been too wrecked to drive straight. The sound of metal grinding against metal had brought a sick sense of satisfaction at the time. Now, it only reminded him of what he'd lost—and what he could still lose if he let his temper slip.

The day Olivia said she was suing for full custody—with no visitation—something inside him broke. He didn't think. Just drove. Straight to the house. The front door splintered under his grip. Chris barely had time to turn before he was airborne—slammed against the wall, feet kicking, a foot off the ground. The growl that tore from Axle's throat wasn't human. And through the red haze, he saw it: Chris's eyes wide, pleading. Terrified.

Axle didn't have fangs. He didn't burn in sunlight. He didn't need blood. But that day, his eyes glowed red like the predator he was. It was the moment he stopped pretending his vampire DNA didn't matter. If he lost control, he was dangerous.

Reid had saved him from himself that night. Later, he'd joked Axle needed a vampire intervention. Both Vincent and Gerard—his old bosses from Lifeblood—had shown up. They'd helped him learn to manage his new talents, though he hadn't tested their limits. Reading mortal thoughts came easily. Implanting them took effort. But at least Chris wasn't afraid of him anymore. He didn't remember what had happened that night. Neither did Olivia. And Bonnie? She didn't even remember she'd ever had a dog, let alone another dad.

Even before Axle rewrote Chris's memory, the man hadn't pressed charges for the damage to his car or the front door. Maybe he'd been in shock. Maybe he knew no one would believe him. It didn't matter. That night no longer existed in his mind. And Axle's secret was safe.

Shoving the memories aside, Axle picked up a car magazine and flipped through the pages. It was going to be a long morning.

#

Haley's fingers curled around the cat collar. Her pulse spiked. How had it ended up in the mailbox? She'd called for Bootsie last night, but he hadn't come. She hadn't reported him missing to Axle on Sunday—it had been too late by the time she got home from church and dinner with her father. But she was damn sure calling Axle now.

Bootsie's collar didn't just fall off in the mailbox. He'd never fetched the mail. Someone had put it there. Why? And what else might be inside?

Haley crouched and peered into the mailbox's shadowed interior. A neatly folded sheet of paper rested against the back wall. She reached in, throat tightening, and unfolded it slowly as she stood beside the parking lot.

When the cat's away, the mouse will play. Stop playing and the cat will come home.

A chill swept through her, freezing her blood. Josh. He didn't need to sign it—she knew. His message was unmistakable. He had Bootsie. And he wouldn't give him back unless she agreed to see him again.

She left the mailbox open and bolted across the lawn. The sales circular she'd pulled out with the collar fluttered to the ground. Let the neighbors pick it up—and report her to the apartment manager. Her address was printed on it. They'd know it was hers. She didn't care. She didn't stop running until she reached her front door.

Her hand trembled as she fumbled with the key. She'd never locked the door just to check the mail before Josh. Now, she didn't even take out the trash without locking up.

Inside, she sprinted through the living room toward the kitchen. Her rubber flip-flops gripped the freshly scrubbed vinyl-plank floor. She stumbled, shoulder slamming into the doorjamb. She righted herself, clutching the collar, the note crumpling in her fist as she darted around the center island. Her phone was charging by the toaster. She'd never leave the house without it again.

As she grabbed the phone, a heavy footstep echoed behind her. The front door thumped softly closed. Haley froze. In her rush, she'd left it wide open.

"Haley?"

Axle. Relief surged through her. Her body sagged. The phone slipped from her hand and landed on the counter with a hollow thunk. She squeezed the collar, the note crumpling around the blue nylon.

"Axle!" She rounded the counter and ran toward the living room. Her flip-flop twisted again. She tripped, falling forward just as Axle stepped into the dining room.

His arms caught her. One hand landed squarely on her breast, the other curled around her waist. Their bodies collided, air whooshing from her lungs. He tightened his grip, pulling her flush against his chest, his hand trapped between them. Their hips touched.

He wasn't wearing a suit. His relaxed-fit jeans hid nothing. Haley felt him swell against her—unmistakable. Her gaze dropped to the open V of his black Polo shirt. A wall of muscle peeked through.

Was his chest smooth all the way down? Or roughened with hair?

Her breath hitched. Pulse quickened.

Axle jerked his hand away, shifting it to her shoulder, his face flushing. She inhaled sharply—an erotic gasp she couldn't suppress.

"What's wrong?" His breath warmed her cheek.

Her heart sank. He was just doing his job. Meanwhile, she was fantasizing about seduction.

What a joke. She wasn't Olivia. Axle wasn't interested now any more than he'd been in high school.

"Josh has Bootsie."

"I knew something was off. You left the front door open." His arms dropped. Reality hit her like a cold shower, dousing her foolish lust.

What was wrong with her? One accidental touch and her hormones hijacked her brain. She needed to focus. Bootsie was missing, and Josh had him.

She raised her balled fist, collar and crumpled note clenched tight. "I found this in my mailbox."

Axle stepped back, eyeing the collar like it was a weapon. "It's a collar."

"It's Bootsie's," she snapped. Her emotions tangled—fear, anger, confusion. Axle was making her crazy. One minute touching her, the next recoiling like it was a mistake. Like that kiss in high school.

She needed a reality check. She wasn't a teenager anymore, and Axle wasn't some untouchable football star. They were adults. Their lives had diverged.

She handed him the collar and note. Instead of reading it, he took her arm and guided her to the couch. He sat beside her.

"Breathe," he said.

She did. Air rushed from her lungs. Her shoulders sagged.

Axle nodded, then looked down at the note.

"Josh took my cat," she said, voice trembling. "He left the collar and that note in my mailbox as a warning."

"I'm sure he did," Axle said calmly. "But you don't have proof."

"My cat is missing. What more proof do you need?"

"Bootsie could've lost the collar. A neighbor might've found it and dropped it in your mailbox."

"With a threatening note?" Was he serious?

"The note isn't a direct threat."

Maybe not to him. But she knew Josh. And she wanted her cat back. Bootsie wasn't affectionate, barely acknowledged her—but he'd shown up after her mother died. He knew when she needed comfort. And he gave it, grudgingly.

Tears welled. She blinked them back, furious. She hated crying in front of people. It made her feel weak. And she didn't want Axle to see her that way.

"So you're not going to do anything?" What the hell was she paying him for?

Axle sighed. "I'll call Gordon Sikes and file a report. But unless he sees Bootsie at Josh's house or business, there's not much he can do. Even then, Josh could say he found the cat. There's no way to prove otherwise. We both know Josh did it. But belief isn't proof."

"But the note—"

"Is just a note. If it were an actual threat—or if you'd found the cat's body in the mailbox—that'd be different."

A flash of Bootsie, broken and bloody, stuffed in the mailbox, seared her mind. She cringed. "That's horrible."

"That's reality," Axle said, voice hard. "I thought you could handle the truth."

"I can," she snapped. She didn't want sugarcoating—but she didn't need graphic images haunting her either. "I just don't understand why you're not taking this more seriously."

"Oh, I'm taking it seriously. And once I reach Gordon, you and I need to talk about what I learned from Patterson's employee today."

#

Deputy Gordon Sikes took Haley's statement, then conferred with Axle on the porch before heading out. Haley cast Axle a wounded look and slipped back inside. His heart sank. He could feel her frustration—her disappointment. She'd been upset before, but now she was furious. She didn't think they were taking the threat seriously, and truthfully, there wasn't much Gordon could do. But Axle had options—ones he couldn't share with her.

Reading minds and twisting thoughts were just the beginning of what Dr. Weldon's genetic tampering had unlocked. Axle had sworn never to use those abilities casually. They weren't gifts—they were violations. He'd kept them holstered, reserved for emergencies. But Haley wasn't just anyone. And this wasn't just a threat.

Josh Patterson had taken her cat. The ransom? Drop the case. Comply, and Bootsie would be returned unharmed. But Axle knew—Gordon knew—that giving in wouldn't end it. Patterson wouldn't stop. He'd keep circling, keep pressing, until Haley broke.

Axle had told her twice already: belief wasn't proof. Not to the county. Not until someone got hurt—or a dead cat showed up in her mailbox. And with the county still bleeding from the hurricane's aftermath, nearly two years on, no one was eager to fund a criminal investigation.

He hated that. Hated how truth had to wear bruises before anyone listened. Hated how his silence felt like complicity. The powers he carried—itched. He could end this. He could make Patterson forget her name. But once he crossed that line, there was no going back. And maybe, deep down, he wasn't sure he deserved to.

After Gordon left, Axle stepped inside. Haley sat on the sofa, looking like she might either fall apart or explode. He hated seeing a woman cry, but he'd take tears over fury. Tears he could comfort. Fury might send him ducking for cover.

"You all right?"

She swallowed hard and shook her head. "No. But I will be."

He sat beside her, gently took her hand, and rubbed the underside of her wrist with his thumb. Her pulse jumped.

"I'm sorry about Bootsie," he said.

She shrugged, avoiding his gaze. "He was just a stray."

"Maybe. But you care about him. Patterson's using that to manipulate you. That's got to piss you off as much as it scares you."

Her chin snapped up, and his heart did a nosedive.

"I'm scared. And pissed. And..." She pulled her hand free, twisting her fingers together. "Confused. I've always followed the rules. But now there are no rules, and I don't know what to do."

"There are rules. He's just breaking them. And we haven't caught him yet." He touched her shoulder, then quickly dropped his hand to his lap. Wanting to protect her was natural—she was a client, after all. But the feelings creeping in? Dangerous. Getting too close could cloud his judgment. He needed to see her as just another case.

Objectivity. Yeah, right. As if that were possible with Haley.

He'd wanted to ask her out in high school but hadn't dared. Then Olivia had asked him out, and he'd felt like he'd finally been accepted despite his upbringing. But Olivia had only wanted a thrill—a walk on the wild side.

When he came back, she'd rekindled things only because she needed a backup dad in case Chris didn't make it home from combat. But Haley was different. She always had been.

Trying to reel himself back into professional mode, he pulled a small notebook from his hip pocket. "Okay. Let's go over what I learned about Patterson today. Maybe you can fill in some blanks."

"You went to the body shop?" she asked. He nodded.

"So, which one of Donald's nephews did you talk to?" For a moment, the shadows lifted from her eyes, and she smiled.

"Donald?" he asked, then it clicked. A grin tugged at his mouth. "Oh, right. The nephews." Her wit hadn't dulled. "I spoke to Louie. Then I did some digging on my own."

"Lou," she corrected with a smile. "He and his twin, Hugh, hate it when people add 'ie' to their names. Probably because of all the jokes since Josh hired Dewey."

But the moment she said Patterson's name, the smile vanished. Axle would've given anything for a joke, a story—anything to bring that light back to her eyes. Instead, he flipped open the notebook and got to work.

Chapter 9

Haley pressed her fingers into the knot forming at the base of her skull. The headache was creeping in again, slow and insistent. "So," she said, voice tight, "how did you get Lou to talk?"

Axle leaned back, one arm draped over the sofa's edge. "Wasn't hard. Lou likes to gossip. He actually opened the door by asking if I knew Josh. I told him my ex-wife had known him—which isn't true, but Louie didn't know that. Then he asked if my ex had been friends with Josh's ex who died, and I said I hadn't heard about her death. Lou filled in the rest."

Haley's pulse kicked. "Josh had a wife?" Her voice cracked. "Why didn't he mention it when I told him about Ben? A normal person would have. But Josh never said a word. Not even about a former girlfriend."

Axle shifted, angling his long legs toward her. Their knees bumped. Haley flinched, then masked it with a slow, casual lean away, pretending to adjust her posture.

"They weren't married," Axle said. "She was his girlfriend. But after meeting you, he told Hugh he'd just broken up with her and wanted to know if you were single. Hugh told him you were divorced. Apparently, we went to school with Hugh and Lou, but I don't remember them."

Haley lowered her gaze. "I know they look young, but they were just three years behind us in school. They were freshmen when we were seniors, but then you moved right after we started senior year, so...." She glanced at him. His face was carved from stone—no flicker of recognition, no warmth. Just silence.

Axle never explained why he hadn't called Geoff or even Olivia after leaving Asheville senior year. He'd still been a minor, so the move hadn't been his choice—but he could've at least let someone know. Unless shame had kept him silent. Shame over whatever reasons had forced his mother and Jefferson Cross to vanish from town. There was still so much she didn't know about Axle—back then, and even now.

Haley drew a deep breath and let it out slowly. "So, did Lou tell you anything about her? Or how she died?"

"Her name was Ashland Clark," Axle said. "She and Josh lived together in Boone."

"And?" He was holding something back—something he didn't want her to know.

Axle exhaled heavily and met her eyes. Her pulse quickened, then plummeted when he said, "She died in a car accident the week after he met you."

A chill crept through her veins. Her throat thickened. "Josh is a mechanic. He could've tampered with her car."

"Lou said her brakes failed. She ran off the side of a mountain. Died on impact." His gaze didn't waver, and Haley couldn't look away. His eyes pulled her in like steel to a magnet. Then he added, "His girlfriend in high school died in a car accident too."

Haley's heart lurched into her throat. Her chest tightened, pulse pounding so hard she could hear it. Had she dated a man capable of killing two women? Was she next?

"What happened to the girl in high school?" she asked, swallowing the lump of fear.

"She crashed into a tree the night before senior prom."

Haley's heart slammed against her sternum. "Let me guess," she said, forcing the fear down. "She wasn't going to be his prom date, so he cut her brakes."

"I don't know yet," Axle said. "But I'm going to Butner tomorrow to find out."

Her heart thudded faster. Sinus tachycardia—just a symptom, not a disease. But knowing fear was the cause didn't help. "Is that where the accident happened?"

"No. The accident happened at night on Cash Road just outside the city limits of Butner. Sharon was a junior. She was heading to the Wildlife Club between Creedmoor and Raleigh to help decorate for prom."

"There wasn't anywhere in Butner to hold prom?" Asheville High had used a fancy hotel near Biltmore Estates.

Axle shook his head. "Butner doesn't have a high school. In 2007, they bused the students to Creedmoor, another small town just six or seven miles away."

"So Butner's not much bigger than Whisper Falls. We don't have our own high school either." Which meant Josh had probably gotten away with stalking there too.

"Well, Butner has its own public safety officers. They don't rely solely on the sheriff's department. I think the highway patrol investigated the accident, but I'll stop by Butner Public Safety tomorrow. I've also got an appointment with the school librarian in Creedmoor to look through yearbooks from Josh's time. Then I'm talking to the auto mechanic who gave him his first job."

"His old girlfriend might be gone, but what about her parents? Maybe they suspected something."

Axle took her hand. "Sharon Davis's mother died a year after the accident. Her father's in a nursing home in upstate New York—early-onset Alzheimer's. Aside from an aunt in New York, she has no other family."

Dread settled in Haley's gut like an anchor. "So her father can't tell you anything, even if he wanted to."

Axle's expression softened. "I'm afraid not."

"What about Josh's parents?" Did they know their son was a sociopath?

Axle released her hand and glanced at the notebook on his knee. "His father still lives in Butner, in the same house Josh grew up in. His sister's in California. His mother left when he was a kid."

"And I bet his father thinks Josh is a saint. He's so damn charismatic, the whole town probably loves him."

"You never know. Cliff Patterson's on my list. I just have to be careful how I approach him."

"Maybe going to Butner is pointless," Haley said, meeting Axle's sympathetic gaze. "It could be a coincidence—two girlfriends dying in car accidents. Just because Josh is a mechanic doesn't mean he killed them. Their deaths were ruled accidental. Right?" She didn't want Josh to be a murderer. The implications were too terrifying to contemplate.

"There's no proof either woman was murdered," Axle said. "But I need to be sure. Yearbooks might help me find someone who remembers something. Maybe a teammate. As for Ashland, Gordon got Boone PD to send over the accident report, but I'll still go there after Butner. Maybe one of the investigating officers noticed something off. Had a gut feeling."

Something was off. Two ex-girlfriends dying in car crashes wasn't just bad luck. Maybe if the deaths had happened in the same county, someone would've connected the dots.

"Well, at least your trip to the body shop wasn't a total waste. Did you make an appointment to fix your bumper?"

Axle tilted his head. "No. I didn't go there to fix my bumper. I went for information."

"But they didn't know that. So what excuse did you give for not booking the repair?"

He raised his brows. "I didn't need an excuse."

Haley would've said something. She couldn't imagine walking out without a reason. Even if they offered free estimates, it still took time. She'd have felt rude not at least saying she wanted a second opinion.

Her gaze dropped to the notebook resting on Axle's knees. "You just walked out without saying anything?"

"I thanked him for his time," Axle said, his voice oddly amused.

She looked up and caught him biting the inside of his cheek. His hooded brown eyes sparkled. What was so damn funny?

"Are you laughing at me?" She wasn't sure whether to be embarrassed or offended.

Axle choked on a low chuckle. "You always were too nice for your own good."

Wasn't that what guys said about girls who weren't pretty? *How's she look? Oh, she's real nice.*

Haley narrowed her eyes. "What's that supposed to mean?"

"Nothing," Axle said, grinning. "I just can't believe you still worry about things most people don't even notice."

She lifted her chin. "Maybe if people worried more about others, there wouldn't be so many assholes in the world."

"Oh, and are you calling me an asshole?" His bedroom eyes widened, sparkling as if he thought teasing her was great fun.

Well, maybe it was a little fun. Haley felt the corners of her mouth curve upward. "If the shoe fits."

His eyes gleamed. His voice dropped. "I do have pretty big feet."

Haley glanced down at his slightly scuffed loafers—size twelves, at least. He did have big feet. Did that mean...

Her chin snapped up and her face flamed as heat warmed her skin, and her over-active imagination conjured up thoughts and images she had no business thinking and conjuring.

"I..." Her throat closed. She had no idea what she'd meant to say. Why flirt with Axle? Hadn't high school taught her better?

Axle let go of her hand and looked down at his notebook, as if avoiding her gaze—but not before she saw the heat in his eyes. Was that a blush? Maybe Axle Travers was just a mortal man after all.

"Well, you know what they say about men with big feet," she said with more confidence than she felt.

Axle's head jerked up, and his eyes widened. He looked a bit like a bug just before it hit the windshield. "They wear really big shoes?" he croaked.

Her confidence soared. "No. They've got a lot more to spit out when they stick their foot in their mouth."

Axle nearly choked on his laughter.

Chapter 10

Axle sat in the high school library, thumbing through old yearbooks. Josh had seemed like a typical kid—football player, auto shop regular, member of both the Key Club and the auto club. He wasn't in many photos, but he smiled in every one. His senior year, he'd even been voted "Most Likely to Be Recruited by the CIA." Axle wasn't sure what that meant, but it suggested Josh's classmates thought he was either tough... or secretive.

After thanking the librarian, Axle returned the yearbooks and headed to Josh's family home. Between Creedmoor and Butner was an area the locals called Butmoor. It was mostly fast food restaurants and a small shopping center just off the interstate anchored by the town's only grocery store. Within the city limits of Butner, the town was less congested, which didn't mean much. The entire population of the town was less than nine thousand.

Once the site of Camp Butner, a U.S. Army base during World War II, the town had housed German POWs. Now it was home to the Federal Correctional Complex—current residence of disgraced R&B artist R. Kelly. Before Butner officially became a town in 2007, it was managed by the state, and a large area of what used to be Camp Butner was now a training center for the Army National Guard. Besides the training center and federal prison, there were several state and federal correctional institutions, a state mental hospital, and a facility for those with developmental disabilities.

The former barracks had given way to private homes laid out in a crosshatch grid. Numbered streets ran northwest to southeast; alphabetical ones cut southwest to northeast. Cliff Patterson lived in a modest brick ranch on one of the numbered streets.

Axle pulled into the driveway and noted an old truck parked under the carport. The truck belonged to Josh's father, but would the old man answer questions about his son? Even if he didn't, Axle could slip into his thoughts and extract what he needed. But he hated doing that. A person's mind was sacred. No one should be able to do what Axle—and however many vampires still walked the earth—could do. It was unnatural. Intrusive. But sometimes necessity overruled ethics. The problem was, Axle wasn't sure he was the one who should decide when that line got crossed.

He squelched the thought and climbed out of his vehicle. On the second knock, a weathered man opened the door. He looked closer to seventy than sixty, though Cliff Patterson was only sixty-two.

"Yeah?" the old man said. "How can I help you?"

Axle smiled. Only in a small southern town did people open the door without asking who was on the other side. "Mr. Patterson?"

"Yeah, that's me. Who are you?"

Axle extended his hand. "Mike Dixon," he lied, borrowing the name from one of the yearbooks. Mike had been one of Josh's former teammates. "Josh and I played football together."

Mr. Patterson grunted and released Axle's hand. "No kidding."

"No sir. I was in town and thought I'd stop by, see if Josh still lived around here. Haven't seen him since the ten-year reunion."

"Where'd ya see him at? He didn't go to the reunion. I told him about it, but he wasn't interested—said the old rumors still bothered him. But that's all they were. Rumors."

Damn. Axle had been too specific. Still, the door was open. His pulse quickened, senses sharpening. "What rumors?"

"You remember when his girlfriend died junior year?" Patterson asked. Axle nodded. "Well, some folks around here thought Josh had something to do with it. But he didn't. It was just an accident. She shouldn't've been driving so fast on wet roads."

Maybe. Or maybe Josh had been tailing her, pushing her to drive faster. Did Cliff Patterson truly believe his son was innocent? Or was that just what he needed to believe?

Axle peered into the older man's rheumy eyes without blinking. He had no trouble reading his thoughts. Cliff Patterson believed his son was blameless.

"Well, I'm sure Josh wasn't responsible," Axle said, briefly swaying as he regained his equilibrium. "If you talk to him, let him know I stopped by."

"He's in Asheville now," Patterson said, stepping onto the porch as the storm door eased shut behind him. "Lived in Boone for a while. Was even engaged. But after he opened his own garage in Asheville, he moved closer to work, and Ashland broke it off. I guess Josh got too busy building his business, and she got tired of waiting. It happens. He says his garage is bigger than Mac Preddy's—that's where he worked during school, you know? So I guess it keeps him plenty busy."

"I'm sure," Axle said, descending the porch. Patterson didn't even know Ashland was dead. This visit had run its course. "Maybe I'll stop by his garage next time I'm in Asheville."

The old man followed him down the steps. "Yeah, I been wanting to go see him, but I don't like driving long distances." He tapped the side of his face. "Even with glasses, I don't see well enough to drive at night. And Asheville's a good four-hour drive. So if you do go, maybe I could hitch a ride."

A pang twisted in Axle's chest. Josh was a lousy son. Cliff Patterson's wife had left him, his daughter lived in California, and Josh might as well have been on another planet. The man was so desperate to see his son, he'd hitch a ride with a stranger.

"Well, it was good meeting you," Axle said, unwilling to offer false hope. "If you talk to Josh, let him know Mike stopped by."

"Sure enough, son. Sure enough, and you drive safe, now. Ya hear?"

Stopping at the Patterson house hadn't been a total waste. The old man didn't know the details, but he'd confirmed Axle's suspicions. There had been whispers about Sharon Davis's accident. The question was: idle gossip... or something darker?

Next stop: Preddy's garage.

Preddy Car Care sat tucked off Central Avenue on a quiet side street in Butner. The public entrance was to the left of three garage doors—two open, one closed. Inside the open bays, mechanics worked on cars raised on hydraulic lifts.

At least Josh had been honest about one thing. His garage was bigger. He had four bays.

Axle shook his head and stepped through the plate glass door stenciled with Preddy Car Care. The waiting room was standard fare—car posters, tire displays, four red vinyl chairs, a vending machine, and a small television. Behind a chest-high counter, two men stood at computer terminals. The older one looked up as Axle entered.

"Mac Preddy?" Axle asked, flashing his PI badge—gold with blue lettering and the North Carolina seal.

"Yeah. I'm Mac. What can I do for you?"

"Axle Travers," he said, slipping the badge back into his coat pocket. "I'm investigating Josh Patterson. I've got a few questions."

"A PI, huh?" Mac exchanged a glance with the younger man beside him, then turned back. "He applying for some government job, or is this about the accident?"

"This isn't about a job," Axle said, eyeing the younger man. "Can we talk somewhere private?"

Mac nodded toward a door on the right. "Follow me. I've got an office in the back."

Axle followed him through the work area to a cramped office behind the first bay. Mac gestured to a battered chair, and Axle sat.

"So," Axle began, "what can you tell me about Josh Patterson's past—and why some folks think he should be investigated?"

Mac settled behind his cluttered desk. "Not me. I liked Josh. But there was talk—some people thought he might've had something to do with the Davis girl's accident. With all the rumors back then, I'm not surprised her dad finally hired someone."

Apparently, Mac didn't know much about Sharon Davis or her family. "Henry Davis is in a nursing home in New York. He didn't hire me."

"Sorry to hear that," Mac said. "I just assumed. After the gossip died down, I figured he'd be the only one who might dig it back up. Her mother passed not long after Sharon did."

At least he knew that much. "How well did you know Josh? I understand he worked for you his senior year and the two years he attended the community college."

"I knew him pretty good, I guess. He didn't have a big circle of friends, but he was a charmer. Folks liked him. Then Sharon broke up with him, and he changed. Got angry. Arrogant. Argued with everyone. I couldn't criticize his work without him storming off, and he wasn't always polite to customers either."

So far, Mac's description checked all the stalker boxes—charming, narcissistic, praise-hungry, and rejection-averse. "Why didn't you fire him?

"He was damn good. Body work, mechanics—top notch. As long as I didn't criticize him, we got along fine. If I backed him in private after a customer complained, he'd smooth things over with that charm of his. Still griped about them behind their backs, but he'd be civil to their face. Condescending, maybe. But his work was so good, they didn't push it."

"So, there were no more complaints? Not a single one?" That didn't seem likely.

Mac flipped a pencil through his fingers. "Not from customers. But just before Sharon died, her dad came in furious. Said Josh wouldn't leave her alone—kept calling, showing up at the house. But no one reported him, and Sharon didn't file anything. Then, right before she died, Josh said they'd gotten back together."

Unlikely. More probable, Josh was already planning her death.

"Besides that incident, why do people think Josh was responsible?" Axle leaned in, ready to press if needed—but Mac didn't resist.

"The night Sharon died, a witness driving a few hundred feet behind her saw another car pull out and latch onto her bumper. She hydroplaned right after Gate 2 Road crosses Highway 15 and becomes Cash Road. Back then, that stretch was less developed, with murky runoff pooling along the shoulders. Sharon lost control in a curve, slammed into a tree, and flipped into one of those swampy pockets backing up to Falls Lake.

"The car that had pulled in behind her didn't stop, but the one trailing that car did. He called 911, waited for paramedics, and gave a partial plate and make. It matched Josh's car. So, yeah—people started asking if he'd run her off the road."

Axle frowned. "Did the cops question him or charge him with anything?"

Unless Josh physically struck her vehicle, it wasn't a hit-and-run. Even if witnesses saw him tailgating and the officer concluded that following too closely caused Sharon Davis's crash, it would've been a misdemeanor at most. And in North Carolina, a driver wasn't legally required to stop at an accident they merely witnessed—even if it was the decent thing to do.

Mac nodded. "They questioned him. Josh said he'd just pulled out behind the other car and didn't know who was driving."

"What was his excuse for not stopping when she crashed?" Legally, he didn't have to. But the cops would've pressed him on why he didn't.

"Said it was raining so hard he didn't see her go off the road. Claimed he had no idea anyone had crashed. That satisfied the cops. And when he found out it was Sharon, he was devastated. So, I doubted the rumors. But since you're here, maybe there's more to it."

"He's stalking my client," Axle said. "I'm trying to establish a pattern."

Mac rubbed his stubbled chin. "Guess that's why he never comes home to see his old man. Maybe he didn't kill her on purpose, but it sounds like he feels guilty. Never mentioned her name again after the funeral."

Sociopaths didn't feel guilt. Sharon's death had likely empowered him—like a serial killer's first rush. Control was his emotional stabilizer. When Sharon broke up with him, he retaliated. Her death gave him satisfaction, not remorse.

"Did he date anyone else around here after Sharon?" Axle asked. If there was another ex, he needed to find her. Sharon was likely the first, but not the last. He'd stalked Ashland Clark. He was stalking Haley. So who came in between?

"If he did, he didn't mention her to me," Mac said. "After Sharon died, he buried himself in school and work. There was talk about him harassing a girl at the college, but he never brought it up. I figured he was still mourning Sharon."

Axle didn't buy that for a second. Sharon was Josh's first victim. Ashland wasn't the second. There had to be someone in between. Maybe more than one.

#

Axle's visit to Butner Public Safety had yielded less than he'd hoped. Though the highway patrol and Granville County Sheriff's Office had responded to the crash, it was Butner's officers and firetrucks that had arrived first. Josh had been questioned by all three agencies, but nothing stuck.

The official report blamed excessive speed and poor weather for Sharon Davis's death.

Her father had pleaded with Butner to investigate, but the accident had occurred just outside their jurisdiction. All they could do was review the report and talk it through with him.

"That girl had to have been going over sixty," said Officer Grant of Butner

Public Safety. "Don't know if you've ever driven that stretch, but Cash Road and Gate 2 Road are narrow and winding with few places to pass. Speed limit's forty-five. If it hadn't been for that one witness, we wouldn't have known to question Josh. And since the guy only saw taillights before Sharon hydroplaned, he couldn't say for sure whether it was Josh's car ahead of him or Sharon's."

"Do you think Josh was following her?" Axle asked. No doubt, the girl had been as terrified as Haley.

The thought of Haley dying in a similar crash chilled his blood. Mountain roads were far more treacherous than anything in Granville County. Josh could ride her bumper, nudge her off the side of a mountain, and there'd be no way to prove he was responsible—just like with Sharon.

"I know that boy was tailing her," Grant said. "My son graduated with Josh—he told me Josh harassed a girl at Vance Granville Community College after Sharon died. Her name was Kate Palmer. She moved to Arizona years ago, but she never filed a report. Neither did Sharon. So, after she died, we had nothing to stand on. We pushed for an investigation, but the car was totaled. Troopers blamed excessive speed. No foreign paint. No signs of forced contact. Still, I'd stake my pension she was running from him. He wanted her to lose control. He wanted that crash. And now he walks free—no charges, no trial. The bastard got away with murder, and the law can't touch him."

Chapter 11

Haley's heart leapt into her throat when she opened the door to Deputy Sikes. "Any updates on Bootsie? Did you find him?"

Gordon sighed and patted Haley's shoulder. "I'm sorry. He wasn't at Josh's garage, and when I asked, Josh said he hadn't seen the cat since the two of you broke up."

"We didn't break up. It was three dates." What part of three dates didn't people understand? Anger surged through her. Josh had told everyone they were dating. Lied about that. Lied about her cat. He was such a consummate liar he could convince someone there were thirty days in February. "I know he took him. Did you search his house? Ask Hugh, Lou, or Dewy if they've seen Bootsie?"

"Haley, honey, I can't search his house without a warrant, and no judge is going to sign one over a missing cat. Bootsie's disappearance isn't a criminal case." He held up a hand to forestall any protest. "And before you ask again, the 'nephews' haven't seen Bootsie either. I asked."

Her heart beat against her sternum. Her face burned. Josh could stalk her, steal or kill her cat, and no one could or would do a damn thing about it.

"Josh took him," she snapped. "And if you can't find him, I will. I'll go to his house and get him myself."

"And risk voiding your restraining order? I don't think so." Gordon gave her a sympathetic smile and patted her shoulder again. "Let Axle handle it. He still has to follow the law, but he can get away with things I can't. He can search the outside of Josh's house without a warrant. Might even spot Bootsie through a window. Then I could probably get a warrant to go in and retrieve him."

"Then why can't you just walk around the house yourself? Axle's in Butner, and I don't know when he'll be back."

"I'm an officer of the law. I need a warrant or probable cause to search private property, and your suspicions aren't enough. For all I know, the cat just wandered off."

"He didn't just wander off," she snapped again. "And he didn't drop his collar off in my mailbox with a typed note either."

Gordon sighed, frustration flickering across his face. Was it the situation—or her?

She took a breath, forcing calm. It wasn't Gordon's fault. At least he'd gone to Josh's garage and asked. "What did Josh say when you asked if he'd taken the cat?"

"Not much," Gordon said, frowning. "He didn't even ask how long Bootsie's been missing. Just denied having him. Said he hadn't seen him since...well, since the last time you dated."

"Thanks for trying," she said, her voice softening. "And I'm sorry I snapped. I know you're doing what you can."

"No need to apologize. I know you're scared and frustrated. And I know he's stalking you. Axle gave me the GPS tracker he found on your car."

So Axle hadn't told Gordon about the second tracker—on her neighbor's car. She wasn't about to mention it either. "And?"

Gordon shrugged. "We can't prove Josh put it there. Only prints on the device were Axle's. It was bought online and shipped to a PO Box in Boone. Whoever's paying the monthly fee is using a prepaid credit card. No way to trace it."

She hadn't expected anything different. "Thanks anyway."

"Is there anything I can do to make you feel safer? Besides arresting Josh?" he added with a smile.

Haley smiled back, reminding herself that Gordon was just following the law and Josh wasn't. "Maybe check my windows and doors. Make sure he can't get in without breaking glass."

"Sure thing." He handed her a business card. "My personal cell's on the back. If you feel threatened, call 911—then call me. Before you call Axle. I can arrest people. He can't."

Gordon left fifteen minutes later, having checked every window and door. Short of breaking glass or prying something open with a crowbar, Josh wasn't getting in. At a loss for what else to do, Haley picked up the remote and put on a movie she'd seen half a dozen times. Axle called about midway through.

"How are you holding up?" he asked when she answered.

"Okay, I guess. Gordon stopped by. Naturally, Josh denied taking Bootsie. He also told me about the GPS tracker you turned in. I didn't correct his assumption that there was only one."

Axle chuckled, and the sound warmed her. "Yeah, I kind of broke the law by placing it on your neighbor's car without permission. But even if I'm caught, it's a misdemeanor. I'd probably get off with a warning."

"They couldn't trace it to you anyway. They can't even trace it back to Josh."

"I'm not surprised. Josh has trackers on his loaner cars and tow truck, but they're all accounted for. I checked with the company. So I figured he used another company and a fake name."

"And had them shipped to a PO Box in Boone," she added. She was so tired of Josh outsmarting everyone.

"Don't lose faith in me yet. We'll get Josh. I promise." His voice rang with conviction, easing some of her fear.

"I know you will," she said with a sigh. "You're a man of your word."

"I don't know about that," he said, less certain.

"I do." She smiled into the phone, picturing him on the other end. "Are you on your way back to Asheville?"

"Leaving shortly," he said. "It'll be too late to stop by tonight, but I'll come by in the morning before heading to the office."

#

Haley clicked off the television, the movie's final scene still flickering in her mind. She checked the locks—twice—then headed toward the bathroom, ready to wash off the day. The doorbell rang. Her stomach dropped.

It wasn't Axle. He was probably only halfway to Charlotte. Her phone was already in her hand—she didn't go anywhere without it anymore. Not even to the bathroom.

She tightened her grip and crept back to the living room, heart thudding. Through the peephole, a familiar face filled the frame. Bootsie.

"That's my cat," she said through the door, praying one of her neighbors had found him. *Please don't let it be Josh.*

"He misses you. So do I." Josh's voice slithered through the door, cold and intimate. Haley's breath caught. He'd taken Bootsie—and now had the gall to bring him back like he was doing her a favor.

"You took him," she snapped.

"I found him," he said smoothly. "Gordon told me he was missing, so I went looking. Just open the door so I can return him properly. I promise not to overstay my welcome."

"I don't believe you. You took him. I know it, and you know it, and you know I know it."

"Let's not do this through the door," he coaxed. "Let me in. Please."

His voice was soft. Reasonable. Manipulative. She wasn't buying it. "Put him down and walk away."

"But he might wander off again. Let me place him in your hands."

"No. Put him down. He can come in through the doggy door." She wasn't fool enough to open the door to Josh. If she did, he'd never leave her alone.

"Okay," he said, sounding wounded. "You know I'd do anything you ask."

"Except leave me the hell alone."

"You know I can't do that," he said—and this time, it wasn't sweet. It was a threat. "You're mine, Haley. Which makes Bootsie mine. But I'll release him. Just remember—I'll never release you. We belong together. I'm proving it by honoring your wishes."

"Get off my porch. Now."

"I love you, Haley." His voice was tender. And terrifying.

"I'm calling the cops." She'd already dialed Gordon. He picked up on the second ring. "He's here," she said. "Josh is at my door. He wants in."

"Call 911. I'm on my way."

By the time Gordon arrived, a patrol unit was already sweeping the perimeter. Josh was gone. Bootsie had slipped in through the doggy door, tail twitching. Haley scooped him up, clutching him until he squirmed. When she let go, he rubbed against Gordon's leg and padded toward his food bowl.

"He looks healthy and well-fed," Gordon said. "At least Josh didn't hurt him."

"Can you prove stalking now?" Haley's voice was sharp. "He took my cat. He came to my house. He jiggled the doorknob." Had he? She couldn't remember. But he'd demanded entrance. He'd sounded dangerous.

Gordon sighed. "I can arrest him for violating the restraining order. But he'll argue he had a legal reason to be here. He'll probably plead out."

"How?" Her voice rose. "He created the reason. He stole my cat. Isn't that enough?"

Her fury surged, hot and wild. "What does Josh have to do to prove he's dangerous? Gut Bootsie? Slit my throat?" The rage curdled into fear.

Gordon wrapped an arm around her and pulled her to his side. It was a bit unprofessional, but she'd known Gordon for years. "Unfortunately, it's a class A1 misdemeanor. No other crime committed. No prior conviction."

Haley stepped away. "But he stole Bootsie to come here. That's a crime."

"A crime no one can prove," Gordon said.

Haley's throat tightened. "But he is going to jail tonight. Isn't he?"

Gordon nodded. "Deputy Kanati's headed to Josh's place now. He'll arrest him. Tomorrow, I want you to go to the magistrate's office."

"Why?" She just wanted to wrap up in a blanket and wait for Axle.

"To file a 50B order. That will protect Bootsie. Tell the magistrate Josh kept you from your cat. That'll add Bootsie to the restraining order."

"Can't we do it tonight?" She didn't want to leave the house, but she didn't want Josh to get away with taking her cat either.

"We can. I'll take you myself." He sighed. "Now block that doggy door. Does Bootsie have a litter box?"

"He does," she said, managing a smile. "He just never uses it."

"Make him. At least until this mess is over."

Haley nodded and went to the kitchen. She'd never needed to close the doggy door before. The sliding panel was in the pantry. She pulled it out and sealed the flap. Bootsie looked up from his food bowl and gave her the stink eye.

"It's only temporary," she said, as if the cat could understand. He turned up his nose and gave her his back before sauntering away. She'd probably come home to shredded pillows.

Shaking off her fear, she went back to the living room. Gordon was waiting for her at the front door. "Ready?"

"As ready as I'll ever be," she said. "I'll call Axle on the way."

"Good. Maybe he'll be back by the time we get the magistrate out of bed and get those papers signed."

#

Axle pulled up to Haley's apartment sometime after midnight. Gordon sat in his patrol car outside her unit, window down, eyes sweeping the quiet street. Axle approached and leaned in.

"Thanks for watching her," he said.

"Serve and protect," Gordon replied with a tired smile. "Part of the job."

"This goes beyond that. Josh is locked up for the night—you didn't have to sit here."

"It felt right," Gordon said. "Besides, I like Haley. Maybe not as much as you do, but she's a friend."

"Haley's a client," Axle lied, too fast.

Gordon chuckled. "Sure she is. Just keep her safe. Noya says Josh used his phone call to contact an attorney."

"Noya Kanati?" Axle asked, recalling the only Native American on their high school football team.

"Yeah. He's been a deputy almost as long as I have. He's keeping eyes on Josh in lockup."

"So Haley's safe—for now." Axle exhaled. First 48 hours, only a judge could set release conditions. If not, the magistrate could. Bond was usually five grand, but Josh only needed five hundred. "Josh is tight with the magistrate," he muttered. "If the judge doesn't intervene, he could walk on his own recognizance."

"And if that happens," Gordon said, "there's nothing stopping him from showing up again."

Axle's jaw tightened. The law was a sieve—too many holes, too many ways for men like Josh to slip through. He'd seen it before. Sharon Davis. Ashland Clark. Both gone. Both dismissed as accidents. And Josh had walked away clean.

Not this time.

"Josh's attorney is already pushing for a bail hearing," Gordon continued. "Since he signed the restraining order voluntarily, the judge validated it without a finding of fact. No judgment entered. That puts the burden of proof on Haley."

Axle snorted. "Innocent until proven guilty—and he's made damn sure she doesn't have proof. Until now. Witnesses saw him outside her door with Bootsie."

"Doesn't mean much," Gordon said. "He claims the cat ran in front of his car. Says he recognized it, scooped it up, and knocked just to let Haley know he was leaving it in her yard. Claims it went in through the doggy door."

Axle clenched his teeth. "And she can't prove otherwise."

Even if it went to trial, Josh wasn't likely to be convicted. First offense. Signed the order. Probation was likely. And Haley—Haley might be in more danger after sentencing than she was now.

Axle's thoughts spun. If Josh had counsel, the hearing could be Friday. The following Monday was a holiday, so it might get moved up to Thursday, or pushed past the holiday weekend to next Tuesday. Either way, the judge would review his criminal history—if there was one. But Josh had kept his record clean.

The Butner officer suspected him in Sharon Davis's death. No charges. Same with Ashland Clark's accident in Boone. Axle had tried to connect the dots before. No one wanted to see the pattern.

But he saw it. And if the legal route failed, he'd take the vampire route—no blood, just truth. The kind that left scars.

He'd sworn never to take that path again. Promised himself he'd never use it for revenge. But this wasn't revenge. This was protection. This was survival.

"Thanks for everything," Axle said, shaking Gordon's hand. "I'm going to check on Haley, then head home. Tomorrow, I'm driving to Boone. If I can establish a pattern, maybe the judge will hold Josh until trial."

"Good luck," Gordon said. "Josh has powerful friends in this town. I doubt he gets more than a slap on the wrist."

Axle smiled—sharp, cold. "Then let's see whose friends are more powerful."

Chapter 12

Haley watched Axle through the living room window, his silhouette tense as he spoke with Gordon. When he stepped onto her porch, she opened the door before he could knock.

"Axle," she breathed.

He folded her into his arms before she could take another breath. "You're safe. And Bootsie's safe." His embrace tightened briefly, then released.

Haley stepped back, breath hitching. Her fingers twisted together. Now what? Invite him in? Beg him to stay? When he crossed the threshold, she shut the door behind him. He was inside—but for how long? The thought of being alone clawed at her.

"Are you okay?" he asked, keeping his distance.

She nodded, then admitted, "Not really."

"Come on." He touched her shoulder but quickly dropped his hand. "Let's sit in the living room so we can go over everything I learned in Butner."

She doubted it was anything useful. Josh was too careful, and this wasn't his first rodeo. He'd stalked at least two other women before her and hadn't gotten caught. Now, he was better at it. Smarter. Deadlier.

In the living room, Axle took the sofa. Haley chose the swivel recliner, angling herself toward him but keeping space between them. Axle sat close enough to touch her. But he didn't.

Relief and disappointment tangled in her chest. If he touched her, she might unravel. But the distance felt like rejection. "So, did you learn anything useful?"

Axle exhaled. "Yes and no. He was definitely stalking Sharon Davis. But he didn't run her off the road. He matched her speed until she panicked, accelerated, and lost control. She died instantly."

"And the cops can't charge him because he didn't technically do anything illegal, and even if he did, they can't prove it." Her hopes dashed, she sagged against the back of the chair.

"Pretty much." Axle leaned forward but still didn't touch her. "I'm going to Boone tomorrow. Even if the police can't prove Josh was responsible, maybe I can establish a pattern that will satisfy the judge enough to hold him until his court date."

"And if you can't?" The resignation settled deep. Until Josh moved on—or she died—she'd have to live with fear.

It wasn't a fun companion.

"Let me worry about that. For now, get ready for bed. I'll stay until you're asleep and check in again tomorrow."

"Promise?" She stood, teetering on the edge of vulnerability. She wanted to ask him to stay the night—on the sofa, maybe—but if he had other ideas, she wouldn't stop him.

Axle smiled, eyes darkening with heat. "If I thought it was a good idea, I'd stay. But..."

"But?" she whispered.

He rose and pulled her into his arms. His chest pressed against hers, solid and warm. His arms wrapped around her, and then his mouth found hers. The brush of his goatee tickled. His tongue teased the seam of her lips, and she opened—her mouth, her body, her heart.

Kissing Axle was like coming home. All those pent up teenage fantasies raced through her mind, filling her heart and fueling her fantasies. After that first kiss back in high school, she'd craved his taste and the feel of his body pressed against her. Perhaps that's why her marriage had failed. Ben wasn't Axle.

His kiss deepened. His hands threaded through her hair, pulling her closer. Her body responded, eager and unguarded. Their hips moved in rhythm, her muscles coiling with need. And then—he stopped. His arms dropped and he stepped back.

Catch and release–like a fish–and damn it, she was already caught.

Her heart sank. Vision blurred. She lashed out. "Is that how you comfort all your clients, or just the women?"

He ran a hand over his head, gaze lowered. "I'm sorry. That was unprofessional. I shouldn't have kissed you."

"So it was a mistake." Her voice cracked. She clenched her jaw, trying to mask the hurt.

"Yes–no. Haley," he took a deep breath and dropped his arms to his sides. His palms turned outward. "Yes it was a mistake to kiss a client. But no, Haley, I don't regret kissing you. Not back then and not tonight."

A gasp escaped her clamped jaw. "What?" She was breathless and dizzy. Her head spun. When Axle touched her cheek, she nearly choked. "You remember kissing me?"

"I remember more than kissing you." His eyes burned. "I remember touching you. Wanting more. But I was drunk, and you weren't ready. And now—because of Josh—you're vulnerable. I won't take advantage."

"Even if I want you to?" she whispered.

He smiled, soft and devastating. "Even then. But when the time is right..." His gaze lingered, hot and full of promise. She trembled.

"I never slept with Josh," she blurted. "We fooled around, but I didn't love him. It wouldn't be rebound sex."

Oh God. Had she really just said that? She was practically begging. She barely knew Axle anymore. It had been fifteen years.

"I know," he said, brushing his fingers down her cheek. "But I think you'd regret it in the morning. If and when we sleep together, it should be more than just sex."

"I'm the girl," she said with a shaky smile. "Isn't that supposed to be my line?"

He chuckled, low and warm. "No. That's just how it should be. And if the time comes, that's how it'll be with you."

If. When. Her heart twisted. Timing was everything, and when it came to the two of them, it was never the right time.

She snorted, trying to mask the ache. "As if saying that makes you any less appealing."

Axle leaned in and kissed her forehead. "I'll make sure you're tucked in safe before I go."

Haley's thoughts took a nose dive straight into the gutter. She had no doubt her idea of getting tucked in was a lot more graphic than his.

#

Axle watched Haley disappear down the hall, her silhouette swallowed by shadows. He was still hard as a damn post, but he wasn't going to treat her like a conquest. She wasn't a one-night fix. She was Haley—bright, intuitive, and far too close to the fault lines he'd spent years burying.

He hadn't lied when he said he wanted more than sex. Not to her. But to himself? That lie had teeth.

After Olivia, he'd sworn off emotional entanglements. Love was a trap. Vulnerability, a loaded gun. Haley might've played it cool, but he knew her tells. She didn't sleep with men she didn't trust. That's why she hadn't slept with Josh. He'd seen it in her eyes—a flicker of something tender when she denied it. She'd wanted to believe in Josh, just like she'd wanted to believe in Ben. And both had let her down.

Haley valued trust like oxygen. And Axle? He was drowning in secrets.

If he gave in—if he touched her the way he wanted—she'd expect more. She'd expect truth. And he couldn't give it. Not without unraveling everything. Some secrets weren't just dangerous. They were corrosive. The kind that didn't just destroy relationships—they rewrote people from the inside out.

If Haley ever uncovered what he was hiding, she wouldn't just lose faith in him. She'd lose faith in herself. And that was unforgivable.

"I'm done with my shower," Haley said, her voice slicing through the silence.

He flinched. Since Dr. Weldon had altered his DNA, no one had been able to sneak up on him. No one but her. She was a blind spot he couldn't afford.

"I see," he said, turning from the window. His voice snagged on the edge of restraint.

Her damp hair glowed auburn in the low light, curling around her face like smoke. She wore plaid shorts and a long-sleeved tee, nipples taut against the fabric. Nothing seductive about the outfit—and yet she looked more dangerous than Olivia ever had in lace.

His breath hitched. He was already halfway gone.

"Were you heading to bed?" he asked, voice low. "Or staying up?"

Her mouth curved, slow and deliberate. "It's two a.m. I'm definitely going to bed. But I don't plan to sleep alone."

His pulse spiked. If she made even a half-hearted move, he'd cave. He'd cave hard. Like the roof of that mountain shack he'd lived in with his mom and Jefferson—buckling under snow, splintering under the weight. That memory—cold, brittle, unforgiving—helped. Barely.

He forced a smirk. "Oh?"

She grinned. "I'm letting Bootsie sleep with me tonight. He's already kneading my pillow. I might have to sleep on the other side unless I want him making biscuits in my hair."

"Making biscuits?" he croaked, the phrase dragging his mind somewhere it shouldn't go.

She giggled. "He curls up at the top of my head and digs in like he's kneading dough. It's cute until the claws come out. Then it's war. Easier to let him have his side."

"Well, as long as you're not alone," he said, smiling—relieved, and aching. He stepped closer, brushed a kiss against her cheek. Her skin was warm, damp from the shower. Real.

"Good night, Haley. Lock the door behind me. Keep your phone close. I'll swing by on my way to Boone."

"Goodnight," she whispered, walking him to the door. "Drive safe."

"Stay safe," he echoed, and against every warning bell in his head, he leaned in and kissed her lips—soft, warm, dangerous. A promise he couldn't keep.

Then he stepped outside before he did something irreversible.

#

Moving with the speed and stealth of a ninja—or more accurately, a vampire—Axle slipped unseen into the Buncombe County Detention Center.

Contrary to myth, vampires had reflections and could be photographed—unless they chose otherwise. They could bend mortal perception, vanish from mirrors, blur in photos, or move too fast for cameras to catch. Axle wasn't a vampire, exactly, but his altered DNA granted him similar advantages, so slipping past the intake desk was effortless.

Inside the holding area, metal doors with shatterproof windows lined both sides of the off-white corridor. Guards made their rounds every fifteen minutes, scanning RFID boxes beside each cell to log time and location. Axle had a narrow window before the guards made their next rounds.

He stopped in a blind spot, just outside camera range, and closed his eyes. A rush of thoughts and emotions flooded his mind—rage, fear, despair—then a void. Josh's mind was disturbingly hollow. A flicker of frustration, but no empathy. No remorse. Nothing had ever kept Josh from sleeping soundly—until now.

The hallway cameras focused on cell doors, not interiors. Axle mentally unlocked Josh's and slipped through. If the camera caught anything, it would be a blur—gone before it registered.

Inside, Axle paused to steady himself. Moving at vampire speed and manipulating matter could be as disorienting as invading someone's thoughts. The momentary bout of vertigo left him momentarily exposed. When the dizziness passed, he glanced around the nine by nine, dimly lit cell. Josh lay sprawled on his stomach, drifting in the twilight of sleep.

Axle smiled. This part, he would enjoy. "Wake up, asshole."

Josh groaned, rolled onto his back, and flung an arm over his eyes. "Just do your damn rounds, Henry. Let me sleep."

"It's not Henry."

That got his attention. Josh bolted upright, eyes narrowing. "Who the hell are you?"

Axle considered saying, "Your worst nightmare," but it was too damn cheesy. "I'm here to give you fair warning. Leave Haley alone."

Josh stood, scoffing. "I don't know who you are or how you got in here, but Haley's mine."

"No," Axle said, voice low and sharp. "She's not. And if you go near her again, I'll make sure you understand that—permanently."

Josh stepped closer, posture aggressive. "So it's like that." He smirked, but his eyes stayed cold. "Haley's mine. I keep what's mine. You understand?"

Axle clenched his jaw. He wanted to wipe that smug look off Josh's face, wanted to leave him broken and bleeding—but he couldn't leave a mark. Not one that might validate Josh's story if he remembered this visit.

"You've tormented her long enough. I'll see you convicted of felony stalking. And when you get out, if you so much as slow down near her house, I'll find you. And I'll end you."

Josh raised his brows. "You think I'm scared of you?" He snorted. "I don't let emotions rule me—not guilt, not fear. Keep that in mind next time you try to threaten me."

Axle didn't answer. He slipped into Josh's mind, navigating the barren terrain of emotionless memories. Without emotions to anchor the memories, he couldn't erase Haley from his thoughts, but he could make her memory hurt. From now on, every time Josh thought of her, his head would throb. It wouldn't last forever—but maybe it would buy Haley time.

But as he planted the psychic trigger, something twisted in Axle's gut. A flicker of doubt. Was this justice—or vengeance? Was he protecting Haley, or indulging the darker parts of himself?

Josh's mind recoiled, twitching under the pressure. Axle felt the resistance, the strain, the pain—and for a moment, he hesitated. He could push harder. Make it permanent. Make it unbearable.

He didn't. Instead, he pulled back, just enough to leave a scar without destroying the landscape—enough to cause pain whenever Josh thought of Haley. Enough to ensure she was no longer his to torment.

Without another word, Axle commanded him to forget—and sleep.

Then he vanished, just as silently as he'd arrived.

Chapter 13

Ashland Clark's car had gone off the road in a remote stretch of the Blue Ridge Parkway—a place infamous for switchback curves, sparse guardrails, falling rocks, and wandering wildlife.

The wide-angle photo of the crash scene looked almost cinematic. The close-ups were brutal: her red car wrapped around a pine at the bottom of a steep ravine, a debris trail marking its descent, a clear shot of the license plate. But no skid marks.

Axle was studying the scene documentation—diagrams, notes, photographs—when the highway patrol officer slid the official report across the counter.

"Her vehicle veered off the road about a hundred feet past the last guardrail," the officer said. "Just beyond a curve shaped like a racetrack bank. No skid marks. No signs of braking. The investigating officer listed speed and wet roads as contributing factors."

"No one checked the brake lines?" Axle asked, scanning the report.

"Why would they?" The officer shrugged. "No foul play suspected. Her mother said Ashland drove the Parkway to clear her head. She wasn't suicidal. It looked like an accident."

"Or a setup," Axle muttered. "A cut brake line. A chase. Who takes a scenic drive in the rain to clear their head?"

"Maybe it wasn't raining when she left. Or maybe she had a blowout. Her family didn't question it—they were grieving. And crashes on that stretch aren't rare. Whatever happened, the result was the same: a woman died, and her car was totaled. A full analysis would've taken months, and no one asked for one. Her family took the insurance payout, and the car went to the junkyard. It's been crushed. Whatever answers it held are gone."

On the drive back to Asheville, Axle veered off course, detouring to the mile marker listed in the report. The speed limit was 45 but dropped to 25 where the road twisted like a serpent—tight corners, off-camber turns, blind switchbacks daring you to misjudge them. The landscape was even more breathtaking than the photographs had captured—lush, cinematic, and treacherous. One wrong move and you weren't just off the road—you were airborne. Josh hadn't wandered into Ashland's path. He'd hunted her—whether by instinct or GPS, it didn't matter. The result was the same.

Axle parked at a nearby overlook and walked the shoulder until he reached the crash site. The underbrush hadn't fully reclaimed the ravine, leaving a jagged scar down the slope. He followed it to the base of a towering pine. Its bark still bore the wounds of impact. No one could have survived that crash. No one human, anyway. And Ashland had been painfully, tragically human.

He couldn't prove it, but he knew: Josh had cut her brakes and then chased her up the mountain. There was nothing scenic about her final drive. She'd been speeding to escape him—and in doing so, sealed her fate.

Axle closed his eyes and pressed a hand to the tree. A jolt of energy zinged up his arm—like the tree was vibrating, remembering. The mountain whispered.

Images flooded his mind. The impact. Ashland's terror. Rain slicking the road. Josh standing at the curve's edge, watching. Satisfied.

The tree pulsed beneath his palm, ancient and aware. It had witnessed the moment. Absorbed the violence. And now, it shared its memory.

Axle felt Josh's vindication. His satisfaction. No sorrow. No remorse.

Josh Patterson wasn't a vampire, but he was no better than the Ekimmu—damned souls who fed on the fringes of society, draining life from the living. Unlike the Ekimmu, Josh had no fangs. He was just a mortal predator who walked in daylight, stalking his prey in plain sight.

Axle's eyes snapped open. His heart clenched. Josh was a killer. He'd killed at least twice. And Haley was next.

Reaching out with his mind, Axle tapped into the power of remote viewing. Haley was in Whisper Falls. Home. Safe. But anxious. Afraid. Worried about him.

He had to get to her. He had to keep her safe.

The descent down the mountain was long. Axle had arrived in Boone mid-afternoon. Now it was nearly seven. He connected his phone to the car's Bluetooth and called Haley.

"Are you back yet? Did you find out anything useful?" Her voice was hopeful. Too hopeful.

"Not really," he lied. Not a full lie. He'd found plenty. Just nothing he could explain without revealing how he knew. "But I'm leaving Boone now."

"And?" she asked, breath hitching.

"And nothing we didn't already suspect. Ashland's car went off a mountain road. Officially, it's an accident. But you and I both know Josh was involved. We just can't prove it."

"Or anything else," she whispered, voice trembling.

Axle's chest tightened. He'd let her down. "I'll be back in Asheville tonight," he said. "If it's not too late, I'll stop by."

He would stop by. Even if she was asleep. He'd sit outside her apartment all night if he had to. Josh wasn't going to get to her—not like he had Sharon. Not like he had Ashland.

"Thank you," she said.

"For what?" He smiled as the sun dipped behind the mountains. Orange, pink, and mauve streaked the sky—colors that reminded him of Haley's hair. Bright. Beautiful. Unforgettable.

"For just being you," she said, barely above a whisper.

Damn. If he wasn't careful, he'd fall for her all over again. And just like before, he couldn't afford to. Not with his secrets. Not with a predator like Josh closing in.

#

Haley checked all the locks and made sure Bootsie hadn't found a way to unlock the doggy door. The cat probably hated her. She hadn't let him out since Josh returned him, and Bootsie was used to going outside whenever he wanted. He kind of owned her rather than the other way around, but she couldn't risk Josh hurting him to get to her.

"Bootsie," she called as she poured fresh water in his bowl and set it down by the half-eaten dry cat food. As a treat, she opened a can of the stinking wet stuff and poured it onto a plate.

"Here kitty, kitty." She placed the plate on the floor, and Bootsie jumped down from the top of the refrigerator, where he'd been perched. Haley jumped and let out a startled yelp.

"You scared the crap out of me," she said when her heart stopped pounding.

Bootsie meowed and wound around her leg a few times. Then he sniffed the wet cat food and sat back on his haunches as if waiting for the maître d' to place a napkin on his lap. Haley shook her head and moved the plate away from the wall. Bootsie cocked his head as if he were reprimanding her and then turned to eat. Unlike the dog she'd had as a kid, he didn't devour his food. He ate delicately, savoring each bite. So why was her kitty so fat?

"Pig," she said with a smile as she turned out the kitchen light. Before she reached the bedroom, the doorbell chimed. Her heart lodged in her throat and her steps slowed as she approached the living room. The moment she looked through the peephole, her heart soared.

"Axle," she whispered as she unlocked the door and opened it wide.

His hot eyes raked over her, and her face flushed with heat. She was wearing a pair of shorts and a t-shirt without a bra. The moment their gazes met, her nipples hardened and pushed against the thin fabric as if begging for his touch.

"Did I wake you?" he asked, his voice low and rough. A shiver passed through her.

"No," she said, her voice slightly hoarse. "I just fed Bootsie and was going to read a bit. Come on in."

"You sure?" he said as he crossed the threshold and closed the door, locking it behind him. She swallowed hard and nodded. Then she turned and without another word, he followed her into the living room.

She sat on the sofa and he sat beside her, making no effort to put any distance between them. Her pulse jumped, and her throat tightened. He sat close as if preparing to comfort her. "You didn't find out anything good. Did you?" she asked.

He met her gaze and shook his head. "Sorry. No. Like I said on the phone, you and I know what happened, and the cops probably suspect him of at least contributing to the accident, but there's nothing anyone can prove. Whether he intentionally killed those two women or simply caused their accidents, he's still responsible, and it doesn't seem to have fazed him at all."

"So, he'll get away with it."

Axle sighed. His arm rested on the back of the sofa and his fingers inched closer to her shoulders as if he were tempted to touch her. From the corner of her eye, Haley saw him curl his fingers into a fist, avoiding contact.

Disappointment warred with relief. If he had touched her, she'd probably do something stupid, like throw herself into his arms and beg for sexual release. Instead, she bit her lip and dropped her gaze.

"I don't think he meant to kill Sharon Davis," Axle said, "I think he was just following her, trying to scare her into taking him back. Then when he saw her wreck and learned she died, he felt vindicated. He saw it as her fault, not his, and it empowered him, but Ashland was no accident, I just can't prove it."

"And now that he's gotten away with it twice, there's nothing stopping him from coming after me," she said, and her breathing hitched.

"He'll have to get through me first," Axle said, pulling her into his arms, and she melted against him.

His caress was soothing, calming. And then it wasn't. It quickly ignited a fire in her belly that had her reaching for him. Without hesitation, he lowered his lips to hers. His hands moved over her body, one dropping to her hip, the other tangling in her hair, holding her steady as the kiss became wilder–unrestrained. Her pulse raced as he dove into the kiss, dragging her from the shallows and into the deep end. She was over her head. Drowning. And she didn't care.

Axle's kiss devoured her, feeding her passion and numbing her fears. There was nothing but the feel of his hard chest pressed against hers, his soft lips pressing her deeper into the back of the sofa. She moaned, and he shifted his hips, pulling her toward him until she was the one on top, pressing against him, driving him into the soft cushions as his hard arms pulled her in deeper–drowning out everything but him.

There was no pulling back this time. He didn't attempt it, and she wouldn't have allowed it if he had. She'd waited too long for this–too long for Axle. This time, she was taking him inside of her, and she would make love to him, even if it was just for the night.

"Haley," he murmured against her throat, sliding an arm beneath her hips. With effortless strength, he rose, cradling her in his arms. Their foreheads met, breath mingling. "I'll stop if this isn't what you want."

She drew back just enough to see him clearly—his strong, caramel-toned face, the kind that lingered in dreams. His golden-brown eyes searched hers, as if trying to read the answer he should already know.

"If you stop this time," she said, voice low and steady, "I'll never forgive you."

A smile tugged at his full lips behind his goatee. "I don't want to stop. But you need to understand—I can't promise anything beyond tonight. My life is...complicated."

"Then promise me tonight," she said, more plea than demand.

He held her gaze for a beat longer, then turned toward the bedroom.

#

The moment Axle reached the bedroom, he lowered Haley to the bed. His knee sank into the mattress as he came over her, his mouth trailing to the hollow of her throat.

He tasted her, savoring the sweet warmth of her pale skin. When his teeth gently nipped, her chest lifted in a gasp. He lowered his hips, pressing her into the mattress, his elbows bracing his weight as he trailed lower, kissing the top of one breast and then the other.

Haley moaned. "Axle," she whispered, her voice thick with longing.

He understood. He'd been dreaming of this moment since that mind-blowing kiss the night her brother graduated. He could barely breathe, barely think as he continued his sensual assault along her collarbones. If he'd taken a moment to think, he would have realized making love to Haley was a terrible idea. It was a bad idea with any woman, but especially her. If anything happened to her because of him, he'd never forgive himself.

He raised his head. His body pulsed, but he had to be sure. If he stopped now without giving her a voice, she'd spend a lifetime wondering what she'd done wrong. He couldn't hurt her like that.

"This is a bad idea," he said, breathless.

"No." Her hands snaked behind his neck, pulling him down. "It's only a bad idea if you stop."

He smiled, touching his lips to hers. He was lost—knowing he couldn't turn back. Not now. Not this time.

Heart pounding slow and hard, he reached for her T-shirt and pulled it over her head. His eyes devoured every inch of her. Her nipples were strained, begging for his kiss, and he wasn't about to deny them or himself.

He lowered his mouth, lost in the hot surge of desire, the feel of her skin. His hands dropped to the waistband of her shorts, pushing them over her lush hips and down her thighs.

He rose, bracing his knees on either side of her, then yanked his own shirt off and tossed it aside. Swinging one leg over her body, he stood, stripped off his trousers and boxer briefs, and hovered above her. The moonlight spilling through the blinds cast her pale skin in a soft, ethereal glow.

Haley sat up, her wide, coffee-colored eyes sweeping over him, memorizing every detail. "You have tattoos."

He drank in the sight of her—more beautiful than he'd ever imagined. "You don't like tattoos?"

She reached out, fingertips brushing the Celtic cross on one shoulder, then the Ankh on the other. Her touch trailed down his biceps to his elbows, slow and reverent. His breath caught.

"I love them on you," she whispered.

Before he could lower her back onto the bed, she slid down his body and took him into her mouth.

He nearly lost himself.

Her hands gripped his buttocks, fingers digging deep, while his own tangled in her hair. She drove him to the edge, and just before release, he pulled back. Their eyes locked. His body trembled. Clinging to the last shred of control, he lowered himself and pushed inside her, holding still, fighting for mastery over the storm inside him.

Haley moved beneath him, wild and unrelenting, matching his rhythm, testing his restraint. He thrust harder, deeper, until she cried out, quivering beneath him. He held himself above her, their breath mingling. He pressed his forehead to hers, wishing the moment could stretch into eternity. For him, eternity was real. For her, it wasn't.

With a sigh, he moved again—slower now, savoring her, holding back. He lifted his gaze to hers and saw it: the same longing he'd carried for fifteen years. He didn't need vampire instincts to read her thoughts. Every emotion he felt was mirrored in her eyes. This wasn't just lust. It was a reckoning. A seduction long overdue. And if he wasn't careful, it would lead to love.

He'd broken Haley's heart once. He knew that now. And damn it, he'd break it again if he didn't tread carefully.

Ignoring the guilt gnawing at his gut, he kissed her—deep, possessive, as if she truly belonged to him. He thrust harder, faster, until nothing short of death could stop them from falling together.

Haley cried out again, then collapsed against the pillows. Spent, Axle rolled beside her, gathered her into his arms, and held her close.

"We didn't use protection," she whispered against his chest, her finger tracing the Celtic cross tattoo.

"It's okay," he said, pulling her closer. "I found out after my divorce that I can't father a child." Vampires were sterile, and thanks to his manipulated DNA, so was he.

"I'm sorry," she whispered against his bare skin.

He shrugged. "It's okay. Really. I'm just glad I didn't find out before Bonnie was born or I never would have had those three years as her father."

"But... couldn't you have stayed in Bonnie's life without confusing her?" she asked, refusing to meet his gaze, even when he shifted up onto one elbow. "People get divorced all the time and share custody. That shouldn't have negated your parental rights, even if you weren't her biological father."

She sounded disappointed and confused. How could he explain the truth without putting her in danger? He wasn't a vampire, but he might as well be, and no human with knowledge of his reality was ever truly safe.

"Bonnie has a father," he said, rolling onto his back to stare at the ceiling. "Chris is a good man, and he didn't deserve what happened any more than I did. Even if he was serving overseas, Olivia should have told him about Bonnie instead of manipulating me. Chris and Olivia are married now, and they seem happy. So does Bonnie. I'm not going to complicate that child's life or make her question her paternity. Chris is her father in every way. I was just a stand-in she doesn't remember."

But he would. He'd cherish those memories until the day he died—no matter how long that life might be.

Haley sat up. So did he. "I didn't mean to sound judgmental. I just want to understand how a man who loves his daughter as much as you love Bonnie could give up his rights so easily when blood has nothing to do with being a parent."

"In this case, it does," he said, swinging his legs over the side of the bed. "Chris is her father. I'm not."

"But you were, and you love her," she whispered, tears glistening in her eyes. "I see the hurt in your eyes whenever you mention her.

"And that's why I don't talk about her," he snapped, rising from the bed.

Haley scooted against the headboard, pulling the sheet up to her chin. "I didn't mean to pry."

"Didn't you?" he challenged.

She looked as if he'd slapped her, but there was no other way. He should have kept her at arm's length instead of giving into desire.

Raising her chin, she sniffed once but held back the tears. Her face was flushed and her voice trembled, but she held his gaze. "Considering how intimate we just were, I assumed personal questions were no longer off limits. I thought we were working our relationship in reverse order. Sex now, get to know one another later. But I guess you don't want me getting to know you at all."

She was hurt, and he couldn't blame her, but this way was better. This way, they could go back to her being nothing more than a client—if she didn't fire him first.

"Look, we don't need this complication," he said as he started to dress. "You hired me to do a job, and I took advantage of your vulnerability. For that, I'm sorry."

"Bullshit," she snapped, drawing his undivided attention.

"Excuse me?"

"I slept with you because I wanted to," she said, her voice firm. "I've wanted you to make love to me since I was sixteen. I got over you once, and I'll get over you again, but don't you dare act as if I had no say in what just happened. I'm not that helpless or gullible."

He quirked a brow, admiring her spunk. "I never assumed you were."

"Really?" she said, folding her arms under her breasts. He quickly averted his gaze. "I hired you to protect me from a stalker. Don't pretend you don't see that as helpless."

"Needing help doesn't make you helpless," he said softly.

"No. It doesn't. And tonight wasn't a mistake either. So don't you dare look at me as if you think it was."

Sighing, he sat on the edge of the bed, but he didn't make the mistake of touching her again. If he had, it would have been game over. "At another time and another place, I'd have no regrets. But you hired me to do a job, and this wasn't part of it."

She shrugged. "No, it wasn't. This was personal. It has nothing to do with why I hired you."

"Doesn't it?"

"Stop responding to everything I say with a damn question!" she snapped.

He held up his hands in surrender. "Okay. Sorry. But the truth is, if not for Josh, you and I never would have reconnected. It's as simple as that. So until this thing with him is settled, it can't get personal. Not again. Neither of us need that kind of drama."

This time, it was she who raised her brows. "Drama didn't draw us together, Axle. Unresolved feelings from the past did. This isn't over between us. It wasn't then, and it isn't now."

"No, it's not," he said with a small smile. "But we can't find resolution now. There's too much at stake. So let's just call a truce and keep things professional until Josh goes to trial. Once he's out of your life, then you and I can talk. Deal?"

She grunted. "Do I have a choice?"

"There's always a choice, Haley," he said, resigned. "You can always tell me to go to hell and never touch you again."

"Not very damn likely," she admitted with a sad smile.

He leaned forward but suddenly straightened before kissing her like a besotted fool. "Stay put and get some sleep. I'll see myself out, and we'll talk more in the morning."

He sat on the edge of the bed to put on his shoes and then stood. Bootsie gave him the side eye before jumping onto the mattress. "Keep an eye on her," he said to the cat.

Bootsie hissed and backed up against the headboard.

Haley grunted. "At least he'll stay the night."

Axle turned to glance over his shoulder as he was exiting the bedroom. "He doesn't have a choice. You're holding him hostage."

"Unlike you," she said with a huff.

"That's where you're wrong," he said, turning to fully meet her gaze. "I may not be locked in, but you still have the power to hold me hostage."

"Ha!" she snorted. "If that were the case, you'd get back in bed."

"Trust me, sweetheart, if the choice were mine, I'd crawl into your bed and make love to you until sunrise. But that wouldn't protect you from Josh, and that's what you hired me to do."

With a heartfelt sigh, she nodded. "Goodnight, Axle."

"Goodnight, Haley."

Axle slipped out of the house. Using the power of his mind, he stood on the opposite side of her locked door and slid the chain into place. In the morning, she might wonder how he'd managed it, but he wasn't about to leave without doing everything in his power to keep her safe.

Chapter 14

Most people would've felt relief walking free after forty-eight hours in jail. Not Josh. Relief was for the weak. He was already scheming—calculating how to get what he wanted without paying the price. Remorse didn't touch him. He'd done nothing wrong. Anger and self-pity were distractions. The past was dead. The future? Malleable. What mattered was now. And now, he was in control.

No woman had ever left him and gotten away with it. He decided when things ended. Not Sharon. Not Ashley. Not that girl from community college. And certainly not Haley.

As he followed the guard down the corridor, a sharp pain lanced through his skull. Hunger, maybe. Or something deeper. The food had been barely edible, but this felt like something clawing at the inside of his mind. He'd eat, then plan. And he'd win. He always did.

His father and sister had been slaves to guilt. His dad defended his mother's cruelty. His sister fled at seventeen, a trembling coward. Josh had leveraged his father's guilt for a house, a garage. He'd manipulated the magistrate too. He wasn't a stalker. He wasn't spending another night in jail.

He rubbed his temple, trying to crush the headache before it bloomed. The guard pushed open the steel door to the processing area.

"He's all yours," the guard said to the deputy behind the counter.

"Thanks, Henry," Josh replied, flashing a smile. The man blinked, confused. People were so easily led.

Henry nodded. "You're not like the rest of these criminals. I hope you work things out with that girl. I'd hate to see you back in here."

Josh smiled. "Just a misunderstanding. It'll be cleared up soon." Even if it went to trial, he wouldn't be convicted. He'd make sure of that.

"Ready to get out of here?" the deputy behind the desk asked.

Josh nodded. "Yes, sir."

"Then sign here." A paper slid across the counter. Josh signed for his belongings, and the deputy handed him a sealed envelope with the items he'd had in his possession when he was arrested. "Just stay away from the Connors woman," the deputy added. "She's not worth risking bail over. No woman is."

Josh nodded. He'd worked on the deputy's vintage truck a few years back. "Don't worry, Donnie. I just wanted to return her cat. I know how much she loves that stupid animal."

Donnie smiled. "Didn't figure you for a stalker, but the law's the law. No hard feelings?"

"Of course not." Not toward Donnie. He could be useful. Noya and that prick Gordon were another story. Josh forced a smile. "Stop by the garage next week. We'll catch up." As if Donnie's wife would let him. She was a hag. He'd be better off if she vanished like Josh's mama had.

His mother hadn't allowed emotion. That suited him fine. People existed to serve or obstruct. Donnie Randolph was a puzzle. What made people like him—and Haley—so eager to please? Josh only cared about pleasing himself. If everyone did that, the world would be less miserable. That's what he'd told the shrink back in grade school—the one who said he needed mood stabilizers.

His dad thought his mom needed meds too. That's why she'd left. Cliff Patterson couldn't give her what she wanted. Josh didn't blame her. He was like her, only smarter. He'd learned to mimic the emotions people expected. He was what he projected. Today, he projected humility.

"How 'bout next Friday?" Donnie asked.

Josh had already forgotten what he'd said, but replied, "Sure," and stepped into the warm, early evening sun.

The bail bondsman hadn't posted bail until after five. It was nearly seven now, and he was starving. By the time his rideshare dropped him at the garage, dusk had settled. Screw food. He needed a beer to dull the headache. Every time he thought about Haley, the pounding returned.

The bar near his garage wasn't up to his usual standards. It was a dive, but it was dark, and the lights didn't hurt his eyes. It also served some of the coldest beer in town. By all accounts, it was a biker bar, and truth be told, he fit in with bikers better than with the suits uptown. Like him, most bikers didn't give a shit about what others thought. The suits, on the other hand, were useful. They paid premium to fix their expensive rides and restore their vintage toys.

Josh took a seat at the bar, watching the mirror behind the bartender. Most patrons were drunk, stoned, or both. He ignored them—until a gorgeous redhead walked in with an equally attractive man. He assumed they were a couple until the man started flirting with the bartender.

"We're not together," the woman said, slipping onto the stool beside Josh like smoke. "Antonio's gay." Her beauty was sharp, otherworldly. She didn't ask—she took. He recognized her instantly. A kindred spirit. Or something more.

She'd be great in bed, but she couldn't be bent to his will. She was too much like him. Or far beyond him.

"I didn't ask," Josh said, glancing at her, though his eyes lingered on her reflection.

The bartender poured her red wine without a word. Either she was a regular, or Antonio had tipped him off. She sipped and met Josh's gaze in the mirror.

"No need to feel guilty. Looking and imagining aren't cheating."

Josh turned toward her, smiling. "I don't feel guilty—about anything. Guilt's a leash. People use it to control you. They think if you feel bad, you won't do it again. But I wasn't put here to please others. I do what pleases me."

"Well, aren't you the enlightened one," she said, her smile hypnotic.

"I try," he said, offering his hand. "Josh Patterson."

"Sonia."

"Sonia...?"

"Just Sonia."

"Well, nice to meet you, Just Sonia," Josh said, reaching for his beer. She was fascinating. She'd made him forget Haley—until he thought of her again. Then the headache returned. He rubbed his temple.

"Girl trouble?" Sonia purred.

"If you only knew," he sighed. "But I'll work it out. I always do."

"You and I are a lot alike," she said, lifting her glass. For half a heartbeat, Josh saw a flicker of loneliness in her eyes. And then it was gone.

"Possibly." He watched her, curious. Was she looking for a hookup? He could oblige. Monogamy was a myth. Even if he married Haley, that wouldn't change.

A sharp pain stabbed behind his left eye. He winced.

"My, my," Sonia said. "You're fighting it. Aren't you?"

"Fighting what? A headache?" Did she expect him to embrace it? Damn. He needed an aspirin. He drained his beer and asked the bartender for a bourbon. Neat.

The bartender looked annoyed—Josh had interrupted his flirtation with Antonio.

"You've been manipulated," Sonia said. "I've seen it before. A mortal with a scrambled mind—courtesy of a vampire."

Josh froze. The air around her shimmered.

Oh, hell. One of those Goth weirdos. He should've known—black nails, leather biker-chic. Asheville drew all kinds—YoPros, socialites, bohemians, activists, Goths. Always had, even before the hurricane.

"Look, lady, maybe find another hookup," he said, trying to sound charming. "It's not guilt that stops me from cheating. Like I said, I don't feel guilt. That gives me an edge. If I'm kind, it's by choice. If I'm rude, it's necessary. And right now, I just need peace and quiet."

"No, sweetie. What you need is me."

Sonia smiled, and her reflection shimmered—then vanished.

Josh turned to face her, and for a second, he could've sworn she had fangs, and her eyes glowed like embers.

#

Haley tried not to feel neglected. Or depressed. But Axle hadn't reached out all day—not really. He'd stopped by yesterday morning as promised, yet said nothing about the night before. Nothing about how her front door had ended up chain-locked from the outside. She'd wanted to ask. She didn't. She was determined to match his aloofness with her own.

He'd told her Josh had made bail the night before, but no one had seen him since. Maybe Josh had come by, seen her with Axle, and finally given up. Or maybe he was lying low, careful not to jeopardize his release. Either way, Haley hadn't heard from him. Maybe—just maybe—she was safe. For now.

Axle had texted earlier, asking if Josh had tried to contact her. She'd replied with a curt "no" and tossed her phone onto the sofa. The rest of the day blurred into reruns and restless pacing, her mind circling the same thought: she needed to do something. But what?

She told herself she wasn't waiting for Axle. Not really. She waited until supper before giving up and turning off the TV. If Josh still posed a threat, surely Axle would've come by. Or called. He might not care for her the way she cared for him, but he'd protect her. Of that, she had no doubt. Axle was a consummate professional—which, in her case, wasn't necessarily comforting.

"Damn you," she muttered, feeding her cat and eating alone. She couldn't stomach another minute of mindless television, so she read until dark and turned in early. It was nearly ten. Still no call. No text. Maybe Axle wouldn't reach out. Maybe he believed Josh wouldn't risk his bail.

The thought should've calmed her. It didn't. Knowing Josh was out made sleep a fragile thing. She tossed and turned, dread gnawing at the edges of her mind, wearing her thin. Eventually, exhaustion dragged her under—until a sound tore her awake.

"Bootsie?" she murmured, rolling over. The pillow beside her was empty.

She sat up. Bootsie perched atop the chest of drawers, growling. Then he hissed, and the hairs on Haley's neck stood on end. Her pulse spiked.

"What's wrong, Bootsie?" she whispered, voice cracking.

"Hello, Haley," said a voice from the darkest corner of the room.

She screamed, bolting out of bed and backing into the far corner of the room. Josh stepped into a shaft of moonlight slicing through the blinds. He stood between her and the door. Her escape.

Her blood turned to ice. "How did you get in?"

He shook his head, clicking his tongue. "Did you really think you could keep me out?"

She blinked—and he was suddenly inches away. No sound. No warning. Just there. Her skin went cold. Her heart thudded against her ribs.

"What do you want?" she rasped.

"You." His voice was low, venomous. "You're mine, Haley. And I keep what's mine."

His eyes gleamed red. When he smiled, his teeth looked sharp. Predatory. Like a wolf. Or a vampire.

Haley blinked again. His teeth looked normal. It had to be a trick of the light. Or else—she was still asleep. "I'm dreaming," she whispered. "This is a nightmare."

"Think what you want." He touched her cheek. His hand was ice. Soft.

Uncalloused. Not the hands of a man who did body work. Not the hands she remembered.

"Please, Josh." She pressed herself into the corner, wedging between the wall and her nightstand. "Please leave me alone."

"I can't. And no one can stop me now." His breath ghosted across her skin. "I will have you, Haley. But not tonight. First, I'll make you suffer. I'll haunt you—and hunt you. I'll keep you waiting. I like the power it gives me—the power that surges through me now. Power that will bind you to me. Forever."

Haley screamed—and he vanished. No door. No window. Just gone. Somewhere between breath and scream, she thought she heard the front door open.

Or had she?

"It was just a dream," she said aloud, legs trembling as she crept into the living room.

The front door stood wide open. Cool night air licked at her bare feet. She ran, slammed it shut, locked it, then sprinted back to her room for her phone.

She called Axle. Then she dialed 911.

#

Axle hadn't been able to track Josh since learning of his release, but that hadn't stopped him from driving past Haley's apartment last night before heading home. He hadn't seen or sensed Josh's presence, but he planned to check her place every night until a court date was set. Tonight, he'd gotten tied up with another case and had left the office late, but he was already halfway to her house when she called. The moment she opened the door, he pulled her trembling body into his arms.

"What happened, sweetheart?" he asked, realizing too late he'd used an endearment—despite promising himself and her that he'd keep it professional.

"He was here," she whispered against his chest. "Josh was in my house. In my bedroom." She pulled back just enough to meet his gaze. "He came and went through the front door."

The bastard must have made a key. He cupped Haley's cheek. "I'll change the locks. Tonight."

"But Axle," she said, her voice shaky and raw, "I changed the locks last week."

"Then he broke in." He stepped away and turned to the front door. The lock and frame showed no signs of forced entry. The side and back doors were clean too, and all the windows were locked. Even the doggy door in the kitchen was sealed tight. So how had Josh gotten in? Unless... he hadn't. Haley was under a lot of strain, and she had been in bed.

Leaning against the kitchen counter, Haley folded her arms and glared. "I know what you're thinking, but it wasn't a dream. It was real."

Axle blew out a frustrated breath and pulled out a kitchen chair. Haley sat. He sat beside her and reached for her hands. "There's no sign of a break-in. And if you changed the locks last week, I don't know how he could've gotten a key."

"He was here, damn it." She yanked her hands free. "I didn't just wake up from a vivid nightmare. Bootsie was growling from the top of my dresser. I got out of bed, and Josh was standing between me and the door. He backed me into the corner and threatened me. When he left, I was still standing there. I wasn't dreaming."

She was so certain. And Haley wasn't prone to dramatics—at least not that he'd ever seen. "I suppose he could have picked the lock. Was the door opened or closed when you came into the living room?"

"Open," she said with a sigh. "But Axle, I never saw him move. He was there—and then I heard the front door open and slam against the wall, the same moment he was gone. Not like someone leaving. Like someone vanishing. No tail lights. No engine. It was like he disappeared. I know it sounds crazy, but I swear, that's what happened."

Her version of events was neither impossible nor crazy, but it wasn't likely–unless Josh was a vampire.

A sense of dread drenched Axle's soul. His heart sank. Josh had been mortal when Axle visited him in his cell, but he'd been out of jail for forty-eight hours. What had happened in that time?

Axle rose and walked through the living room, down the hall to Haley's bedroom. Inhaling deeply, he cataloged the scents like a bloodhound. Haley followed, but he ignored her. Lemon-scented dust spray. Plug-in air fresheners. Soap, shampoo, dish liquid, laundry detergent. Takeout from a sub shop. Bootsie's litter box—recently used. But beneath all that was something else. The scent of a man. But not a man.

Haley touched his shoulder. "What the hell are you doing?"

He brushed her off. He had to concentrate, but he smelled it—cold, thick blood. Vampire blood. His heart slammed against his ribs. Fear congealed in his veins. Josh was now Utukku—one of the undead. He'd been dangerous as a mortal. Now he was immortal. Deadly. An Ekimmu, the deadliest of vampires.

"Axle." Haley stepped in front of him. "What's with the bloodhound routine? You're scaring me."

"Josh was definitely here. I don't know how," he lied, "but he was, and you're not safe. Pack a bag. We're leaving. Now."

"What about Bootsie? I can't just leave him." Her voice trembled. He understood better than she might think. If Josh was a vampire, someone had turned him. Axle didn't know who—but the scent was old, powerful. Not just any vampire. An elder. Which meant there were vampires in Asheville again—and this time, they weren't playing nice.

"Princess has never been around cats, and Bootsie's bigger than she is. You can't stay at my place." Besides, he'd be too busy hunting vampires to keep her safe.

"I can go to my dad's," she offered. "He likes Bootsie. Sort of," she added with a smile.

Axle shook his head. "No. Josh knows where your dad lives. That'll be the first place he looks."

"Maybe I can stay with my friend, Sandy. We work together, and she has a spare room."

"No," Axle said. "I'm taking you to my dad's. Jerome's off at college, so his room's empty. You can stay with my folks for a few days."

"What about your stepmom? What's she going to think?"

"If I tell LaDonna we're dating, she'll be thrilled." But he wouldn't be. He hated lying to his family. And he didn't want to lead Haley on. But damn, they'd already had sex. It wouldn't be hard to convince LaDonna they were a couple. They kind of were.

"I won't lie," Haley said, voice quivering. "You told me point blank you weren't interested in a relationship, and I believed you. So I won't lie to your stepmom and say we're a couple."

He smiled, and against his better judgment, said, "Then it doesn't have to be a lie. It's not like we haven't already had sex. And I wouldn't mind doing it again."

"Be still my heart," she quipped, dripping sarcasm.

"It makes sense."

"No. It doesn't. I won't pretend we're dating when I honestly wish we were. I'm not that good of an actress."

"It doesn't have to be an act." Cursing himself, he pulled Haley into his arms. Their gazes locked seconds before his lips met hers. The first touch of her tongue sent a jolt through his body. He cupped her face, deepening the kiss. Gentle at first, then desperate. Urgent. His hands dropped to her waist, skimming her skin beneath her tee shirt. No bra. He touched a taut nipple. She moaned. He growled—low and feral.

His heart stilled. So did his hands. He lowered them to her hips and gently eased her out of his arms.

Making love to Haley again would be a mistake. But letting her go could cost her life. If he wanted to keep her safe, he had to keep her close. But if she discovered his secret, she'd fear him. Even if she didn't, keeping her close put her in more danger than she already was. He'd seen what happened when mortals learned the truth. The fear. The revulsion. The threat of exposure. He couldn't go through that again–not with Haley.

"I'm sorry," he said with a frustrated sigh.

Haley's lips trembled on a smile. "I'm not. I've been waiting two days for another kiss."

Axle laughed despite himself. "Sorry it took so long. Keeping you safe isn't easy."

"Apparently not," she said, fear flickering in her eyes.

He lowered his forehead to hers. "I won't let him get that close again. I promise."

The fear faded, replaced by confusion. "I'm not sure what just happened. Was that pretend so we can tell your stepmom we're dating—or was that real?"

He raised his hand to her face, then dropped it. "Oh, it was real. A real kiss. Real emotions. But Haley, it probably wasn't a good idea."

"Well, that was clear as mud," she said with a snort. "You know you're sending mixed signals, right?"

"Not intentionally," he said, scrubbing a hand over his head. "I'd love nothing more than to take you to bed again, but I don't need the distraction."

"Well, I damn sure do." Her bluntness caught him off guard. The old Haley had never been that direct.

He smiled. "Nothing much has changed in fifteen years. The timing for us is still all kinds of wrong. But we'll make this work. I don't know how, but we will. Now go pack and put Bootsie in a carrier."

"What about his litter box?"

Axle smiled. "I don't think he'd enjoy traveling in it."

She snorted. "No, but I still need to bring one."

Seeing her smile warmed his heart. For a second, he thought maybe a life with her was possible. Then he remembered why he was taking her to his dad's.

"I'll get the litter box," he said.

"I just changed the litter, so you can probably slip the whole thing in a garbage bag," she said, heading out of the kitchen.

"I don't think so," Axle muttered, shaking his head. The downside to vampire-like senses was the smell. And Bootsie's litter box reeked of piss.

As Axle loaded Bootsie's litter box, litter, and cat food into the trunk of Haley's hybrid sedan, a patrol car rolled up to the curb. Two deputies stepped out. One headed for Haley's front door, the other made a beeline for Axle.

"Show me some ID," the second deputy said, his hand resting on the grip of his gun.

Axle slowly raised his left hand and then reached into his back pocket with his right. He pulled out his wallet and PI badge. "I'm a private investigator. Ms. Connors hired me to look into her stalking case. She called me tonight after Josh Patterson broke into her house."

The deputy took his ID's and radioed the information back to the station. The radio crackled. Less than a minute later, someone from the station radioed back. "He's legit."

"Any outstanding warrants?" the deputy asked into his shoulder mic.

More crackling. "That's a negative."

He handed Axle's wallet back. "How long you been here?"

Axle looked at the name on his uniform. "Well, Deputy Hines, I got here right after she called."

Hines nodded to Haley's car. "This your vehicle?"

"No, sir. It's Haley's." Hines gave him the side eye and grunted. Axle hated to jump to conclusions, but he could read some mortal's thoughts without delving into their minds. Apparently, the mere color of his skin made Deputy Hines suspicious.

"Where's your car?" Hines asked, hand drifting back to his weapon. "I need to take a look inside."

"Of course you do," Axle said, unable to resist sarcasm. "It's the black SUV," he said, pointing to the space beside Haley's car.

"So why are you taking hers?" Hines' fingers curled around the grip, ready to draw.

Axle leaned casually against the bumper. "I'm loading it so she can follow me to my parents' house. If I drove her there, she'd be stranded while I investigate Patterson."

"She's staying at your parents' house?" Hines sneered, dragging out the "your."

"Why wouldn't she?"

"You smart mouthing me, boy?" Hines asked.

Axle raised his brows. "Boy?" Hines was probably younger than he was.

"Turn around and put your hands on the trunk."

Axle complied. No point escalating. So far, only one neighbor's light had come on since the patrol car arrived.

Hines frisked him and then pulled Axle's arms behind his back. As he was cuffing him, Haley emerged with the other deputy, who carried Bootsie's carrier. The cat caterwauled, furious at confinement.

"What are you doing?" Haley shrieked, rushing forward. The first deputy held her back with a free hand.

"What's going on, Dwayne?" he asked.

"This prick was giving me lip," he said, stepping back and allowing Axle to stand up and turn around.

"I called him here," Haley said, shrugging off the deputy's hand.

"He says he's your PI," Hines said, voice thick with doubt.

Even with her mortal senses, Haley must have gotten the same vibe from Hines Axle had. She briefly met his gaze before turning her attention back to the deputy. "He's also my boyfriend."

Hines raised his brows and gave Haley the once over, his disapproval evident. "You're dating *this guy*?" He snorted. "Is he stalking you?"

"No, you moron. He's protecting me—from my actual stalker. And doing a better job than the cops."

Axle cringed. Hines was a moron, but Haley was skating on thin ice.

"Why's he cuffed?" the other deputy asked

Hines cocked his head toward Axle. "He was getting smart with me, so I figured he had a gun to back up that mouth."

"Let it go, Dwayne. If Mr. Travers has a gun, it's registered. He's legit."

Axle stepped forward. "Have we met?"

"Yeah. Hank Baskerville." He extended a hand. Axle glanced at the cuffs behind his back.

Hank glared at Hines. "Damn it, Dwayne. Uncuff him."

Grumbling, Hines complied. Axle rubbed his wrists, then shook Hank's hand. "Axle Travers. You look familiar."

"I graduated a couple years before you. We met later—during the manhunt when you disappeared from Lifeblood Labs. You were unconscious when they found you. I stopped by the hospital later, but the FBI had already spoken to you and you'd left AMA. I wasn't officially on your case, but I visited your dad. You didn't want to talk, so he asked me to leave. But you thanked me for my service."

Axle nodded. Vincent Maxwell's wife, Dr. Megan Harper, had urged him to leave the hospital before his bloodwork raised questions. The samples had vanished—thanks to one of the vampires–Vincent or Gerard, he wasn't sure which. Weldon had used Gerard Delaroche's cloned blood to turn him. Megan carried the XP gene and had created an mRNA vaccine using her own blood and her husband's vampire blood to cure Axle of the virus's side effects—before he ingested human blood. If those samples had been tested, they might have exposed everything.

"Sorry. I don't remember," Axle said. He'd been too busy adjusting to his new reality and the knowledge that vampires were real–and that had been before Olivia told him she was pregnant. "I'd already been grilled by Asheville PD and the FBI. I didn't want to talk anymore."

"I get it," Hank said.

Axle glanced at Haley. Her eyes shimmered with pity. He looked away.

"If you two are done reminiscing," Hines snapped, "we've got a call to wrap up."

Besides looting after Helene, crime in Asheville had surged—especially violent crime. Axle suspected a vampire was behind the more violent crimes since one was obviously in the area. Hines, of course, wouldn't be taking a bite out of crime—pun intended.

Hank gave Hines a look, then turned to Axle. "Haley told me about the intruder. No sign of forced entry, but we'll check the perimeter."

"He might've picked the lock," Axle said. "He also planted a tracker on her car while it was in his shop." He didn't mention transferring a second tracker to a neighbor's vehicle. No need to give Hines ammo. "I turned it in to Gordon Sikes."

Hines snorted. "You got proof Josh put it there? Or just guessing?"

Axle held his gaze. It would be easy to plant a suggestion, twist his thoughts—but he didn't. "He had access. He's shown up wherever Haley goes. It's a logical assumption."

"I believe you," Hank said. "But without proof, there's not much we can do. I'm sure Sikes told you that."

"He did," Haley said, voice rising. "But Josh broke the restraining order again. He's out on bail for it. Shouldn't he go back to jail?"

"Got proof he broke in?" Hines asked. "Or are you just making sure he stays locked up?"

"I saw him," Haley snapped. "I'm not making anything up."

Hank placed a hand on her shoulder. "We'll put out an ABD and take him in for questioning, but he'll bond out again. Without evidence, it's your word against his. I'm sorry."

Hines smirked. "Maybe it was just a bad dream."

"It wasn't a damn dream," Haley said.

Axle stepped beside her, draping an arm around her shoulders. "I know, sweetheart. That's why I'm installing cameras and alarms tomorrow."

Haley looked up, eyes somber. "I thought I was staying at your dad's."

"You are," Axle said. "But Josh doesn't know that." If Josh was a vampire, cameras wouldn't catch him anyway. And even if Josh didn't show up on video, Axle would recognize the recorded blur for what it was.

Axle's pulse thudded in his ears. If Josh had turned, he wasn't just dangerous—he was untraceable. Unstoppable. And Haley was a beacon.

His skin prickled. The air felt wrong—too still, too heavy. Like static before a lightning strike. He scanned the tree line, heart hammering against his ribs. Shadows pooled thick as oil, and for a split second, he saw movement. Not a shape. A shift. Like something watching. Waiting.

He pulled Haley closer. The gesture felt instinctive, yet hollow. She believed he was her shield, her safe place. But what if he was only glass—transparent, fragile, already splintering with cracks?

He'd been turned against his will. Cured by a miracle. Left in a body that no longer felt like his own. The vaccine had saved his life, but it hadn't erased the virus. It had altered it. Driven it deeper. Quieter. A predator in remission, waiting for the right trigger.

Could rage blind him? Could the act of protecting Haley awaken something feral—something that didn't care who it tore apart?

He told himself no. Swore it. Yet the fear gnawed at him—not fear of Josh, but of himself. Of what he might become if pushed too far. Of what he might already be.

He looked into Haley's eyes and forced the spiral to stop. She saw strength in him. Safety. He couldn't let her glimpse the fracture lines. Couldn't let her feel the tremor in his hands or the way his thoughts circled back to blood, to teeth, to the memory of a nurse's pulse hammering beneath her skin.

He remembered the hospital—the sterile light, the copper tang of blood, the way his vision tunneled until all he could see was his nurse's throat, pulsing. He'd gripped the bedrail so hard it snapped. Megan dosed him with another dose of the antiviral seconds before he lost control. Would he have attacked? He didn't know. Had he tasted blood in Weldon's lab? He couldn't remember.

All he knew was that Haley could never learn the truth. If she discovered how close he'd come to becoming the thing he feared... she might not look at him with trust in her eyes. She might not look at him at all. And if Josh had already crossed that line—if he was out there, changed, hunting—then Axle wasn't only fighting to protect Haley. He was fighting to keep himself from becoming the very thing she needed protection from.

He didn't know which terrified him more. But he wouldn't let fear win. Not again. He was more than he had been before. Not less. He had to believe that. Had to cling to it like a lifeline.

Haley trusted him. And he would not betray that trust. Not to Josh. Not to the thing inside him.

She'd be safe at his dad's tonight. Tomorrow, he'd move her to his place. After a few calls. After a meeting with Reid. After he figured out how to fight something already dead.

The stakes weren't just higher now. They were closing in. And if he didn't hold the line—if he cracked—Haley would be left unprotected.

Chapter 15

Haley's heart lodged in her throat when Britt Travers opened the door in a bathrobe and bedroom slippers. It was nearly three in the morning—Axle had clearly dragged him out of bed. Behind the imposing Black man stood a petite, birdlike woman with luminous light brown eyes set in a dark, elegant face.

"What's wrong?" Britt asked, glancing briefly at Haley before ushering her and his son inside. "It's the middle of the night."

"I need a favor," Axle said. He looked from Haley to his father, then leaned around Britt to address his stepmother. "Sorry to wake you, LaDonna."

"It's okay, Sweetie. How can we help?"

LaDonna stepped beside her husband. Britt wrapped an arm around her shoulders, his stern tone softened by the adoration in his eyes. "I thought I told you to stay upstairs."

"You tell me a lot of things." She smiled, slipping out from under his arm to take Haley's hand. "I'm Axle's stepmother, LaDonna, and that big brute is my husband, Britt. Ignore his bluster—he's really just a great big teddy bear."

"Haley Connors," Haley said, her voice catching on the lump in her throat. "I..."

"She's a client," Axle interjected. "We were friends in high school. A guy she dated a couple of times is stalking her, so she hired me to investigate. We're kind of dating now," he added with a crooked smile and a soft glance in Haley's direction.

Her heart melted—and clenched. Leave it to Axle to shape a lie so it wasn't quite a lie. "Sort of dating" was a far cry from calling her his girlfriend, and it left her more tangled than ever in the question of what they really were. The warmth in his eyes made her ache, but the ambiguity twisted her emotions into knots.

"Oh, my." LaDonna gently patted Haley's hand. Somewhere between introductions and Axle's explanation, she had looped her arm through Haley's and pulled her close. Haley towered over the tiny woman, yet still felt protected—like she had when her mother was alive. The memory hit like a bruise. She hadn't realized how much she missed that feeling.

"Why don't you come with me into the kitchen? I'll make us some hot tea," LaDonna said, guiding her toward the back of the house before Haley could respond. "We'll get acquainted while Axle brings his dad up to speed. He's a lawyer, you know," she added, flipping on a light and settling Haley at a small table tucked into a kitchen nook. "Mostly corporate law now, but if you need him to look into your case, he'd do it for Axle. He'd do anything for that boy."

Haley nodded, her throat too tight to speak. The kitchen smelled faintly of cinnamon and lemon soap. It felt warm, lived-in, and safe, but she didn't belong here. Not with her hair tangled, her hoodie damp from the night air, and her nerves frayed to the edge of breaking.

As LaDonna busied herself with the tea, Haley told her about Josh—ending with the latest incident. "I don't know how he got into my house. Axle thinks he picked the locks, but I... just don't know."

LaDonna placed a blue floral cup in front of her that matched a porcelain tray with a sugar bowl and creamer already on the table. Catching Haley's gaze on the delicate pattern, she smiled. "I love my Polish pottery. A gift from Britt—he bought it on our honeymoon in Europe."

"It's beautiful," Haley murmured, adding sugar with the tiny, matching spoon. Her hand trembled but LaDonna didn't seem to notice.

She stirred her own tea, then took a sip. Setting the cup down, she asked, "How do you think Josh got in?"

Haley shook her head. How could she explain the fear churning in her gut, or the way Josh had moved—without her actually seeing him move? She couldn't very well tell Axle's stepmother he'd appeared and disappeared like a magician. She'd sound unhinged. "I don't know," she whispered.

LaDonna patted her hand again. "Don't worry about it tonight. Axle and Britt will figure it out. You're safe here, and you can stay as long as needed."

Safe. The word landed like a lie. Haley wanted to believe it, but the fear was coiled too tightly inside her. She swallowed hard. "I have a cat. He's in a carrier in the car." If Bootsie wasn't welcome, she wasn't sure what she'd do.

LaDonna smiled. "I like cats. Britt, on the other hand..." She laughed. "The two can ignore each other for a short time, I suppose. The cat might be better at it than Britt."

"If your husband doesn't like cats, I wouldn't want to—"

"Nonsense." LaDonna reached across the table and patted her hand again. "Britt's more bluster than bite. He'll probably end up loving the cat as much as he likes Princess Paw Paw." She paused, smiling. "Believe me, he claimed he didn't like that little ball of fur either. Says he prefers real dogs with purpose. But every time we visit Axle's house, guess who ends up with that little dog curled up in his lap?"

Haley managed a laugh, but it cracked at the edges. LaDonna was treating her like family—offering warmth, comfort, a place to land—while her own family had no idea where she was or what was happening. She hadn't told her dad. Or Joe. Or Amy. Or Geoff. No one knew anything except that she wasn't seeing Josh anymore. She hadn't wanted to worry them—or disappoint them. All they'd ever wanted was for her to be happy, and they'd liked Josh. She was sure they'd all expected an engagement by year's end.

Instead, she was hiding out in a stranger's kitchen, staring down a court date just to get him out of her life.

"Thank you," she said, her voice barely above a whisper. Her smile trembled, and LaDonna nodded, as if she understood more than Haley had said.

Once again, Haley's life was a tattered, hot mess—and this time, it was worse than when she'd gotten divorced and moved back home. At least her divorce had been civil. This? This was anything but. And for the first time since this nightmare began, she let the quiet sting of tears fall from her eyes. Not from fear. From the quiet, aching relief of being believed.

#

Axle and Britt sat in his father's office, nursing expensive bourbon as Axle recounted everything that had happened. Britt was one of the few who knew Axle's secret—alongside Reid Sheridan and the strange mix of vampires and mortals who'd helped rescue him from Dr. Weldon's lab. Convincing his father hadn't been hard. After years working for Vincent Maxwell and Gerard Delaroche, the oddities Britt had witnessed over the years finally made sense.

"I've never told LaDonna or Jerome," Britt said, swirling the amber liquid in his glass. He took a slow sip, then met Axle's gaze. "It's not that I don't trust them. I do. But they don't need to know—and I'd prefer they never did. No one else needs their world turned upside down."

Axle's chest tightened. "So, you don't think I should tell Haley?"

"I'm saying she doesn't need her life turned upside down, but..." Britt swirled the bourbon again before downing the rest. "Her life has already been upended. Keeping this from her could put her in more danger."

"So I should tell her?" Axle's head throbbed. A dull, pulsing ache behind his eyes. The first headache he'd had since waking up in the hospital. Vampires didn't get headaches. But he wasn't exactly a vampire. Not fully. Not mortal either. Megan Harper had called him a comic book hero. He wasn't sure what he was—only that he was afraid to test the limits.

What if he couldn't control his powers? What if they warped him, hollowed him out from the inside? He'd spent most of his life as a lowlife. It hadn't taken much for Enrique to rope him into selling pot, or for his redneck friends in Richmond to drag him into illegal street racing. With power came responsibility, and he wasn't sure he was responsible enough to handle whatever powers he might have.

Britt stood and poured them both another bourbon. "What I'm saying, son, is that if you care about this woman as much as I think you do, you'll tell her everything."

"It's not like that," Axle said, knowing it was a lie the moment it left his mouth. The words tasted bitter, like ash.

"Isn't it?" Britt raised his brows. "You love her."

"Why in hell would you say that?" Axle snapped. But his heart wasn't in it, and Britt knew it.

"Because you never looked at Olivia the way you look at Haley."

Axle flinched. He hadn't meant to. But the truth hit harder than expected. He drained his glass, throat burning, and tried to redirect. "You love LaDonna, and you've kept my secret from her."

"It's not my secret to tell. It's yours. But if what happened to you had happened to me, LaDonna would kill me if she found out before I could tell her. You don't want to crash and burn before telling Haley how you feel."

Axle's heart sank. "What difference does it make? Either way, I'll lose her. Why start something I know will end badly?" He stared into the glass, watching the light fracture through the bourbon. "Look how things ended with Olivia. After I told her, she looked at me like I was a monster. Like I was already gone."

Britt shook his head. "Sometimes life takes things away. Sometimes it gives them back. I got you back, son. Do you really think being a non-blood-sucking, day-walking vampire changes that?"

Axle rolled his eyes and groaned. "That's not a little thing, Dad."

"It's better than being locked up like your mother. Or dead. I'm proud of you, son. Despite everything, you're still a good man—the man I would've raised you to be, if I'd had the chance. That's on you. Not me. Not Shannon."

Axle's throat tightened. "I just wanted to make you proud, even when I thought you'd abandoned us. But it wasn't easy. I sold pot for one of Mom's boyfriends. Got into street racing. And now I'm some freak of nature. I guess I let you down anyway."

Sorrow flickered in Britt's eyes. "You're not a freak. With the way you were raised, it's no wonder you stumbled. But you're a man now. A man who makes me proud."

"I can't blame Mom for the choices I made after I turned ten. That's on me."

"And you've taken responsibility."

"Unlike Shannon." Even after her conviction on multiple drug charges, his mother blamed him and every boyfriend she'd ever had for her downfall. If Enrique hadn't gotten arrested, if Jefferson hadn't died, if Axle hadn't left...

Britt smiled, sadness lingering in his eyes. "I know your mom's a piece of work. But Shannon wasn't all bad. She gave me you."

Axle snorted. "And then took me away."

"But you came back. And all good things come back," Britt said, raising his glass. "So here's to life, love, loss—and fighting like hell to hold on to what truly matters."

Axle raised his glass and nodded. They drank, then set their glasses down.

Britt met his gaze. "If she matters, son, don't let her go. Tell her everything. Have faith. She might surprise you."

Axle's pulse jumped. "What makes you say that?"

Britt sighed. "Because she looks at you the way LaDonna looks at me—the way your mother never did. Trust me, that girl's in love with you."

Axle didn't respond. He couldn't. The words lodged somewhere deep, tangled in the part of him that still didn't believe he deserved love. He stared at the empty glass in his hand, wondering if Haley would still look at him that way once she knew the truth.

And if she didn't—if she looked at him like Olivia had—he wasn't sure he'd survive it.

Chapter 16

Axle had just returned from installing cameras and a security alarm at Haley's house when the doorbell rang. Princess, convinced she was a Doberman, bared her teeth and growled. Axle scooped her up in one arm and opened the door with the other.

Reid Sheridan stood on the porch dressed like he'd just stepped off the set of a Men in Black reboot—black suit, black tie, white shirt, dark shades. He quirked his mouth. "You're gonna need a bigger dog."

"Don't disrespect Princess Paw Paw," Axle said, stepping aside. "Her teeth may be tiny, but they're sharp. She won't take you down, but she'll draw blood if I tell her to."

Reid chuckled and ruffled the dog's fur. Princess melted instantly, licking his hand with giddy enthusiasm.

"Traitor," Axle said as he put the dog on the floor and led Reid into the kitchen.

Princess followed and made herself at home under the kitchen table to await falling food as she had done when Bonnie lived in the house. Axle ignored the ache that thought triggered. He opened the fridge, grabbed two beers, and handed one to Reid before sitting across from him. Then he twisted off the cap, took a long pull, and set the bottle down.

"There's an Ekimmu in Asheville," he said without preamble. "One of my clients was being stalked by a mortal. Now that same man can vanish into thin air and smells like a vampire."

Reid took off his sunglasses and slipped them into an inside coat pocket but still didn't make eye contact. Instead, he took a long pull on his beer, set it down, and sighed. "So. Just one?"

Axle's gaze narrowed. "What aren't you telling me? If you want me reporting vampire activity to the BBTF, then you don't get to keep secrets. What do you know?"

Reid raised his hands. "Hey, if there's a fledgling, there's a creator. Right? And I'm only interested in hunting Ekimmu. You don't drink blood, so you're not really a vampire. And as far as I'm concerned, Carl and the BBTF don't need to know about Vincent, Gerard, or Amber's father, Nicolas.

They've left the country. They take antiviral injections. They don't feed on people, and they live like mortals. If that ever changes, they won't be able to hide—from me or the task force."

The BBTF—Blue Book Task Force—was a covert government agency charged with identifying and eliminating vampires. Reid had once fought alongside Vincent, Gerard, and Nicolas when he and Amber Buckley rescued Axle from Dr. Weldon's lab. He kept their secret, but trust never followed. Not after Amber left for Austria with Gerard and her vampire father, Nicolas. His feelings for Amber were why Reid joined the BBTF—to keep her safe. It was why he hunted the Ekimmu, bloodthirsty predators like the monsters in horror films, and spared the Utukku, vampires who struggled to live as humanly as possible.

Carl Matheson, Reid's BBTF supervisor, had forged an uneasy alliance with Surratt, leader of the Shedu, to track the Ekimmu. The Shedu were Utukku who had sworn never to kill, despite their hunger. Surratt's brother, Ashmada, commanded the Ekimmu. Because the Shedu refused to kill and most Utukku avoided the war altogether, Surratt leaned on Carl and the BBTF to strike the Ekimmu during daylight, when vampires slept. Carl, in turn, depended on Surratt to identify and locate them. Their alliance was symbiotic, born of necessity, never trust.

Axle leaned forward. "So. What do you know about a vampire hunting in Asheville?"

Reid hesitated. "I think it might be Sonia."

Axle frowned. "I thought she moved to Alaska after the hurricane."

Bat Cave, a small community about thirty minutes from Asheville, had been devastated by Hurricane Helene. Sonia had been swept from her home, but because she'd created Vincent—who created Gerard—whose blood altered Axle's DNA, Axle had been able to locate her buried under rubble. He'd rolled her in a tarp, dragged her out, and kept her safe until nightfall. The next night, she vanished. Axle hadn't seen her since. Apparently, Reid had.

"She did move," Reid said. "For a while. Then she went off grid."

Axle's fingers tightened around the bottle. A slow pulse of unease throbbed at the base of his skull. "She disappears for over a year, and now she's back—just as an Ekimmu shows up?" His voice dropped. "That's not a coincidence."

Reid didn't respond, and a silence settled between them, heavy and electric. Princess snored softly beneath the table, oblivious to the storm gathering above her.

"If she's back," Axle said, breaking the silence, "it's not for nostalgia. Sonia created Vincent. That bloodline runs through Gerard. Through me. If something's stirring in Asheville, she'd feel it. Hell, she might be the reason it's stirring."

"Or maybe she came back because she lost everything," Reid snapped. "It wouldn't be the first time."

Axle's tone sharpened. "You think this is like Austria? When she helped Gerard and Nicolas?"

After the cloning operation collapsed, the survivors scattered. Vincent and mortal wife, Dr. Megan Harper, fled to Amsterdam. Nicholas took over a luxury ski resort in Austria. Gerard and Amber, Reid's former partner in the Asheville PD, joined him. But the Ekimmu followed. That first winter, vacationers began dying on the slopes at night. Sonia and Reid helped eliminate the threat, dragging themselves deeper into the war.

"She went into hiding after that," Reid said. "Killing her own kind wrecked her. She came back a year later. Maybe this is the same. Helene took her home. Almost took her life. She left to heal. Now she's back."

"So, you think it's just a coincidence that after Helene destroyed all the vampires in Buncombe County, another vampire who isn't Sonia, just happened to show up at the same time she did and turned Josh Patterson into a vampire?"

Reid flushed. "She might be a vigilante and a vampire, but she's never taken an innocent life or turned anyone against their will. She would have gotten consent first."

Reid wasn't speculating—he knew. And that certainty had to come from somewhere. Axle leaned in, not probing his mind, not yet. "If she left Alaska last spring, where's she been for the past year?"

Reid drained his beer, set it down hard. "She was with me. In Colorado. Okay? Satisfied?"

Axle drummed his fingers on the table. "And?" Sonia? Seriously? Vampire or not, that woman was dangerous.

"Don't," Reid growled. "We hooked up. What do you think happened? You've seen her. She's sex on a stick, and I was the idiot who took a bite."

Axle studied him. "You bit—but did she?" A sip of blood could bind a mortal to a vampire's will. A full drain followed by a taste of vampire blood before death? That turned them.

"I was speaking figuratively, asshole," Reid snapped, face flushing crimson.

"But I bet she offered you immortality." Vincent had accepted her offer—though he'd been bleeding out on a Revolutionary War battlefield at the time. Reid, as far as Axle knew, wasn't leaking from a single orifice.

"You're not wrong," Reid muttered, grabbing Axle's beer and finishing it too.

"But you turned her down," Axle said, finishing the thought.

Sonia had that biker-dominatrix vibe—raw, unapologetic. Axle had known the type back in Richmond. That kind of overt sexuality didn't do it for him anymore. Not that he was into the bougie model types like Olivia either. Fake was fake, no matter the packaging. He preferred natural beauty with a soft sensuality. Something a bit more real.

Like Haley?

Get a grip, Travers. She was more out of reach now than ever.

Axle leaned into Reid's mind, probing for truth. Not knowing could get them both killed. He had to be sure Sonia hadn't implanted thoughts or wiped memories. But Reid's mind felt intact.

Sonia had been dynamite in bed—no denying that. But Reid hadn't trusted his own feelings, and that uncertainty had ended whatever they'd had. Luckily, Sonia hadn't retaliated. Not yet. For now, Reid was still mortal. Still himself.

"Yeah. I turned her down," Reid said, unconsciously pushing Axle from his thoughts. "Besides not trusting her, she's still hung up on Vincent, and I wasn't about to step into eternity with someone chasing revenge sex."

Axle snorted. "You still know how to step in it, though. Don't you? You don't trust your boss not to wipe out every vampire, and you don't trust Sonia. Maybe steer clear of both."

"I would if I could. But we need the BBTF. And we need Sonia." He raised a hand before Axle could interrupt. "Not like that. I need her tech skills. She's the best at covering vampire tracks. That protects them—and the public."

Guilt tugged at Axle. He shouldn't have invaded Reid's thoughts, but Sonia was a wildcard, and Reid was vulnerable because he genuinely cared. That should've been obvious without digging through his mind.

"Could she be the one who turned Josh Patterson?"

Reid's gaze darkened. "It's possible. She feels rejected—by Vincent, by me. She's lonely. I think she just wants someone who won't die or leave. I just can't imagine what kind of man would accept her terms."

"I can," Axle said, and the thought chilled his blood.

He stared at the empty beer bottle in Reid's hand, heart thudding harder than it should. Sonia turning someone—anyone—was bad enough. But turning someone now, in Asheville, and it just happened to be the asshole stalking Haley? That wasn't coincidence. He didn't believe in coincidence.

His gut twisted.

Haley thought cameras and alarms would keep her safe. That Axle could keep her safe. But if Sonia was back—and if she'd turned Josh—this wasn't just external. It was personal. Bloodline-deep.

"She's not just lonely," Axle said, voice low. "She's strategic. Calculated. If she turned Josh Patterson, it wasn't for companionship. It was for leverage."

Reid frowned. "Leverage against who?"

"Against you. Against Vincent. Against me. Against anyone who ever made her feel disposable."

Axle abruptly stood and paced the kitchen. Princess stirred beneath the table but didn't rise. "She knows Haley's connected to me. She knows I'd do anything to protect her. That makes Haley her target as much as Josh's. Maybe that's why she turned him—to get to me."

Concern flickered behind Reid's usual stoicism. "You think this is about you? Why? Sonia helped save you. You saved her. Why would she come after you now?"

"She's hurt. You said it yourself. Vincent turned Gerard—so it wasn't just Sonia and Vincent anymore. A century later, he's still tight with Gerard, married to Megan, and Sonia's on the outside looking in. Then you turned her down but stayed friends with me—a mutant freak in her eyes. So yeah, I think she'd turn Haley into bait if it served her purpose."

Reid shook his head. "You're chasing the wrong lead. Sonia's not about revenge."

Axle gripped the counter, knuckles white. "Haley's already on edge. Her sense of safety is gone. If Sonia drags her into this war, she won't survive it. Not emotionally. Not physically."

Reid stood. "I know you care about her. But maybe you're not thinking this through."

Axle didn't answer. He turned back toward the table, eyes shadowed. "I installed every sensor I could. Reinforced the doors. Set up remote monitoring. But none of that matters if Sonia decides Haley's useful."

Reid hesitated. "Haley's innocent. Sonia wouldn't hurt her. I'm sure of it."

Axle's voice cracked. "But I'm not. If she turned Josh, it's not a coincidence. It's strategy."

Silence fell, heavier than before. Princess whimpered softly, sensing the shift.

Axle straightened, shoulders rigid. "I need to know if Sonia turned Josh. Because if she did, Haley's not just in danger—she's in play. And I won't let that happen."

Reid nodded slowly. "Then we find out. But don't jump to conclusions. Even if she turned him, it doesn't mean it's about revenge. And her being in Asheville isn't a stretch. She lived here for years before Helene."

Axle didn't respond. His mind was already racing through every possible way Sonia could get close to Haley.

And every way he'd stop her.

Chapter 17

Using the bloodline connection that ran from Vincent and Gerard, Axle tracked Sonia to the far edge of Cherokee, an hour west of Asheville. He drove while Reid slept off jet lag. Before flying in from Colorado, Reid had been in Austria, following up with his old partner, Amber.

Sonia's cabin clung to the mountainside like a secret. Below, the river shimmered beneath the rising moon, its beauty a deception. Helene had stripped the land bare, leaving scars and splintered trees in her wake. A new deck jutted from the house, but the structure itself stood mostly untouched. That detail alone made Axle's gut tighten. Sonia had survived the hurricane—but had she emerged unchanged? Was turning Josh an act of vengeance, or had she truly been blind to his bond with Haley, as Reid insisted?

"Where are we?" Reid asked, squinting at the terrain as they stepped from the vehicle. "This place looks familiar."

"About an hour west of Asheville," Axle replied, scanning the tree line as they approached the house and climbed the front steps. Something about the place felt wrong. He didn't trust it—the location, the timing, and least of all, Sonia.

On the porch, Reid shifted uneasily, keys jingling in his pocket. He had every reason to be nervous. Sonia wasn't just a vampire—she was a jilted lover. And Reid was the one who had done the most recent jilting.

"Hey," Axle said, clapping a hand on his shoulder. "I've got your six."

Reid smirked, though his voice carried a shadow of unease. "That won't help when I'm sleeping alone tonight."

"You don't have to stay in a hotel," Axle said. "I've got a spare room."

If Reid stayed with him, Axle could keep watch—on Reid, and on Haley. He'd just have to leave her at his dad's a little longer—especially if Sonia was shielding Josh. If that was true, he wouldn't just need backup—he'd need Vincent and Gerard.

The door creaked open, and Sonia stepped into the frame—not in her usual leather armor, but in a fitted top and jeans. She looked... almost human. Almost. Then she smiled. No fangs, yet the menace in her expression was unmistakable. She wasn't startled; she was composed, deliberate—like someone who'd just scrubbed down a crime scene and now dared them to spot the bloodstains.

"I'm under no illusion this is a social call," she said. "So—how did you find me, and why are you here?"

"I've missed you too, Sonia," Reid said, voice laced with false bravado. Axle felt the fear behind it.

"Have you now?" she said, staring him down. Reid looked away. Smart. Avoiding a vampire's gaze was the best way to avoid mental manipulation.

"We need to talk," Axle said, stepping forward. "And no—Vincent didn't tell me where to find you. Not directly. Bloodline tracking. You made Vincent. He made Gerard. Gerard's DNA ended up in me. You know how that works."

Her eyes flickered—surprise? Calculation? Axle shifted, ready for anything.

"I see you brought backup," Sonia said, gaze narrowing on Reid. "Planning to turn me over to that weasel Carl Matheson the second I fall into the day sleep?"

"It's not like that," Reid said. "We just want to talk."

"And yet you couldn't come alone," she said, voice edged with betrayal.

Reid bristled. "I didn't even know where you were, damn it. If not for Axle, I still wouldn't."

"Exactly," she snapped. "So why now?"

"I needed to see you," Axle cut in. "Not Reid. Me. He's helping with a case. We need your insight." And the truth. He had to know if she'd turned Josh knowing he was stalking Haley. Vampire or not, he'd know if she was lying.

She turned her full attention on him, eyes blazing red fire. "Then why bring Reid? You clearly didn't need him to find me. Don't tell me you're scared."

Axle offered a tight smile. "I'm not. But you're friends with Reid, not me. I figured you'd be more willing to help if he asked."

She tossed her sable hair and glared at Reid. "So you think we're friends after everything? Is that all I am to you now, darling?"

To his credit, Reid didn't flinch. Much. "I do consider you a friend,

Sonia—a good one. I just can't be what you want me to be."

„Vai, te rog!" she muttered, rolling her eyes.

Axle and Reid exchanged a glance. "Huh?" Reid said.

"Oh please," she said, translating. "If you say we can still be friends, I think I'll puke."

"I thought we could be," Reid snapped.

She snorted. "Really? I never asked you to marry me. Never even asked for fidelity. But you practically threw me out when I had nowhere else to go."

"You asked for eternity. I can't give that." Reid's voice hardened. "I have no desire to live forever."

Axle cleared his throat. "Can we take this inside? You might not have neighbors, but I feel awkward as hell standing here while you two hash things out. And it's not why we came."

"By all means," Sonia said with a snort. "Step into my lair."

Axle entered first, scanning the interior like a crime scene. Reid followed, halting just past the threshold. "Whose house is this?" he asked.

Sonia smiled. "It used to be Vincent's—before Megan hauled him off to Amsterdam."

Damn. Reid had dodged a bullet when he turned down Sonia's offer. She'd clearly moved into her ex-lover's house as a jab at Megan—his mortal wife.

Sonia's eyes flicked toward him, sharp. "It's not like that," she snapped, reading his thoughts. "Vincent never sold this place. He hired a caretaker. Designed it to survive anything—buried in the mountain, just the entrance and front windows exposed. Safe. Remote. Practically indestructible. Megan won't live forever, and he wanted it waiting for when she's gone."

She paused. "The night you saved me from the hurricane, I called Vincent. He offered me this place. I couldn't take it then—too soon. So I went to Alaska. Ran into Reid in Juneau where he was tracking an Ekimmu killing the Auke, part of the Tlingit tribe. I helped him find the lair. He dispatched her while I was in regenerative slumber. I left a week later when the BBTF came snooping. Reid owed me, so I paid him a visit. Let's just say we were more than friends last summer."

"So you're fine being friends with Vincent, just not me?" Reid snorted. "Did it ever occur to you that I didn't want to compete with him for your affection?"

She shrugged. "As if you could. You're still mortal. Now, if you'd joined me in eternity..."

"Damn it! How many times do I have to say I'm sorry?" Reid snapped.

"Just once."

"What the hell, then?"

Sonia sighed. "That was the first time you've ever said it. So, apology accepted."

Reid looked so stunned Axle couldn't help laughing. "Damn, Reid. Don't you know anything about women?"

Reid huffed. "Apparently not. Hell, I guess if you're a man in a straight relationship, you apologize even when you're not wrong."

Sonia's eyes shimmered, but she didn't cry. "I never said you were wrong, *pula*. But you still hurt me."

"Fair enough," Reid said. "So—where can we talk? You're right. This isn't a social call."

"Well, I'm definitely not inviting you to my bedroom. I'm not up for a *ménage à trois*."

Reid gulped, probably picturing it, and Axle snorted. "Don't even think about it, bro."

Reid laughed, breaking the lingering tension. "With you? Not a chance. I was picturing Sonia and another woman. If I ever did do a three-way, it wouldn't be with a guy more buff than me. I don't need the competition."

Ignoring them, Sonia led the way into the great room. An archway opposite the front door opened into an eat-in kitchen and dining area. On either side of the room were closed doors. A sectional sofa faced a stone fireplace with a wide-screen TV mounted above the mantle. Sonia curled into the center of the sectional. Axle and Reid took seats on either side, careful not to invade her space.

"So," she said, once they were settled, "why have you dragged me from my slumber so early in the evening?"

Axle didn't waste time. He needed the truth, and he needed it now. "Do you know Josh Patterson?"

"Why?" she asked, instead of answering.

"He's stalking my client."

"And?"

"He wasn't a vampire before." Axle's tone sharpened. "Now he is. And as far as I know, you're the only vampire in Asheville who survived Helene."

Sonia probed his mind. Axle blocked her. She pushed harder—then smiled. "She's more than a client, isn't she?"

She'd read his thoughts—but he'd read hers too. The one thing he'd learned about vampire abilities is that one couldn't protect one's own thoughts while attempting to read another's–at least not between two vampires. It was a two way bridge from one mind to the other.

"And Josh betrayed you," Axle said, voice like ice. "Even after you gave him immortality."

Her eyes flared. Fury. Not denial. "Nice trick for a mutant," she said.

He smiled. "Aren't all vampires mutants?"

"No. We're infected. Ask Reid's friend, Dr. Harper. She's been pushing that damn vaccine on me since day one. But you?" she said with a sneer. "You're a genetic mistake. A mutant. Not human. Not vampire. You don't even know what you are."

Axle's heart slammed against his ribs—not with fear, but rage. "I'm the man who saved your ungrateful ass. The same man I was before—just enhanced. Don't mistake that for weakness."

Sonia flushed and spared a quick glance in Reid's direction before smiling a faint but genuine smile. "I guess I'm more like Reid than I thought. He has trouble with apologies, and I apparently forget to say thank you." She redirected her gaze to Axle. "Thank you for saving my life. I suppose I couldn't say it then—because I was disappointed to still be alive."

Axle's pulse quickened. He'd never considered Sonia might have wanted to die. When Vincent called from Amsterdam after hearing about the hurricane, Axle hadn't hesitated. He'd found her and pulled her out.

"There's a reason you're still here," he said. "And if you turned Josh Patterson, you didn't crawl out of that hurricane to start over. You crawled out with a plan." But was it revenge? Or something more personal?

Reid slid closer, leaned forward, and took her hands despite her half-hearted protest. "You're tired. Lonely. But death isn't the answer. Reconsider Megan's offer. Take the anti-virus. You won't be human again, but you'll age—slowly. You'll stay awake for most of the day. Just avoid peak sun, and you can take your life back."

She pulled away, shaking her head. "It's too late for me. I am what I am. I don't know how to be anything else."

Reid sighed. Axle met her gaze, pushing to see her thoughts. She tried to block him, but he caught a glimpse—heartbreak. Betrayal. Pain. But not a hint of vengeance.

"You knew Josh was dangerous before you turned him, didn't you?" he said, verbally pushing when she blocked his mental invasion.

"What the hell do you know?" she snapped, rising.

Reid sprang up, instinctively placing himself between them. Axle gave him points for bravery—then docked a few for stupidity. If Sonia wanted, she could rip out his throat before Axle had time to blink.

"Enough," Reid snapped. "We didn't come to hurt you. Or blame you. We just need to know—did you turn Josh Patterson?"

Sonia sank back down onto the sofa, legs crossing with practiced grace. "What if I did?" she said. "Is it so wrong to want steady companionship?"

"No," Reid said, lowering himself back into his seat. "But you already have that—with me. With Vincent. We're your friends. What's Josh?"

"My lover," she replied, smiling. Seductive. Hollow.

Axle saw the truth: loneliness, pain, and the sharp edge of regret. Maybe she'd slept with Josh, but he wasn't her lover. That bastard had his own agenda. She hadn't known he was dangerous when she turned him, and she hadn't known he was stalking Haley.

"You and Josh... you're not the same," he said quietly.

Her eyes narrowed. "What's that supposed to mean?"

"I mean," Axle said gently, "he used you. Not the other way around. You didn't turn him for some sick purpose. You didn't even know who he was. Or how he connected back to me. Did you?"

"I don't know what you're talking about," she said. Honest.

Axle met her gaze. "He betrayed you."

"'Betrayed' is a strong word," she snorted, looking away. "It's not like I loved him. He just seemed like someone who'd appreciate immortality."

"But he'd rather be immortal with my client," Axle said. "She's terrified of him—and she doesn't even know what you turned him into. Imagine her fear when she finds out."

"How do you know she won't be tempted?" Sonia asked, taunting him with a possibility he'd already considered—and rejected.

"Is that really the point?" Axle said.

"He's dangerous," Reid added. "He slipped into Haley's house last night. Taunted her. Threatened her. She's terrified, and he seems to enjoy her fear."

Axle glanced at Reid. He hadn't told him about the taunting. Or that Josh fed on fear. Reid wasn't just astute—he was a damn good judge of character.

"He's killed two other women," Axle said, locking eyes with Sonia. "I just don't have proof."

Sonia cocked her head. "Why do you need proof? If you know it, act."

Reid shot Axle a look. He didn't need to read minds to know Reid was pissed—Axle hadn't told him about Sharon and Ashland.

"Unlike vampires," Reid said, "mortals need proof."

Sonia rolled her eyes. "Please. Josh isn't mortal anymore. Neither is Axle. So what's the problem?"

"There's a fine line between justice and vengeance," Axle said. "I try not to cross it unless I have no other choice."

"You won't have a choice," Sonia said quietly. Then, with a sigh she added, "I looked into his mind before I turned him. I swear—I didn't see anything. No hatred. No jealousy. No remorse. Not even fear. Nothing that suggested he'd turn Ekimmu so fast."

Axle studied her. He'd never seen her so humbled. Her voice had lost its edge. Her posture, once feline and poised, now sagged with something closer to shame.

"You couldn't see it because it wasn't there," he said. "Josh doesn't feel emotions like most mortals. That's why you couldn't access them. I don't know if he's a sociopath, a psychopath, or just broken—but he lacks a conscience. That makes him dangerous. More so now that he's a vampire."

Sonia looked at Reid. For the first time since Axle had met her, he saw vulnerability.

"I'm sorry I turned him," she said. "But I was hurt. First by Vincent. Then André. Then you. I just wanted someone I didn't have to lie to—someone who understood why I seduce men for blood. I don't make a habit of turning mortals. I don't kill when I feed. Taking blood is survival. I don't enjoy it. I want you to know that."

Reid stood and gently pulled her to her feet. Holding both her hands, he said, "I know. You gave me a choice when you didn't have to. And when I said no, you let me go. I never meant to hurt you."

A tear shimmered in her eye. Her smile wobbled. "I know. But you know what they say about a woman scorned."

She pulled away. Chuckled—humorless, hollow. "My hands aren't clean. But I swear—I've never taken the blood of an innocent. Never turned anyone against their will. Besides Vincent and Josh, I've only turned one other. That didn't end well either. I should've learned my lesson then."

Axle stepped forward, voice low. "You were looking for connection. That's not a crime. It's human."

She blinked. Startled.

"I don't condone what happened," he added. "But I get it. You were trying to survive. To feel something. To not be alone."

Sonia looked away—but not before he saw the flicker of gratitude in her eyes.

Chapter 18

LaDonna handed Haley the last plate. She slid it into the dishwasher, shut the door, and pressed start.

"Thanks again for supper—and for letting Bootsie and me stay here."

"Thanks for helping with the dishes," LaDonna said, wrapping an arm around her waist. "And Bootsie isn't a bad cat, no matter what Britt says."

Haley flushed. She'd tried keeping the beast upstairs, but after two days as guests, Bootsie had other plans.

Britt had been deep into a NASCAR race when Bootsie leapt into his popcorn bowl. Britt had launched both the popcorn and the cat into the air, cursing loud enough to make Haley blush—and LaDonna laugh.

"I'm really sorry about the popcorn," she said for what felt like the thousandth time.

LaDonna chuckled. "It was hilarious. Britt thinks he's Joe Cool, so watching him jump and scream like a girl? Highlight of my day."

"Still..."

"Please," LaDonna said. "The race is over, and I am not spending the rest of the evening watching highlights. Basketball season is bad enough, but race season is practically year-round."

Racing was often seen as a white man's sport, especially in the South. But the Travers weren't your stereotypical Black family. They reminded Haley of the people she'd grown up with—most of whom were white.

Did thinking of the Travers as "non-stereotypical" make her racist? Or just naïve?

She'd had a crush on Axle all through high school, but most of her friends had been white. Was that because she'd grown up in a predominately white area? Or was it just a birds-of-a-feather thing? She felt at ease with Axle's family. Unless she made a conscious effort to think about it, race and religion didn't even cross her mind. In fact, she had no idea what religion Axle practiced.

"Does Axle go to church?" she asked, instantly regretting it.

LaDonna hesitated. "Not very often. But that doesn't mean he's an atheist. He just doesn't attend church."

Haley's pulse spiked. "I didn't mean to imply anything," she stammered. "It's just that we've never... I mean, I haven't... It doesn't really matter, it's just—"

"He believes in God," LaDonna said gently. "And Lord knows, if I could get that boy in church, I would. But he doesn't believe in organized religion. Don't let that fool you—he's a moral man. A just one."

"I know," Haley whispered. "I..."

"You love him, don't you?" LaDonna asked, cutting straight to the heart of it.

Haley's breath caught. She couldn't love Axle. Could she? They barely knew each other. And yet... her heart knew his.

She sighed and met LaDonna's gaze. "Is it that obvious?"

"Girl, a blind man could see how much you care for that boy. Personally, I couldn't be happier—even if you're not Black," she said with a wink that loosened the knot in Haley's chest. "I never cared much for Olivia, and it had nothing to do with her being white. The moment I laid eyes on Bonnie, I knew Olivia had lied to Axle. That baby wasn't his—but that little girl was easy to love. Olivia, though, was easy to dislike. She thought she was better than Axle. Used him. Hurt him. He bounced back from his kidnapping faster than he ever recovered from what that woman did to him."

Haley's pulse jumped. "I know what it's like to be betrayed by someone you love—or think you love. It's devastating."

LaDonna snorted. "Losing Bonnie is what hurt, not losing Olivia. I don't know why that boy didn't fight harder to keep his parental rights. Doesn't matter if he was the biological father or not. For three years, he was that girl's daddy. And she loved him."

"And Axle loved her. He still does," Haley murmured. No matter his reasons for cutting off contact, his love for Bonnie hadn't faded. He'd made that painfully clear when Haley raised the subject the other night.

LaDonna sighed. "Our little Bonnie is almost seven now, and I haven't seen her since she was three. I don't even know what she looks like anymore," she added in a strained whisper.

Haley's throat tightened. She couldn't ease a grandmother's pain, so she gave LaDonna a hug before the two women headed into the family room.

After watching a movie with Britt and LaDonna, Haley found Bootsie hiding on a bookshelf in Britt's study and carried him up to bed. She hadn't been asleep long when the doorbell rang. She jolted awake, heart hammering. Axle wouldn't show up in the middle of the night unless something was wrong. Even with the cameras and security system he'd installed, he wouldn't drag her out of bed without a reason.

Still breathless, she stepped into the hall just as Britt emerged, tying his robe. LaDonna followed, locking eyes with her.

"Stay up here, both of you," Britt ordered, shooting them a look.

LaDonna clutched her phone. "I've got 911 queued. All I have to do is hit send—and I'll be on the landing to see who's at that door."

"And I'll be right beside her," Haley said, voice tight around the lump in her throat.

Britt grumbled his way down the stairs and threw open the door without checking the side glass. "What?" he snapped.

Haley couldn't see who it was, but Britt's shoulders tensed before Gordon stepped inside. "Sorry to wake y'all," he said, "but I need to see Haley."

Haley's knees buckled, and she nearly collapsed against the railing. Britt cast a sympathetic glance up and over his shoulder. Then she and LaDonna descended the stairs to meet them in the foyer.

"What's wrong?" Haley asked, her voice thin with fear. LaDonna wrapped an arm around her in a side hug that felt like home.

"We got a call just after midnight," Gordon said. "Your front door was wide open—and your convertible was on fire."

Haley's heart nearly leapt from her chest. Her beautiful classic car. She remembered riding in it as a child. Her dad had taught her and Joe to drive in that car. And Axle—Axle had kissed her on the hood. She'd fallen in love with him that night. It hadn't lasted, but what she felt then, she felt now. And it was more than friendship.

"It was Josh," she said, tears spilling. "You know it was."

Insurance might cover the cost, but it couldn't replace what the car meant. Even if she found another like it, it wouldn't hold the same memories.

"We'll question him," Gordon said, sighing. "But there were no witnesses. None of your neighbors saw anything—before or after."

"What about the security cameras Axle installed?" Britt asked.

Gordon flushed. "I reviewed the footage with Axle and his friend Reid—he works for a division of Homeland Security. There was no one there. It was like the fire started on its own."

Haley jolted. "Axle knows?" He hadn't called. Not once in two days.

Gordon nodded. "He and Detective Sheridan went with Deputy Kanati to question Josh. I came here to talk to you. Make sure you're safe." He exchanged a look with Britt. "I told Axle I'd sit out front until Josh is in county lockup again. We can hold him for twenty-four hours without charges… if we can find him." He locked eyes with Britt. "You understand?"

"Shit," Britt muttered, rubbing his neck. "Damn right, I understand. This is worse than I thought—worse than Axle thought."

Gordon grunted. "He's in over his head. But we're taking over now. Arson's serious. Even without a solid case, we've got enough circumstantial evidence to arrest Josh."

Haley's face burned. So did her eyes. "So stalking and catnapping weren't serious enough?"

"We were building a case," Gordon said, voice tight with frustration. "Josh doesn't follow the rules. But we have to."

Haley exhaled, eyes closed. Until now, it hadn't felt like anyone believed her—except Axle. He'd never made her feel like she was overreacting. Well… maybe once.

LaDonna stepped away and fixed Britt with a glare. "What's going on? I know you, and I know you're holding back. Spill it."

"If you know something, Britt, you need to tell me," Gordon added.

Britt looked from Gordon to LaDonna, then to Haley. "I know Josh is more dangerous than anyone thought. And I know he's an imminent threat to Haley. So we're all staying together in the living room until Axle gets here."

Gordon smirked. "I'm a trained officer of the law. I'm armed. Don't you think I can handle this?"

"Not alone," Britt said, steady as stone.

#

"Stay here. I mean it," Deputy Noya Kanati said, stepping away from his patrol car toward Josh's house. The lights were off. The place was empty. Axle had already slipped in and out before Noya confirmed it.

"He's not here," Axle murmured, reappearing beside Reid. "But he's definitely a vampire."

Reid watched Noya circle the house, flashlight beam slicing through the dark. "How long before he goes after Haley?"

"Twenty-four hours. Maybe," Axle said as Noya headed back. "He's still figuring out his limits. He'll need to feed. But first, he'll find a lair—secluded, dark, probably in the mountains. Once he feels safe, he'll come for Haley. And anyone who gets in his way."

"Sorry, guys," Noya said, holstering his weapon. "No one's home, and without a warrant, I can't go in. But I'll post a man outside tonight, and we'll get that warrant first thing in the morning."

"You won't find anything," Axle said. "He's not leaving evidence behind. This isn't his first rodeo." Josh had been good at staying off the radar even before he turned.

"We're not giving up," Noya promised. "The warrant covers the body shop. Asheville PD will serve it. I'll tag along. Josh won't want to draw attention, so I bet he shows up tomorrow like nothing's changed. Bastard thinks he's smarter than us."

Axle knew better but didn't argue. Josh wouldn't be back. He didn't care about appearances or crafting a new identity. He'd been a psychopath as a human. Now he was an immortal one—with no leash.

Reid stuck out his hand. "We appreciate the assist, Deputy Kanati."

"Professional courtesy, Special Agent Sheridan," Noya said, shaking his hand. "Wish I could've done more. But don't worry—between us and Asheville PD, we'll have him by morning."

He gave a half-salute and returned to his cruiser. Reid slid behind the wheel of his black SUV—nearly identical to Axle's—minus the damaged rear bumper. Axle climbed in beside him. As soon as the door shut, Reid turned. "Josh's hunting before he goes after Haley, isn't he?"

"Yes," Axle said, sighing. "And he needs a lair. That house gets too much sunlight—no safe place to sleep."

"And the night after he was turned?" Reid asked, voice neutral. Still protecting Sonia.

Axle gave him a sidelong look. "You know where he slept."

Reid exhaled. "With Sonia."

"Then why ask?" As if he didn't know. Reid had a hero complex. Thought he could save Sonia—even from herself. Axle knew better. Some people couldn't be saved. He'd tried with his mother, and she was now serving ten to twenty in federal prison for prostitution and multi-state drug trafficking. Sonia? No one could save her if she didn't want saving.

"Shit." Reid smacked the steering wheel. "I'm gonna have to kill another damn bloodsucker." He glanced at Axle. "No offense."

Axle shrugged. "None taken. I'm not a vampire. And Josh was a psycho before Sonia sank her fangs into him. Now he's an immortal psycho. If you don't take him out, I will."

"This one's off the books. Carl sniffed around Asheville after your abduction, and I can't risk him finding Sonia now—not when she's so vulnerable. And before you say anything—this isn't about our history."

"I know," Axle said. "She's unpredictable. Maybe even dangerous. But we need her—for now."

"And when we don't?"

Axle felt Reid's tension like it was his own. He still cared for her.

"When we don't, I'll talk to Vincent and Gerard. For now, she's not a direct threat to mortals. But if she turns anyone else..."

"You'll end her," Reid finished.

Axle nodded. "I won't have a choice."

Reid put the SUV in gear. They cruised past Patterson's Auto Body. No scent. Nothing fresh. When Axle climbed back in, Reid asked, "Time to get Haley?"

"Yeah." Axle stared out the window, watching the lights blur. He could get there faster if he ran, but that was one vampire trick he avoided. Moving that fast was disorienting—and terrifying. He didn't trust himself not to slam into a tree or get lost.

Vampires had some kind of internal GPS. They could move like bullets. But it didn't feel natural, and he was still learning how to live with what he'd become—without feeling like a freak.

When they pulled up to his dad's house, Axle hesitated. Reid leaned against the hood, arms crossed. "So, what now?"

Axle exhaled. Damned if he knew. Josh had Haley's scent. No matter where he took her, Josh would find her.

"My parents can't stay here," he said. "Dad will get it. But LaDonna's going to ask questions I can't answer."

"Maybe I can," Reid offered.

Axle turned. "Go on."

Reid shrugged. "I work for DHS. Sort of. BBTF's a black-ops division under Homeland Security. Very hush-hush. But I am a special agent."

"And?" Axle hated when Reid got theatrical.

"I can tell your stepmom Josh is a national security threat. Then I can move your folks to a safe house."

"What about Jerome?" His half-brother was pre-med at Duke, living off-campus. Josh probably wouldn't target him—but Axle couldn't take that risk.

"Med school doesn't take summer breaks, does it?" Reid said. "Knowing your brother, he wouldn't leave Durham even if he knew the truth."

He wasn't wrong. Jerome had that same iron-stubborn streak. Axle would be lucky to get his dad to a safe house. If not for LaDonna, Britt would insist on staying and fighting. But he'd die before shattering her world.

How the hell was he supposed to protect his family—and Haley—without telling them monsters were real? That he was either one of them...or a comic book hero destined to fight them.

"I'll send two of my best men to Durham to keep an eye on him," Reid said.

Axle snorted. "I thought you were the best."

"I am," Reid said with a grin. "That's why they'll listen. All they need to know is Jerome's an endangered mortal. They won't ask questions. They know better."

Axle nodded slowly. "So what's our cover story? Just saying Josh is a national security threat won't cut it. Gordon's going to need details. So will LaDonna and Haley."

"Let me make a call," Reid said, already pulling out his phone.

Axle didn't need to wait for the call to end. With his enhanced hearing, he caught both ends of the conversation.

"I'll be in touch," Reid said, hanging up. He looked at Axle. "That good enough for you?"

Axle sighed. "It'll have to be. Flimsy's better than nothing." He pulled out his own phone. "I'll call Dad. If he can convince LaDonna, she'll go to a safe house—as long as she knows Jerome and I are safe. And Maybelline."

Damn. He'd almost forgotten about LaDonna's mother. If anything happened to any of them because of him, he'd never forgive himself.

If anything happened to Haley...

He couldn't even finish the thought. And that told him everything he needed to know. His dad was right. He was in love with her.

Chapter 19

Haley sat curled at one end of the sofa wrapped in a blanket that did nothing to stop the chill crawling up her spine. LaDonna occupied the other end, arms folded, eyes sharp. Britt and Gordon moved through the living room like sentries, checking every door and window in rotating shifts. Their vigilance felt performative. Whatever was happening—it went deeper than Josh's stalking.

"What aren't you telling us, Gordon?" Haley asked as he returned from another interior sweep.

"Besides the fact that Josh is a stalker and an arsonist, and we can't prove either?" Gordon's voice was tight. "Isn't that reason enough to protect you and catch the bastard?"

"So I'm bait?"

Gordon flushed. "No. I mean—not exactly. But he's targeted you, and someone has to keep you safe while Noya and half the sheriff's department are out hunting him. Asheville PD's involved too. It's a multi-jurisdictional manhunt. You're safe as long as you stay inside. We've got people on it," he added, but his voice lacked conviction.

Haley didn't think he was lying. She realized with a jolt—he didn't know. Someone higher up was pulling the strings.

"What do you know that Gordon doesn't?" LaDonna asked as Britt reentered the room, sliding his phone into his shirt pocket. He was now dressed like a cowboy from a modern western—jeans, button-down, boots, and a sidearm slung low on his hip. All he lacked was the Stetson.

"Nothing," he said, avoiding her gaze.

LaDonna stood, letting the blanket fall. She stepped over it and squared up to Britt, arms akimbo. "Don't lie to me. I don't need that kind of protection, and neither does Haley. We can defend ourselves better if you stop keeping us in the dark. Spill, buddy—or you're sleeping alone for the next six months."

Despite the tension, Britt cracked a smile. "You drive a hard bargain, woman."

LaDonna glanced at Haley, then back at her husband. "Damn right. Now talk."

Britt sighed. "Sit."

LaDonna returned to her seat. Gordon folded his arms, clearly waiting for answers too. Britt nodded at him and took the chair opposite the sofa.

"Josh has murdered two women," Britt said, like it was new information.

"We know that," Haley and Gordon said in unison. They exchanged uneasy glances.

Britt exhaled. "What you might not know is that he's also under investigation by Homeland Security."

"He's a terrorist?" LaDonna asked, skeptical. Haley felt the same doubt.

"Not in the traditional sense," Britt said. "He's a serial killer. That makes him a domestic terrorist."

"Serial killers are usually handled by the Behavioral Analysis Unit or the Child Abduction and Serial Killer Unit," Gordon said. "I ran Josh's name through ViCAP and his prints through CODIS. No hits. So where's this intel coming from?"

"Axle," Britt replied. "You know he consults for Homeland Security sometimes."

"And?" Gordon snapped. "What does Homeland Security have to do with a domestic serial killer—if that's even what Josh is? There's no proof."

Haley's throat tightened. "Did Axle tell you this?" Why hadn't he told her?

"Yes," Britt said, turning to Gordon. "The info came straight from Special Agent Reid Sheridan. He helped Axle get his PI license. After Axle brought Haley—and that damn cat—over, he called Reid for a background check. Turns out, Josh is wanted for questioning in the death of a diplomat's daughter in D.C. That's how Homeland Security got involved."

LaDonna leaned in, eyes locked on her husband. "Is that the truth? You're a terrible liar, Britt. And something still doesn't add up."

"I'm telling you what Axle told me," Britt said, voice low. "I don't know more than that. But if Reid Sheridan's involved, Josh is more dangerous than we thought."

Haley looked at LaDonna. Britt's answer satisfied his wife—but it terrified her. Her heart lodged in her throat. She'd dated a serial killer. "When did Axle call you? Why didn't he call me?"

Britt checked his phone, then met Haley's gaze. "You can ask him yourself when he gets here." He held up the screen, showing a blinking green dot on a neighborhood map. "Axle's been sharing his location on my family tracker app. He and Reid just pulled up."

Gordon reached the door first, opening it before Axle could knock. A man in a black suit stood beside him—FBI written all over him.

"Special Agent Sheridan," Gordon said, stepping aside. "Nice of you to let me know you were coming," he added, voice dripping sarcasm.

"Sorry," Sheridan said, extending a hand. "Things moved fast after Axle's call. I updated Deputy Kanati—he informed the sheriff."

Gordon glared. "This is our case. No one invited the FBI." He glanced at Axle. "Sorry, bro, but you're not part of the Buncombe County Sheriff's Department or Asheville PD. This is our jurisdiction."

"Axle?" Haley pushed past Gordon and the agent, reaching Axle's side. He pulled her into his arms.

Resting her head against his chest, she looked up at Axle, but he was looking at Gordon. "Can we take this inside? Haley and LaDonna need to sit."

"I don't need pampering," LaDonna said, voice firm. "I need answers. Britt's kept us in the dark long enough."

Gordon grumbled as they filed into the dining room. Before anyone sat, Axle introduced Reid Sheridan to Haley. The agent gave a silent nod—cool, unreadable. There was something about him that didn't quite fit the suit. Something coiled beneath the surface.

"We appreciate your help, Sheridan," Gordon said, his tone suddenly territorial. "But there's no way in hell you're taking over my case."

Haley blinked. Gordon was posturing like a peacock—bold talk from a man who'd recently told her they couldn't do anything without witnesses or proof.

"This isn't about ego," Sheridan said. "And for the record, the sheriff officially requested our help. It's our case now."

"I'm not standing down," Gordon said, steel in his voice. "I'm taking point."

"You can assist. Hell, you can make the arrest," Sheridan said. "But you don't know shit about this case."

"I know Patterson probably killed two other women before he started stalking our Haley," Gordon said, as if she were some kind of community property. Haley bristled and shot him a glare, but he kept going. "He's broken into her house twice. Now he's committed arson—ransacked the place and torched her car."

"And you can't prove any of it," Sheridan countered, and Haley's heart sank.

Axle reached under the table and took her hand. "We will stop him," he murmured, just for her. Then, louder: "Reid's been investigating Josh for years. He has enough to issue a warrant. You don't. We need his help."

"We?" Gordon looked between them. "You're not even officially part of this investigation. I let you in as a courtesy—because Haley's a friend. But it's time to step back and let the professionals handle it."

"Gordon!" Haley snapped. "I hired Axle. You told me to. Now you're telling him to back off? Why?"

His face flushed. "I did what he asked—came here to watch out for you while he called in the cavalry and hijacked my investigation. I don't appreciate being told how to do my job by someone with less training and less experience. I'm done taking orders from him. Now that the FBI's involved, we do things my way."

"No. You'll do things my way," Sheridan said coolly. "So we've come full circle. I'm working with Axle."

"Enough with the pissing contest," Britt said, his booming voice cutting through the room like a blade. Silence fell. "This is about protecting Haley—and catching a killer. So what are you going to do about it?"

He locked eyes with Gordon, who flushed and looked away.

"You're right," Gordon muttered. "This is about stopping a killer before he strikes again. We need to keep civilians safe."

"Exactly," Reid said, turning to Britt. "Which is why you and LaDonna need to pack a bag. I'm placing you both in protective custody in a hotel under assumed names."

LaDonna gasped. "What about my mother? And Jerome?"

Britt stood without protest and moved to the head of the table, his hand settling on LaDonna's shoulder with a calm that didn't match the moment. He patted her gently. "I'm sure Axle has that covered."

Haley blinked. That was it. No pushback. No clipped questions about duration or logistics. Britt—who'd taken charge like a general the second Gordon walked in—was just... agreeing. A slow, cold knot formed in Haley's stomach. Britt already knew all of this. So why pretend otherwise?

She looked at Axle, but his eyes were fixed on his stepmother.

"Already handled," he said. "Reid sent two agents to Durham. Jerome won't even know he's under surveillance—it's round-the-clock. Two more agents are picking up Maybelline from her assisted living center. I spoke to her. She'll be at the hotel before you and Dad arrive."

Haley's pulse jumped. She reached for Axle's hand and squeezed. He finally met her gaze, and the worry etched into his brow made her breath catch. If anything happened to his family because of her, he'd never forgive her. And she wasn't sure she'd forgive herself either.

"What about me?" Gordon challenged. "You sending me packing too?"

"No," Reid said. "You and a BBTF agent will be on protection detail. You'll stay at the hotel with the family."

Gordon frowned. "And how does that help the investigation? You're assigning me to babysit."

Britt leaned across the table, eyes hard. "I don't need a babysitter. I need a law enforcement officer who'll protect my wife. If you're not up to it, I'm sure Deputy Kanati can handle it."

"We need you on the inside," Reid said, cutting off Gordon's reply. "You know Josh—his voice, his mannerisms. I'd have to brief another agent from scratch, and they'd only have a photo. If Josh alters his appearance, you'll still spot him before he gets close enough to hurt the family. It's that simple."

But it wasn't simple at all.

Haley's pulse thudded in her ears. The tension in the room felt staged, as if Axle, Reid, and Britt had rehearsed their lines like actors in a police drama. She scanned their faces and saw the same thing in each of them: restraint. Whatever script they were following, they weren't telling her everything.

"This doesn't feel right," she said, her voice low but steady. "If there's no proof Josh killed his exes, stalked me, broke into my house, and torched my car, how is there suddenly enough evidence to justify all this—multiple agencies, protective custody, a manhunt? Where was this help when Gordon needed it?"

Gordon nodded. "Damn good question. It's not like I didn't run his name through every database I had access to. Where was Homeland Security then? And why no mention of the diplomat's daughter?"

"Josh was never officially a suspect in Sharon or Ashland's deaths," Axle said. "So his name wasn't flagged in ViCAP."

Haley's stomach twisted. She didn't know what unsettled her more—Josh slipping through the cracks, or the gnawing possibility that those cracks had been carved on purpose... or never existed at all?

"What about the diplomat's daughter?" Gordon pressed. "Isn't that how Sheridan got involved?"

Reid hesitated. Just for a second. But Haley caught it.

"Josh was questioned in the vehicular death of Rita Milan Zozaya—the daughter of a Mexican diplomat stationed in D.C. The medical examiner ruled it a CUPPI. The investigation raised more questions than answers, but the DA wouldn't indict on circumstantial evidence alone," he said. "When Axle called for help in his investigation, I recognized Josh's name—even though I wasn't on the task force. My supervisor sent me here to look into it. Quietly."

The word landed like a rock.

Haley narrowed her eyes. "Quietly," she echoed. "Why?"

Reid's jaw flexed. "The murder of a diplomat's daughter is politically sensitive. Homeland was running an undercover operation in coordination with DC Metro. I remembered Josh because he lived in Asheville, and I was a detective here nearly a decade ago. He was questioned, but it didn't go anywhere. The Milan Zozaya case is still open, but with her father back in Mexico, it hasn't been a priority for the Bureau."

"And I guess since no other foreign diplomat died, DHS didn't care either," Gordon muttered.

Haley looked at Reid. "So you knew. You knew Josh had a history. You knew he was dangerous. And you waited."

Reid's gaze dropped to the floor, then flicked to the door like he wished he were anywhere else. "I followed protocol," he said finally—but it sounded like an apology.

Haley still wasn't sure she believed any of it—until she met Axle's gaze. It grounded her. As long as he was near, she felt safe.

But what happened after Josh was caught? After the case was closed? Where did she stand with Axle then?

"So everything's settled," Haley said, drawing every eye. "Except for one minor detail. No one's said a word about me—or where I'm supposed to go during this manhunt."

"You're not leaving my side," Axle said, and the promise in his eyes was all she needed.

Chapter 20

Axle hated lying. His dad understood—but would Haley or LaDonna? It didn't matter. Josh wasn't just a stalker who'd murdered two women. He was a vampire. That made him a thousand times more dangerous—and nearly impossible to prove—or stop. Axle's priority was clear: keep Haley and his family safe.

Once Gordon got his parents and Maybelline settled in the hotel under an assumed name, Axle and Reid took Haley and Bootsie to Axle's house. Princess Paw Paw met them at the door, yipping and wagging her tail. She'd met Haley and Reid before, but the moment she spotted the cat carrier, she growled. Inside the crate, Bootsie hissed—a sound so fierce it sent Princess yelping from the room.

"Well, I guess Bootsie doesn't like dogs," Haley said with forced cheer, but Axle caught the tremor beneath her voice.

"It'll be okay," he said, gently taking the carrier from her hands. "Princess is used to ruling the house. So, we'll keep Bootsie and his litterbox in the bonus room upstairs and pray he doesn't shred the felt on my pool table."

Haley laughed, but it was hollow. "Your pool table's doomed. Bootsie once dropped a live rat—rat, not mouse—at my feet while I was on the toilet. I couldn't exactly jump up, you know?" She blushed crimson. "The rat hissed. I screamed. Bootsie sat back, licking his paws like he expected a thank-you. All I had was a toilet plunger. So I beat the rat with it, screaming between swings. Bootsie was impressed when I killed it, but disappointed I didn't eat it. I tossed it out the back door. Found its corpse on my kitchen floor the next morning."

Axle burst out laughing. So did Reid.

"And that's why I'm a dog person," Reid said. "Princess Paw Paw would never pull a stunt like that."

Haley raised an eyebrow. "She couldn't. That rat was bigger than Princess."

"Lucky for me, I don't have a doggy door," Axle said with a grin. For a moment, they were all thinking about something other than Josh. "Bootsie will be fine in the bonus room. I'll put you in the bedroom next door."

"I'll sleep down here," Reid said. "There's a guest room with a private bath, right?"

"Second door on the left," Axle confirmed.

Reid headed down the hall with his duffle bag. Axle carried Haley's suitcase and the cat carrier upstairs. Haley followed, gripping her purse strap like a lifeline. At the top of the stairs, Axle hesitated. If he put Haley next to the cat, she'd be two doors away. If he put her next to his room, he could protect her better. Yeah, right. If he had his way, she wouldn't just be in his room—she'd be in his bed. The thought was tempting. Too tempting. He squashed it and turned left.

The bonus room door was open. Haley stepped inside and froze. "You have a bar in your house?"

Axle set the carrier down and moved past her to shut the door. "Bootsie doesn't have a drinking problem, does he?" he teased.

She didn't answer. Her gaze stayed fixed on the liquor collection behind the six-foot mahogany bar, flanked by four matching stools. A foosball table lined the far wall. A pool table—also mahogany—anchored the center of the room between the bar and a plush sectional facing a massive flat-screen.

Haley smiled. "No, but I might pick up the habit. I could spend months in here watching movies and drinking my troubles away. Who lives like this?"

His heart twisted hard enough to bruise. "Before the divorce, it was Bonnie's playroom." The words scraped out of him. He'd built this room for a child he no longer had—measured the walls, picked the paint, and imagined her laughter echoing off the hardwood. Then he'd gutted it, poured money into a redesign meant for friends he'd never made. A shrine to a life that had collapsed under him. "I don't live like this. Even if I knew enough people to invite over, I don't have the time." He heard the hollowness in his own voice, the loneliness he never let anyone else catch. "Honestly, I usually just watch TV downstairs with Princess."

"What about Reid?" she asked softly, and the pity in her tone hit him like a slap.

"What about him."

"He's been here before, right? Don't y'all ever just hang out?"

"Once." The memory rose uninvited—the week after Austria, the cold that seeped into his bones even after they left the mountains. They'd helped

Nicolas and Gerard hunt the vampire who'd killed three tourists at the ski resort. Two men pretending they weren't bleeding inside: Reid still pining for Amber, Axle mourning the family he'd lost and the man he'd been with them. "We played pool." Reid got drunk. Axle tried, but with his altered DNA, the best he could manage was a dull, useless buzz. Even his vices had been taken from him.

"It's a great man cave," she said gently, letting the subject drop. "When all this is over, can we watch a movie in here and have a drink? I've never had a private screening in a private theater with a bar."

"Sure," he said, forcing a smile that didn't touch anything inside him.

He turned away before the urge to pull her close could betray him—before she could feel how hollow he was up close. He crouched and unlatched the carrier. Bootsie shot out like a launched arrow, hissing as he bolted across the room. He scrambled onto the leather couch, claws sinking deep, claiming the space with frantic, territorial defiance.

"Bootsie, no!" Haley cried, rushing after him.

"He's not declawed, is he?" Axle asked, wincing at the gouges.

"Sorry. He used to be an indoor–outdoor cat, remember?" Bootsie squirmed in her arms, all muscle and indignation. Haley cringed. "Maybe I should just keep him in my room?"

"No. Don't." Axle shook his head. "Maybe I should lock Princess up and let Bootsie explore. He might be less destructive that way."

He took her arm—gentle, guiding—and led her and the cat through the adjoining bathroom to the guest room. He set her suitcase on the bed, then stepped out to grab the litter box. When he returned, Haley sat on the edge of the mattress while Bootsie prowled the perimeter, tail twitching like a fuse.

Axle opened the bathroom door and set the litter box in the corner between the commode and the wall. Bootsie sauntered in behind him and promptly marked his territory.

Haley sighed. "Maybe he can just stay locked in my room if I leave the bathroom door open."

"No. Let him explore," Axle said. "If he has full run of the upstairs, maybe he'll stay out of Princess's way."

She nodded, though doubt flickered across her face as they headed back downstairs.

In the living room, Reid sat on the sofa, leaning over files spread across the coffee table. Princess snuggled beside him, perfectly content—until Bootsie strutted down the steps and leapt onto the table. Reid yelped. Princess barked. Bootsie planted himself in the middle of the paperwork, licking his paw with regal indifference.

"Bootsie, no!" Haley shouted, reaching for him.

Axle caught her wrist. "Wait."

"What the hell?" Reid said. "That's not a cat. That's a damn mountain lion."

"I'm sorry," Haley said. "I'll take him upstairs."

She reached again. Axle stopped her a second time. He looked at Princess, locking eyes with the dog. She froze, then settled instantly, barking cut off like a switch had been thrown.

Surprised, Axle turned to Bootsie and locked gazes.

The cat hissed, fur lifting, and backed away—then toppled off the table in a scramble of claws. With a startled yelp, he bolted up the stairs.

"Since when did you become a cat whisperer?" Haley asked. "The only time I've seen Bootsie act like that was when Josh broke into my house."

Axle went still. His gaze met Reid's. He'd only meant to break up the fight—but maybe cats really could sense vampires. Not that he was one. Not exactly. But the truth of his altered DNA sat heavy in his bones.

The thought clawed at him. In Egypt, cats had been revered as protectors of the dead, guardians of the threshold between this world and the next. In old stories, they watched tombs, kept spirits from slipping free, and saw what mortals could not. Maybe there was truth in all of it. Maybe Bootsie wasn't reacting to chaos or dogs or strangers. Maybe he recognized the part of Axle that belonged to the dead—the part that wasn't fully human anymore.

"Axle does have a pretty mean stare," Reid said, forcing a smile. "Keeps this killer in line."

He scooped up Princess and ruffled her fur. She acted perfectly normal—but Axle knew she wouldn't bark at Bootsie again.

#

Reid and Axle had barricaded themselves in the office, leaving Haley to drift through the house like a ghost. By noon, hunger nudged her into the kitchen. She scavenged through Axle's fridge, cobbling together lunch—slicing potatoes for chips, frying them until golden, stacking sandwiches with cold cuts and cheese.

They didn't even come out to eat. So she carried the plates to the office where Reid and Axle sat hunched over the desk, eyes locked on the computer monitor. Haley took the lone chair across the room, balancing her plate in her lap, her drink on the floor. The men devoured their sandwiches in silence, already turning back to the screen before she'd finished her chips—like she was invisible.

"Thanks for lunch," Axle said, wiping his mouth and turning back to the glow of his monitor. Maps. Listings. Coordinates. Lines of text flickered in the gloom.

Haley stood, gathering the dirty plates. Apparently, she'd been dismissed—like the help. She stepped closer, trying to glimpse the screen. "What are you looking at?"

Axle slid his chair sideways, blocking her view. "Nothing. Mind feeding Princess and letting her out?" He glanced back with a smile. "She doesn't have a doggy door or a litter box."

Haley frowned. "Sure. No problem. It's not like I'm being stalked or anything."

"Thanks, sweetheart," Axle said, ignoring the sarcasm entirely.

After taking care of the dog, she fed Bootsie and cleaned the kitchen. No one offered to help. No one asked how she was doing. No one seemed remotely concerned—until the sun dipped below the trees.

Then everything changed.

Suddenly she couldn't take a step without one of them shadowing her. Axle loitered outside the bathroom like a guard posted at a door. Reid hovered in the hallway, stiff and alert. The second time she opened the door to find Axle standing there, arms crossed, she snapped.

"What the hell?" she barked, brushing past him.

He followed so closely she could feel his breath on her neck. When she dropped onto the sofa, he sat beside her—practically in her lap.

"You ignored me all day, and now you're glued to my side like a bodyguard. What gives?"

"Nothing's changed," Axle said—too fast, too defensive.

"This is what protective custody looks like," Reid muttered, avoiding her gaze.

Haley scoffed. "Is Gordon tailing LaDonna to the bathroom too? Or just after sunset?"

Before either man could answer, a knock rattled the front door.

Axle and Reid exchanged a look. Reid drew his sidearm. Haley barely had time to react before he yanked her to her feet and shoved her behind him. Axle—unarmed—moved toward the door.

That was wrong. Axle wasn't a cop. He didn't carry. So why was he the one opening the door?

The tension thickened like fog. The door creaked open.

A tall, thin man stepped inside, draped in an Arabic-style robe and ghutra. His skin was pale, his presence both ancient and ageless.

"Surratt," Axle and Reid said in unison.

Axle slammed the door shut and stormed toward Reid. "What the hell is he doing here?"

Reid holstered his gun, face draining of color. "I didn't call him."

"You called Carl?" Axle snapped, grabbing Haley's arm and pulling her away from Reid. The old man—Surratt—glided closer.

"I didn't call Carl either," Reid argued. "He doesn't even know I'm here."

Surratt's voice was smooth, low, touched with an accent. "Detective Carl Matheson is unaware of my visit—or the circumstances that necessitated it." He looked pristine, but smelled faintly of mildew and dust.

"So why are you here?" Reid asked.

"Sonia contacted me. The man she turned has been...active. Turn on the news."

"Turned?" Haley echoed, eyes darting to Axle. But he was already across the room, grabbing the remote.

The TV flickered to life. Emergency lights strobed behind a reporter as police cordoned off an alley near a grimy nightclub.

"Just after sunset, witnesses discovered two bodies in an alley outside Hobo's," the reporter said, her somber tone edged with excitement. "Both victims' throats were slit and their bodies drained. Detectives found little blood at the scene—reminiscent of the Lifeblood Labs murders eight years ago."

Haley's pulse stuttered. Her heart slammed against her ribs.

"Axle," she whispered. "I thought the man responsible for the Lifeblood murders—and your abduction—was dead."

"He is," Axle said, but he was looking at Reid, not her.

Reid nodded once, jaw tight. "Josh did this."

Axle wiped a hand over his head and sighed. "It's started."

"What's started? Why would Josh do this? How?" Her voice cracked. "How can you slit someone's throat and leave no blood?"

"Because he can't find you," Axle said gently, taking her hands. "But he will. Once he calms down, he'll pick up your scent. He'll come here. And when he does, we'll be ready."

Haley's blood turned to sludge. Her thoughts thickened. Surratt seemed to drift across the room like a mirage. Axle released her hands and pulled her to his side, his gaze meeting Surratt's.

"Scent?" she whispered. "What...what does that mean?"

No one answered or even looked at her. Surratt's gaze was locked on Axle. "She must be told," he said.

"No," Axle growled.

Surratt held his gaze. "We can erase her memories later."

Erase my memories? The fear snapped. Fury surged in its place. She turned toward Axle, grabbed his arm, and forced him to face her. "I don't know what the hell is going on, but I want answers. Now."

"And answers you shall have," Surratt said, serene as a prophet.

"Back the hell up, Yoda," Axle snarled, but Surratt stepped closer.

She felt the pull of his gaze. Her pulse slowed. "Axle?" Her voice thinned. Her vision tunneled. The room tilted.

Then everything went black.

#

"What the hell, Surratt?" Axle barked, cradling Haley's limp body as he rushed her to the sofa. His pulse thundered in his ears.

Surratt didn't flinch. "Now isn't the time for hysteria," he said coolly. "We need a plan." He nodded toward the door, where Sonia had slipped in without a sound. She didn't bother locking it — not that it mattered. Locks were meaningless to vampires.

"You called Surratt?" Reid asked, voice tight.

Sonia nodded. "I called Vincent first. He told me to call Surratt."

"So you called the cavalry," Axle muttered, guilt gnawing at him. He should've done that yesterday. If he'd called Vincent and Gerard, when he should have, they'd already be here. But he'd thought he and Reid could handle one lone vampire. He'd been wrong.

"I did this," Sonia said, her voice low, almost broken. "I created Josh. Now he's killed two people and he's after your girlfriend."

Axle looked at Haley, her chest rising in shallow rhythm. Surratt had put her in a trance-like sleep — she wouldn't wake until he allowed it, or until sunrise. Either way, when she opened her eyes, Axle would have to erase her memory or explain everything. And if he did the latter, she'd never look at him the same.

"It's better this way," Reid said, watching Axle with quiet dread.

Axle shook his head. "Is it?" The question slipped out before he could stop it. Haley hated when he did that — answered with a question, like he was dodging the truth.

Sonia nodded. "Gerard, Vincent, and Nicolas are flying in tonight. They should be in Asheville by ten. But we can't wait. Josh will find her soon," she said, dipping her chin toward Haley.

"What about Amber?" Reid asked.

Sonia snorted. "She's in love with Gerard. The sooner you let go of your childish infatuation, the sooner you can move on."

"Says the woman still in love with Vincent after two hundred years," Reid shot back, his voice cracking with something raw and wounded.

Surratt raised a hand, silencing them. "We cannot wait. My brother, Ashmada, is drawn to blood and violence. The mortal Sonia turned has stirred him. If we don't end this now, he'll come. And when he does, he won't stop at Haley."

The room fell into a taut silence.

Axle clenched his jaw. "Then we stop it." He turned to Surratt. "But first, I need to talk to Haley. Wake her up."

Chapter 21

Haley's eyes fluttered open to find Axle perched on the edge of the bed, watching her. Her heart slammed against her ribs, breath catching in her throat. How had she ended up in Axle's bedroom and how long had she been here?

She pushed herself upright to lean against the headboard. The room tilted. Her stomach churned. Axle kept his distance, giving her space. She inhaled deeply, then exhaled, slow and steady.

"What happened?" she asked. "The last thing I remember was you opening the door to some Egyptian-looking guy in a robe."

"You fainted," Axle said—too quickly. A lie. But why?

She searched her memory. Her pulse spiked. "There was a murder in Asheville," she said, pressing a hand to her chest as if she could steady the erratic thudding. "Two people had their throats slit. Reid said Josh did it."

Axle exhaled slowly. "He did. And he'll kill again if we don't stop him."

"Why would he do that?" She tried to meet Axle's gaze, but he looked away. "Josh is a stalker. He kills women who reject him. Sharon, Ashland, maybe that diplomat's daughter. But he always covers his tracks. He thinks he's too smart to get caught. Slitting someone's throat is messy. You can't make that look like an accident."

Especially with no blood at the scene.

"He's not worried about getting caught anymore," Axle said, finally meeting her eyes. But something in his stare made her wish he hadn't.

A chill crawled up her spine. "Why not?"

"Because he's a vampire."

She blinked. Once. Twice. Her brain rejected the words outright. "Do you really think now's the time for jokes?" Her voice shook. Axle wasn't delusional. He used humor to defuse tension, but this—this wasn't humor. This was something else. Something he'd been carrying like a bruise he didn't want touched.

"It's not a joke." He sat at the foot of the bed, careful not to touch her, as if even proximity might break her. "You want to know why I never talk about the kidnappings or the murders at Lifeblood? Because no one would believe the truth."

Her pulse jumped so hard it hurt. "And what is the truth, Axle? Vampires?" She laughed, but it came out thin, brittle, wrong. "Come on. That's—"

"Crazy?" he asked quietly.

But the look he gave her wasn't wild or unhinged. It was steady. Certain. He believed it.

Her stomach dropped.

"Axle, vampires aren't real," she said, clinging to logic like a lifeline. "I know you went through hell, but keep it in perspective. Your coworkers were murdered by an ex-military doctor trying to create super soldiers. He wasn't a vampire."

"No. He cloned vampires. And he created me," Axle said, dead serious. "Vincent Maxwell and Gerard Delaroche—my former employers—are vampires. They founded Lifeblood Labs to avoid feeding on the living. Everyone thought they had Xeroderma Pigmentosum, a genetic disorder that makes sunlight deadly. Megan Harper's sister died from it. Vincent hired Megan to find a cure. But really, he wanted her to cure the vampire virus. And she did. Sort of."

Haley's hopes for a future with him crumbled. "Oh, Axle," she whispered, touching his cheek. His skin was warm—not clammy. His pulse steady. His eyes clear. But the words... the words were delusional. "Are you on medication? Do you want me to call your doctor?"

"I don't need a damn doctor," he snapped, pulling away.

She folded her hands in her lap, forcing herself to stay calm. Assess the patient. Stay objective. He was alert and oriented, but his thought process was fragmented, fixated. A psychotic break? PTSD? Something had tipped him over the edge. She needed to keep him grounded until she could get him help.

"Axle, vampires aren't real," she said softly. "You have to know that."

"They are," he insisted. "Dr. Weldon injected me with cloned vampire blood. He tried to recreate Megan's vaccine, but my blood wasn't fully drained first. I wasn't a normal vampire, so the vaccine didn't work. After I was rescued, Megan perfected the vaccine, and it worked better on me because I'm not a typical vampire."

Haley's chest tightened. Injected with cloned blood? He actually believed this. The murders at Hobo's must have triggered him. Delusional disorder? Trauma-induced psychosis Yet the conviction in his eyes made her falter. What if he wasn't sick? What if—

No. Not possible. Stay rational.

Her heart ached. She opened her mouth, but Axle kept going.

"Gerard and Vincent are vampires. The vaccine lets them eat food and survive on minimal blood. They can tolerate sunlight with strong sunscreen, as long as they avoid it between ten in the morning and two in the afternoon. That's when they enter regenerative sleep. But the vaccine affected me differently.

"After months of injections, I don't need it anymore. I don't suffer from vampirism's side effects. I don't need blood—though I crave rare meat sometimes—and I don't avoid the sun. Weldon didn't know it, but he succeeded. He actually created a super soldier. Me."

"Enough." Whatever pity she'd felt curdled into anger. Did he really expect her to believe this nonsense?

She slid away, one leg over the edge of the bed. "You don't drink blood. You don't sleep in a coffin. That sounds human to me, Axle. Because that's what you are."

"I am human," he said. "But I have vampiric abilities."

He stood—and vanished. Reappeared across the room. Vanished again and reappeared at the foot of the bed.

Haley's pulse spiked. Her heart lurched. "What the hell?" she whispered. He'd moved like Josh—silent, fast, unnatural. "Reid!" she shouted, scrambling off the bed. "Detective Sheridan!"

Reid, the Egyptian man, and a curvy redhead rushed in. Axle blurred again, suddenly beside them.

Reid arched a brow. "Parlor tricks, now?"

It had to be a trick. Sleight of hand. Misdirection. Something. Maybe Axle had dabbled in magic since high school. It would've been impressive—if it hadn't terrified her.

"That's not funny, Axle. I don't care how you did it, but don't do it again."

"I'm not trying to be funny." He stepped toward her, stopping when she backed into the corner. "I'm telling you the truth. Vampires are real. Weldon cloned one and used its blood to create me—a soldier for the military. He never knew he'd succeeded because Reid and his partner, Amber Buckley, uncovered the truth—and Gerard killed him. Vincent and Gerard are Utukku vampires, good ones. They don't kill to feed. Amber is Nicholas's daughter. He's a vampire too. He fathered her before becoming fully turned—and sterile. Amber's a dhampir. Half mortal, half vampire. Megan injected herself with Vincent's blood to create the vaccine. Because of that, she has dhampir abilities too."

This wasn't PTSD. This was a full-blown break. The murders, the stress, the comparisons to Lifeblood—it had pushed him over the edge. But was he dangerous? Or just delusional?

Haley swallowed hard, forcing herself into professional mode. "You're safe from Weldon. He's dead. You were protecting me from Josh. Remember? He's a stalker. He killed Sharon and Ashland. But he didn't kill those people in Asheville tonight. And he didn't kill your coworkers eight years ago."

"You're right," Axle said. "He didn't kill Richard Baxter or Tina Gallagher. But he did kill those two tonight. And if we don't protect you, he'll come for you. He won't kill you. He'll turn you."

"Listen to yourself," Haley said, edging around the bed. Why wasn't anyone helping her? Why were they just watching, like spectators at a premiere? And who was the woman with the reddish-brown hair Reid kept eyeing? "Vampires aren't real. So Josh couldn't turn me even if he wanted to."

"He's definitely a vampire. Who do you think turned him?" the redhead said, her voice tinged with a Slavic accent.

"Stay out of this, Red. You're not helping," Haley snapped.

The woman's eyes flashed. "My hair is brown, not red. And the name is Sonia," she said—cold, defensive. And Haley could've sworn she had fangs.

She blinked. Looked again. Still there. Sharper. Longer than Bootsie's.

Haley gasped, stumbling backward, breath hitching as her spine struck the wall. Axle snapped at Sonia. Reid's eyes narrowed. But the Egyptian man stepped forward, calm amid the chaos.

"There is an easier way," he said, voice low, resonant. His gaze locked onto hers—steady, unblinking.

Haley's pulse slowed. The storm in her mind unraveled into eerie stillness. The room fell silent. Her vision dimmed—not into darkness, but into something else. She was seeing, though not with her eyes. Her body remained rooted in Axle's bedroom, yet her mind slipped elsewhere, drifting outside herself.

Mist curled around her ankles. The air grew thick, ancient. Surratt stood beside her, unmoving. Before them stretched a town that looked biblical—sunbaked stone, narrow alleys, silence that felt sacred.

She knew, without knowing how, that this place no longer existed. She was inside someone else's memory. Thousands of years old. And somehow, it belonged to her now.

Surratt nodded, though she hadn't spoken.

"Vampirism is no curse," he said, though his lips never moved. She heard him inside her head.

She couldn't speak. Couldn't move. But she wasn't afraid. Not yet.

"It is a virus," he continued, "born in Mesopotamia, in the village you see before you. The Sumerians ruled this land. They built the first cities, the first temples. But war and death were constant companions. Young men died violently—on battlefields, in plagues.

"Legend says those who died in torment awakened in their graves. Their desire to live was so fierce it pulled their souls back into their broken bodies. They rose at night, seeking blood to survive."

Haley's breath caught. The mist thickened. The town flickered like a mirage.

"The sickness killed the body, but not the soul," he continued. "It lingered as flesh decayed. Without blood, the afflicted withered—but they did not die. They became the Utukku: spirits, demons, men. Some were merciful. Others were monsters."

Monsters echoed in her mind. She wanted to scream—to shut her eyes—but the images kept flickering like a silent film she couldn't look away from.

"To hide their sickness, they emerged only at night," he said, voice hypnotic. "The sun drained them. But blood reversed the wasting. At first, they took only small amounts from loved ones, leaving behind peaceful dreams to ease their guilt. But guilt fades. Hunger does not. Soon, they learned killing enemies was easier. And some stopped distinguishing between enemy and innocent."

Haley's throat tightened. She tried to speak, to scream—Enough—but the words froze inside her.

Surratt's eyes softened. "As the Utukku regained strength, they tried to return to the living. But the sun scorched them. Blood remained essential. They adapted to darkness. For a time, they were content. But loneliness is a cruel thing. Some infected their lovers—their friends. The thirst grew insatiable. The only way to silence it was to drain a body completely."

Centuries pressed against her chest. Her throat burned. Her eyes stung with visions older than language.

"The Utukku divided," Surratt said. "My brother and I were both infected. He sought power. I sought peace. Those who resisted the bloodlust became the Shedu. I am their leader. All Shedu are Utukku. But not all Utukku are Shedu."

Her thoughts stirred. I don't understand, she whispered in her mind.

Surratt heard her.

"Axle's former bosses at Lifeblood are Utukku, not Shedu. They took no vows against killing—though they do not kill indiscriminately. Vincent Maxwell and Gerard Delaroche founded the blood bank to help vampires feed without harming mortals. Vincent recruited Dr. Megan Harper to study his condition. She created a vaccine, and in the process they fell in love. Married.

"The vaccine worked—partially. Vampires who take daily injections need little blood. They need only avoid the sun at its peak when they're forced to sleep. But the vaccine weakens them. Colonel Timmons knew of Dr. Harper's research, yet he wanted more. He hired Dr. Weldon to create vampires without side effects. Soldiers who could not die.

"Weldon captured Gerard, cloned him, and nearly succeeded. Timmons was stopped, but Weldon escaped. He built a new lab to continue the work. He captured Axle, killed his co-workers, and altered his DNA."

Surratt's voice deepened, resonant. "Both Timmons and Weldon are dead. Gerard was freed, and the vampire cloned from his cells destroyed. Axle is the only living proof their experiment worked."

Haley's heart pounded. Her thoughts raced.

"Axle can't be a vampire," she whispered—unsure if the words left her lips or stayed trapped in her mind. "He eats normal food. He walks in the sun.

He sleeps at night."

"He is neither vampire nor mortal," Surratt replied. "He is something more. Something better. But he does not know the limits of his power. He does not trust them. Perhaps you can help him."

The mist surged. The ancient village dissolved. Her body numbed. Her thoughts blurred. She was falling into darkness. Drifting. Dissolving.

Then—light. Warmth. A hand.

She opened her eyes.

She was in Axle's bed.

And he was holding her hand.

Chapter 22

"Hi, sweetheart." Axle's voice was soft, edged with caution, as though one wrong word might send her fleeing. Haley wanted to bolt—but her body refused to move.

"Was I drugged?" she whispered. "Or did that actually happen?" Her voice trembled, disbelief threading every syllable. She couldn't begin to explain what she'd seen—what she'd learned, or thought she'd learned.

"It happened," he said. "I'm sorry you had to find out this way. Hell, I'm sorry you had to find out at all. But at least you believed him. You doubted me. You even doubted my sanity." His smile was sheepish, fractured, almost broken.

Haley cringed, guilt, fear, and disbelief colliding inside her.

"I still don't know what to believe." The words felt hollow, echoes from a dream she from which she couldn't awaken. She pulled her hand from his and sat up in bed. "I mean—how can vampires be real? How have they stayed hidden so long, dismissed as myths, if they actually exist?"

"That's exactly how they've survived—by becoming folklore. They live in shadows, avoiding attention. The vaccine helps the good ones, the Utukku, blend in."

"Unlike the redhead," Haley said. She didn't know how she knew, but Sonia was different. The fangs were undeniable, but it was more than that—an aura that felt sharper, darker. Dangerous.

"You're right. Sonia doesn't take the vaccine," Axle admitted. "But she protects the Utukku, and she helps the Shedu shield mortals from the Ekimmu."

"And yet she turned Josh." Her voice cracked under the weight of it—revulsion, disbelief, fury. The image of Josh's fangs flashing in his smile chilled her to the bone. "She turned a predator into an unstoppable monster."

"She made a mistake," Axle said. "When she realized Josh had no moral compass, she contacted Surratt. She reached out to Vincent, Gerard, and Nicolas—the vampires who rescued me after the Lifeblood murders. They're flying back tonight. They'll be in Asheville before sunrise."

"They can't just turn into bats and fly here?" Sarcasm bled into her voice.

This felt like an alternate universe where unicorns grazed beside ponies.

"Vampires don't fly," Axle said. "They move fast—unnaturally fast. Like Josh, when he blinked in and out of your room. Like I did, when I tried to explain. I'm not one of them, but I share their strengths—speed, resilience, heightened senses. Not their weaknesses. I don't need blood. I don't fall into regenerative sleep at sunrise. And sunlight doesn't burn me. It doesn't even sting."

"Is that how Josh set my car on fire without being seen on the cameras?" she whispered.

"Yes." Axle reached for her, pulling her into his arms. She let him, if only to absorb his warmth and stop the tremors. She couldn't stop shaking.

"We're not alone anymore," he murmured. "Besides Vincent, Gerard, and Nicolas, there's the agency Reid works for—BBTF, Blue Book Task Force. It's a division of Homeland Security. Reid's boss, Carl Matheson, runs the U.S. office. Once we destroy Josh and the vampires he's created, Carl's team will handle the cover-up."

Haley lifted her head, meeting his gaze as she pulled away. He was still hiding something. "That makes sense—except you seemed angry when you thought Reid called him. Why?"

Axle exhaled. "Because Carl doesn't distinguish between Utukku and Ekimmu. If he learns Gerard, Vincent, and Nicolas are vampires, he'll kill them. I owe those men everything. And if Carl learns what I am, he'll lock me up—or worse. He wanted Weldon dead because he couldn't control him, not because Weldon was dangerous. If Carl knew what I've become, he'd recruit me. Failing that, he'd eliminate me."

Haley's breath caught—not because she doubted him, but because she didn't. The cold logic of it settled over her like a shroud. Carl Matheson wasn't hunting monsters. He was managing assets. And if Axle couldn't be managed, he'd be eliminated.

Her stomach churned. She'd seen what Axle could do—how fast he moved, how easily he vanished. And yet here he was, trembling at the thought of a man with a badge and a mandate. Not because Carl was stronger—but because Carl had the power to turn the world against him.

What terrified her most wasn't the idea of Axle being hunted. It was how easily the world would justify it. He wasn't vampire. He wasn't human.

He was something in between—something nameless. And in a world that feared what it couldn't categorize, that made him dangerous by default. If Carl Matheson—or anyone in the government—discovered the truth, Axle wouldn't just lose his freedom. He'd lose everything.

"If Surratt knows Carl's true intentions, why work with him? And why would Carl work with Surratt at all—why not just kill the head vampire and be done with it?" None of it added up. A vampire bound by a vow not to kill, tethered to a man who killed vampires indiscriminately. It was a dark, twisted alliance. And somewhere in the middle stood Axle, caught between monsters and men, between loyalty and survival.

"It's not that simple," Axle said, his sigh heavy with weariness. "Carl uses Surratt to identify vampires, but Surratt only identifies the Ekimmu—the dangerous ones. Then Carl's team kills them in their sleep. Surratt sleeps when they do, so he can't act. And he and the Shedu have sworn never to kill. So he relies on Carl. But once Carl thinks the threat is gone, he'll destroy Surratt."

"So what's stopping Surratt from killing Carl first?"

"Surratt's honor. He took a vow not to kill. And he's trying to stop his brother, Ashmada—an Ekimmu who'd wipe out humanity if he didn't need them to survive."

"Wiping out your food source is bad strategy," Haley muttered, masking fear with gallows humor.

Axle's smile was humorless. "Surratt hopes Carl can kill Ashmada. But Carl needs Surratt to identify him."

"Because mortals can't recognize vampires," she finished.

"That's how they've stayed hidden. If a mortal uncovers the truth, the vampire can kill them, convert them, or erase their memory. That's probably what Surratt will do to Carl once Ashmada's gone."

"Will you erase mine?" she asked. If he did, she prayed he'd leave the memories of their love. Or maybe forgetting him would be mercy.

"No," he said softly. "I've erased memories before, and I never want to do it again."

Had he erased hers before? How would she know? The thought hollowed her out. Still, she couldn't blame him. If mortals knew vampires existed, they'd destroy them all. And they wouldn't stop with vampires.

They'd kill Axle too.

"Does the BBTF know about you?" Reid did—but did Carl?

"No. Surratt altered Carl's memories after my rescue. As far as he's concerned, I'm just one of Reid's assets. He has no idea what I can do. Hell, I don't even know my limits. Vincent, Gerard, and Nicolas know what I am, but aside from Reid, no one in the government does. The only mortals aware are my father, Megan Harper, Amber Buckley... and now, you."

"Olivia," she whispered.

Axle flinched, as if the name carried voltage.

Haley felt the ache ripple through him—sharp, involuntary—and it struck her with a tenderness so fierce she could barely breathe "You told her the truth. She couldn't handle it. So you erased her memory. That's why you didn't fight for Bonnie."

His voice cracked. "It wasn't just Olivia and Chris. It was Bonnie too."

Haley's chest tightened. Tears blurred her vision. "But you'd already agreed to stay out of her life."

"I felt her pain," he said, sorrow flickering in his eyes. "Chris wanted me to keep my visitation rights, but Olivia knew what I was—or thought she did. She threatened to expose me if I didn't give up my parental rights. The last time I saw Bonnie was the day after Olivia sued for full custody. She was already calling Chris 'Daddy.' But she called me daddy too, and she missed her dog. She clung to me like I was the last thread of something real. Chris asked me to leave, and I snapped. And Bonnie saw. Olivia made sure of it."

His voice was broken. Haley felt the fracture inside him as if it were her own. She clasped his hands, but he didn't seem to feel it.

"I couldn't be the ghost haunting her childhood," he said, eyes red, voice raw. "And I couldn't trust that the beast in me wouldn't surface again. So I erased Olivia and Chris's memory of my visit and signed the custody papers. Then I held Bonnie, told her I would always love her... and erased everything—me, our home, the dog. She wasn't quite four. Her memories were soft. I just... made them dissolve faster."

Haley's throat burned. Her heart felt wrung out. She had never ached for anyone the way she ached for Axle.

"King Solomon," she whispered. "You'd rather lose your child than see her torn apart."

He closed his eyes, a tremor running through him. "It was the hardest thing I've ever done. But I didn't think anyone would understand."

"I do." She saw him clearly now—not just a man caught between cultures, but a bridge between worlds. His biracial heritage had always made him a threshold where identities collided. His father, a successful Black man who moved with ease through the upper class, had given him stability, discipline, pride. His mother, a white woman lost to addiction, had dragged him into her chaos, raising him in shadows where survival meant mistrust and hunger.

He had grown up straddling those worlds—privilege and poverty, order and ruin—never fully belonging to either. That fracture had shaped him, carved him into something resilient. And now she saw the echo of that fracture in the supernatural truth before her. He was more than a man. He was the fault line between realms: shadow and sunlight, mortal and immortal, humanity and something beyond.

If anyone could survive being neither vampire nor human, it was Axle. He had lived his entire life as a blade balanced on its edge, a doorway between worlds. He had always carried two truths within one body—and now, impossibly, two natures within one soul.

"Are you immortal?" she asked. For his sake, she hoped not. Watching everyone you love die, again and again, was a fate worse than death.

"I don't know. If I'm like them, destroying my brain or heart would kill me. But I heal from almost everything else."

"What about cancer?" she asked, voice reverent.

"I doubt it," he said, stepping back. "Since Weldon's lab, I haven't had so much as a cold. Before you, I'd forgotten what pain even felt like."

She rose, closing the distance. "So I'm the reminder?"

Their eyes locked, and the air thickened—charged, suspended—as if the world itself held its breath.

Haley's pulse fluttered painfully, a tremor running through her as she lifted her hand. Her fingertips grazed the hard line of Axle's jaw, the softness of his goatee, and the contact sent a shiver through her—want tangled with fear, need tangled with the terror of what he was and what she was becoming to him.

In his gaze she saw the fracture beneath the surface: sorrow threaded with desperate need, a reflection of her own ache... and the terrifying truth that she was falling for someone who might be immortal. When he bent toward her, his lips brushed hers—tentative, searching—then deepened into hunger. The kiss hit her like a collision of grief and longing, binding them in a tether spun from loss and fragile hope. It scared her how much she needed it—how much she needed him.

Her hands moved to his shirt, slipping over buttons until fabric gave way to skin—smooth, taut, unmarred. Her breath caught at the ink etched into him: a Celtic cross over his right shoulder, an Ankh on the left. Death and eternity, tattooed onto flesh. The sight tightened her chest, a cold whisper of everything she didn't understand, everything she might lose.

His arm locked around her waist, pulling her against him. Her palm slid across his chest, up the thick cords of his neck. She traced the line of his goatee, the shape of his mouth, then curled her fingers over the back of his head. His cropped hair was velvet-soft beneath her touch. He groaned, kissing her again—deeper, more urgent—until the room tilted and the outside world dissolved into shadow.

They kissed until time unraveled, until breath itself forced them apart. Their lips moved with aching urgency, hunger tangled with hope, as if each kiss was both surrender and salvation. And beneath it all, fear throbbed in her chest—fear of losing him, fear of losing herself, fear of what waited outside this fragile moment.

When they finally broke apart, their eyes met—wide, searching, raw. Recognition flickered there: something rare, something that would linger long after this moment.

Then pounding shattered the silence.

Haley gasped, heart lurching violently. The spell snapped. Before she could breathe, Axle had already crossed the room. In a blink, the door swung open—Reid frozen on the threshold, hand still raised mid-knock.

"What?" Axle snapped.

"Sorry, Bro, but we need to move." Reid stepped inside, his gaze cutting to Haley—sharp, knowing. Heat flared in her cheeks, chased by a spike of dread. He gave a single nod before turning back to Axle.

"Looks like you two patched things up," he said evenly. "But if she hasn't accepted her new reality yet, we wipe her memory. We're out of time."

The words hit her like ice water. Wipe her memory. Her reality. Her stomach dropped. She crossed the room on instinct, fear propelling her. Axle pulled her to his side, shielding her. "What's happened?"

Reid's eyes held hers. "Okay, then. Acceptance it is."

Beside her, Axle's jaw clenched. "Did we really give her a choice?"

"I guess not," Reid said. "But you both need to come downstairs. There's been a complication."

Axle didn't release her hand as they followed Reid down the stairs. Haley's pulse hammered, dread coiling tighter with each step. In the living room, the television was muted, but the massacre at Hobo's still dominated the news. Blood. Bodies. Chaos. Her chest cramped, tears blurring her vision.

"Ashmada is here," Surratt said, voice low. "I have no choice now but to call Carl. Reid won't stand a chance against my brother—especially now that he's recruited a vampire who lacked a conscience even as a mortal."

Fear iced Haley's veins. Her body trembled. Axle's hand tightened around hers, grounding her. His voice was steady, low. "I won't let anything happen to you."

She gave him a weak smile, clinging to his promise even as doubt gnawed at her. She wanted to believe him. She needed to. But the world was unraveling faster than she could catch her breath.

Surratt looked grim, Reid anxious. Sonia wasn't in the room. Haley's stomach dropped. Had she gone to warn Josh? "Where's Sonia?"

Axle's eyes swept the room, narrowing. "I didn't even notice her absence. Where is she?"

"She went after Josh," Reid said. "We couldn't stop her."

Haley's breath hitched. Gone after Josh? To join him—or stop him? Her eyes locked on Axle. "Do we trust her?"

He hesitated, glancing at Reid, then Surratt, then back to her. The silence chilled her. Finally, he met her gaze. "Yes. The remorse in Sonia's eyes when she saw the news was real. And she did reach out to Vincent and Surratt. She's trying to make things right."

"Will she be able to find him?" Haley whispered. And if she did—would she tell them, or protect Josh?

"She created him," Axle said. "If anyone can find him, it's her."

"Exactly," Reid added. "And once she does, she can relay the location to

Vincent—personally if she needs to, telepathically if she has to." He looked between Axle and Surratt. "So we're agreed. No Carl until the nest is destroyed."

"He'll have questions," Surratt warned. "He'll know you couldn't have done it alone. He'll want to know who helped."

"Then use your vampire voodoo," Reid snapped. "Convince the men I sent to Durham to protect Axle's brother that they were with me. Implant false memories—whatever it is you do. Carl doesn't need to know about Axle's family. All he needs to know is that Axle had a client who needed my help. He knows I use Axle's services. He knows Axle knows about vampires. He just doesn't know what Axle is—or what he can do."

Axle's voice dropped, quiet, haunted. "Hell, I'm not sure of that myself."

He looked at Haley then, his fingers tightening around hers. The weight in his eyes stole her breath when he said, "But we're about to find out."

Chapter 23

Vincent, Gerard, and Nicolas arrived earlier than expected. After landing in Asheville, they moved vampire-fast, dragging Megan and Amber with them. If Amber hadn't been a dhampir—and Megan hadn't injected Vincent's blood—neither woman would've survived the trip. Traveling at vampire speed was like enduring sustained negative G's; mortals would've been crushed under the force.

"Welcome to the vampire convention," Axle said, forcing a smile as he opened the door wide enough for the entourage to enter. Haley stood behind Reid and Surratt. Reid would die before letting anything touch her. Axle still wasn't sure about Surratt—his loyalties lay with the Utukku and stopping his brother, not protecting mortals.

"Such a smartass," Gerard muttered, shouldering past. The big man made Axle feel like a welterweight.

Amber and Megan stumbled in next, Nicolas close behind. Vincent brought up the rear, all business. "How many vampires are we dealing with?" he asked immediately. "And are we certain they're beyond redemption?" He'd kill a mortal who threatened vampires without hesitation, but he was fiercely protective of his own kind. Axle figured it was guilt—for turning Gerard all those years ago.

Megan and Amber collapsed onto the sofa. Megan groaned, her skin a sickly green. "I hate traveling like a vampire. It makes me nauseated."

"Don't worry, my love," Vincent soothed. "We'll return home the mortal way."

Amber shot him and Gerard a glare. "Damn right we will—even if I have to drive you three back to the airport in the trunk. I'm never doing that again."

"Don't look at me," Nicolas said, nodding toward Vincent and Gerard. "Traveling on foot was their idea. I got stuck with the luggage." He slid three duffle bags off his shoulder and dropped them by the door.

Gerard eased down beside Amber, the sofa groaning under his weight. "It was unavoidable, *mon amour*."

"Never again," she repeated, steel in her voice.

"You shouldn't have come," Vincent said, tone hardening. "I told you to stay home."

Amber arched a brow. "I came for Reid."

Megan smiled. "And you should've learned years ago to stop giving me orders."

They'd aged since Axle last saw them—Amber mid-forties, Megan a few years younger—but both striking, easily passing for women in their thirties. Vincent, having been on the vaccine over ten years no longer looked twenty-something, though not two hundred and fifty either. Gerard, turned during the French Revolution, appeared mid-forties at most. Nicolas, the youngest, could pass for thirty though he was closer to seventy. As far as Axle knew, he hadn't been with anyone—mortal or vampire—except his wife the night Surratt turned him in Germany in the eighties, and the mortal woman killed by an Ekimmu in Austria years later. Before reconnecting with Amber eight years ago, he'd spent his life protecting her. Now that she knew vampires were real—and that she was a dhampir—he protected her from the Ekimmu and mortals like Carl. Legend said dhampirs were vampire hunters, and Amber's ability to detect vampires, even those on the anti-virus, was as sharp as Axle's.

Axle nodded to the room. "Glad you're all here. I could use your help. Again." His half-smile didn't soften the tension as Reid, Haley, and Surratt joined them.

Amber stiffened. She'd never forgiven Surratt for creating the vampire who killed her mother and later her friend in Germany—or for turning her father on his deathbed. "Do we need him?" she asked coldly.

Surratt inclined his head. "I wish only to help."

"Just don't turn anyone," she snapped.

Gerard pulled her close. "He's one of the good guys. Don't forget it."

"Do all vampires have accents?" Haley asked suddenly, drawing every eye.

Axle quirked a brow. Fair question. Surratt was Middle Eastern, Sonia Romanian, Gerard French. Vincent, though American, had been turned during the Revolutionary War and carried a faint British lilt. Only Nicolas sounded modern-day American.

"No, sweetie." Axle pulled her close and made the introductions.

Vincent frowned. "So you've told another mortal our secret?"

He'd been furious when Axle told his father. Britt had been Vincent's attorney for years and hadn't known a thing. Vincent had wanted to keep it that way.

"I'm aware vampire knowledge is on a need-to-know basis," Axle said, sarcasm edging his voice. "But since she's being stalked by a psychopath who's now a vampire, I figured she needed to know."

"Vincent," Megan cut in sharply, standing. She glanced at Amber. "I, for one, am glad to have another woman I can talk to without lying." She turned to Haley. "Why don't you, Amber, and I open one of Axle's best bottles of wine? I could use a drink."

"So could I," Amber said, stepping away from Gerard to follow Megan, who practically dragged Haley from the room.

Once the women were gone, Reid spoke. "We need to find Josh's lair. He wreaked havoc solo, but now he's either joined a group or created one in the last forty-eight hours."

"Sonia's already located it," Vincent said. "She contacted me telepathically as we arrived. The lair was vacant, but she found signs of vampires in an unmapped section of caves near her former home in Bat Cave."

Bat Cave was home to the 186-acre Bat Cave Preserve—the largest granite fissure in the United States. Its main chamber stretched more than 300 feet and soared 85 feet high, while countless side passages remained unmapped. Once alive with bat colonies, the caverns fell silent after white-nose syndrome decimated the population, prompting the North Carolina Conservancy to close them to visitors. But locked gates and warnings wouldn't stop vampires from moving in and staying hidden.

"Is she tracking their movements?" Axle asked. "Or searching the lair?"

"She's here," Sonia said, suddenly appearing. Axle hadn't heard her enter. She scanned the room. "Where are the mortals?"

"In the kitchen," Reid said. "Well, all but me," he added with a smile. "So why don't you tell us what you know."

"I won't put Megan in danger," Vincent growled, already aware of what Sonia knew.

Gerard nodded. "Amber, Megan, and Haley can stay here with Reid and

Axle to protect them. Mortals don't need to be involved. We'll handle the vampires."

Axle cleared his throat, loud enough to command attention. "Hate to break it to you, Conan," he said to Gerard, "but I'm not exactly mortal."

"And do you trust mortals to protect your woman?" Vincent asked, clearly guessing Axle's relationship with Haley—even if he didn't say it outright.

Axle glared. "No. But I don't have a limited window after sunrise to go after them either." He met every vampire's gaze. "Reid and I can go in at high noon and stake every last one of the bastards."

"And what if they awaken?" Surratt asked. "Ashmada is ancient. He doesn't need the vaccine to rise during the day. He just needs protection from the sun."

"You're sure Ashmada's with them?" Nicolas asked.

Surratt nodded. "I am sure."

"How's he going to awaken before sunset without the anti-virus?" Gerard asked. "He'd need—"

"Total darkness," Sonia interrupted. "Like in a cave. Ever hear of total cave darkness?"

Axle had. He'd visited Linville Caverns in high school. In total darkness, the eyes lose their ability to see, and the brain exaggerates sound. Without sight, sound could trigger hallucinations—but vampires had night vision, like bats.

Axle glanced from Sonia to Surratt. "Total darkness can disrupt a mortal's circadian rhythms, throwing off the sleep cycle. But what does it do to a vampire?"

"Nothing," Gerard said. "Before the antivirus, I couldn't wake before sunset, no matter how hard I tried."

"Nor could I," Vincent added. "But—"

"You never lived in a cave," Nicolas interjected, and all eyes turned to Surratt for confirmation.

He nodded. "Before the Middle Ages, most vampires lived in caves. A few were privileged enough to own castles or hide in dungeons, but caves were the norm. Over centuries, we developed the ability to awaken in total darkness—whether underground or during a solar eclipse. Have you never wondered about the spike in violent deaths during eclipses before modern electricity?"

"That wasn't covered in the police academy," Reid said dryly.

"I have experienced it," Sonia said. Her voice was quiet, steady—yet Axle caught a flicker in her eyes. Something primal. Fear. It flashed and vanished so quickly he almost doubted it had been there at all.

"I was turned during a total eclipse," she continued. "Long before I even knew what an eclipse was."

Silence rippled through the room. Vincent—her creation, loyal for two centuries—looked stunned. She had never told him. Never told anyone.

Surratt didn't react.

Axle felt his pulse tighten. "What happened?"

Sonia's gaze drifted toward the window, though it showed only blackness. "It was midday. The light dimmed. Birds went silent. The world held its breath. I thought it was a storm, but then the sun vanished. And something else... stepped in."

Her voice trembled—not from weakness, but from the strain of holding the memory back. "I wasn't bitten. I wasn't seduced. I was claimed—ravaged. The eclipse opened a door. And whatever came through didn't ask permission."

A chill crawled up Axle's spine, cold and instinctive.

"You were turned by the eclipse itself?" Reid asked, doubtful.

"No. A man in a robe turned me. He didn't drain my blood. Didn't feed me his. He took me violently on the ground and shoved something between my teeth, forcing me to swallow. Blood. Human liver. I gagged and my vision faded. When I awoke, I was in a cave."

She shook her head as if trying to dislodge the memory. "It was furnished like a palace, lit with candles, and he was seated on a throne, surrounded by four women tending to him. Feeding him. He drew me closer with nothing but his gaze, and then I saw what he was eating."

Her breath hitched. "A human liver—like the one he'd fed me."

The revulsion rolling off her hit Axle like a physical force—fear, shame—bleeding straight into his nerves. His stomach tightened in sympathy. A tear slid down her cheek. She swallowed and continued.

"You never told me," Vincent whispered, stepping toward her.

She lifted a hand, stopping him cold. Compassion clouded his eyes, but she didn't let him near. "I never told anyone. Unlike you—unlike Gerard—I had no guidance. I had to learn of my nature alone. Afraid. And the one who turned me never came after me or tried to link his thoughts with mine." She shrugged. "There is no psychic connection."

Surratt stepped forward, voice low. "Some vampires are born of chaos. Others of ritual. But those turned during an eclipse... they are marked. Their blood carries something older. Wilder. Ashmada may have turned you, but he did not give you his blood. He took your body, but he took your soul by feeding you the liver of a rival vampire."

"That's not possible," Reid snapped. "When vampires die, they turn to ash."

"The liver is not the heart or the brain," Surratt replied.

"The vampire was still alive," Axle said before he could stop himself.

The memory slammed into him—Weldon's lab, restraints cutting into his wrists, garlic sedative burning through his veins, the scalpel slicing into his abdomen. The agony of feeling his own liver removed while semi-conscious. Weldon's voice. The smell of blood. The cold table. The helplessness.

His knees weakened.

A heavy hand landed on his shoulder, grounding him. Gerard.

"I know," he murmured. "He tortured me too."

Surratt nodded. "It seems Dr. Weldon knew the legends and attempted his own ritual."

"Is that why I have no connection to the one who created me?" Sonia asked, wiping away the tear as if it had never existed.

Surratt nodded. "Part of the ritual requires ripping the heart from the one whose liver was used. That severs the bond."

"How do you know this?" Sonia asked, suspicion edging her voice like a blade. "Were you there?"

"No," Surratt said with a sigh. "But like all vampires, I have a psychic connection to the one who turned me. That is how I knew Ashmada turned you through ritual."

Axle's breath caught. Ashmada turned Surratt?

The room froze. Everything clicked—why Surratt couldn't kill Ashmada, why he worked with Carl, why he tolerated the BBTF. He wasn't bound by loyalty. He was bound by blood. By creation. By genetic law.

Reid glared at Surratt. "If Ashmada created you, then you should be able to tell if he's with Josh."

Surratt shook his head. "Too dangerous. If I search his thoughts, he can search mine. If I find him, he finds me."

"He still turned me," Sonia said. "If the sacrificed vampire was of his lineage, I should still be able to find him."

Axle stepped forward, the logic clicking into place. "I agree. It should be possible if he created the vampire whose liver he used. Weldon used Gerard's DNA to create me. Gerard didn't turn me, but I still have a connection to him. I can track him. And because of that bond... I don't think I could kill him."

Gerard snorted. "As if you could."

Axle ignored him. "If Ashmada used one of his own to turn Sonia, she should still have a connection. Weak, but there."

"If police can use familial DNA to find a suspect, why can't Sonia use her genetic link the same way? Not with computers—through her mind." Reid said.

"He's right," Nicolas added. "DNA doesn't lie."

"I could help," Vincent said. "And Gerard. We're from her lineage. Together, we could strengthen the link."

Gerard nodded. "Exactly. Could it work?"

Surratt exhaled, the sound heavy. "Possible. But dangerous. If Sonia reaches for him, he could sense all three of you. The connection does not exist now. Do you truly wish to create one that could lead him to you—and to those you love?"

Vincent and Gerard exchanged a look, their worry for Megan and Amber written plainly across their faces. But Axle felt the weight settle harder on his own shoulders. He had more than Haley to protect. His family was still alive, and except for his father, they had no idea what hunted mortals.

Sonia's jaw tightened. "But if I did it alone—"

"Even a weak connection to Ashmada is perilous," Surratt said, his voice sagging with centuries of exhaustion. "Protecting you from Carl Matheson is challenge enough. If Ashmada learns I work with Utukku who have not taken the Sheddu pledge, everyone here is at risk."

"Because he's taken no such pledge," Sonia said.

"Exactly."

"And neither have I," she added, steel sharpening her tone. "If I find him, I will destroy him—and anyone who tries to protect him."

Axle looked at her—really looked. Not just at her power, but at the wound beneath it. At the violence that shaped her. At the fire that refused to die.

She wasn't dangerous because of what she'd done. She was dangerous because of what had been done to her.

And for the first time since meeting her, Axle trusted her.

Chapter 24

Haley poured herself another glass of wine, the stem of the glass slick against her damp fingers. Her hand trembled just enough to betray the storm inside. The wine sloshed slightly, ruby-dark and glinting under the low pendant light. Across the table, Amber and Megan exchanged a glance—one of those silent, loaded looks that carried years of shared secrets. Haley had barely had hours to absorb the truth.

"So, recapping," Haley said, after a decidedly unladylike gulp of wine, "Amber's father, Nicolas, and her not-legally-wedded husband, Gerard, are vampires."

Amber nodded, her expression unreadable. "So far, you're right on track."

Haley met her gaze, noting the faint amusement flickering behind Amber's eyes. "And the three of you live at a luxury ski resort in Austria where you pretend to be Nicolas' sister instead of his daughter because he looks younger than you—even though he's seventy-something and you're—"

"Forty-something," Amber interjected, her voice dry. "But you're getting it."

"Okay." Haley took another swallow, the wine burning slightly down her throat, and turned to Megan—the brilliant, unflinching doctor whose presence felt like steel wrapped in silk. "Vincent's a vampire too, but you cured him with the vaccine."

"Not cured, exactly," Megan said, her voice low and precise. "It's more like managing diabetes. Vincent, Gerard, and Nicolas take daily injections to suppress the worst of the virus. They rarely need blood now. With sunscreen, they can go outside—except when the sun's at its peak. They still fall into regenerative sleep around noon, but it's more like a siesta. So yeah, they live semi-normal lives."

Haley blinked, trying to process the avalanche of information. The room felt too warm, the wine too strong, the air too thick. "And the Utukku are the only ones who can help the Shedu keep Ashmada—the brother of the morally rigid Shedu leader, Surratt—from unleashing hell on mortals. Right?"

"With help from Reid and the BBTF," Amber added, swirling the last of her wine.

Megan raised her glass in a mock toast, the crystal catching the light like a blade. "And let's not forget Detective Carl Matheson, who thinks he's in charge of Surratt—when Surratt's just using him to defeat his brother."

Haley exhaled slowly, the wine warming her chest but doing nothing to settle her nerves.

"And once Ashmada's defeated," Megan added, "Carl will try to kill Surratt, and Surratt will either erase Carl's memories of vampires or sic an Utukku on him and have him killed."

Haley closed her eyes for a moment, trying to ground herself in reality. It didn't help. Her reality was now flipped on its ass. "So, a group of vampires and vampire hunters who don't trust each other think they can destroy Ashmada and stop a war between good vampires, bad vampires, and mortals—while secretly planning how to destroy each other when it's all over."

"Pretty much," Amber said, finishing her wine with a final, deliberate sip.

Haley reached for the bottle again. Her third? Maybe? "So while everyone in the other room is planning a commando raid in a nearly 200-acre cave deep in the mountains to destroy Ashmada and his vampire army... what about Josh? We don't even know for sure he's with them."

"Sonia says he is," Megan replied, unfazed. "She tracked him through the shared blood link. She sensed other vampires there—one ancient. Surratt believes it's Ashmada."

Haley stared at the wine, watching the way it clung to the glass like blood. "Vampires were relegated to myth status thousands of years ago. They should've stayed myths." Her voice softened. "Or maybe, once the bad ones are gone, the rest can take the vaccine and go back to being human. Maybe they can lobby Congress to get Medicare or insurance to cover the injections—like insulin. Why do they have to involve mortals? Or Axle?"

Amber looked at her like she'd just suggested they fight a wildfire with a garden hose. "Because mortals need the Shedu, and the Shedu need the Utukku. I don't think you've grasped how dangerous Ekimmu vampires really are."

Haley took a long sip and carefully lowered her glass, the weight of it grounding her. "I know you're right—in my head," she said, tears burning like acid behind her eyes. "But I'm terrified. Josh didn't have a conscience when he was mortal. As a vampire... when he came into my room... I've never been so afraid. And now, I'm not just scared for myself. I'm scared for Axle. For his family. For all of you."

Amber leaned forward, her voice steady. "Axle's probably our best chance against Ashmada—and Josh. Gerard and Vincent are powerful, but they're pretty much worthless for three or four hours mid-day. And Reid's a good detective and a good cop, but he's not superhuman like Axle."

"Exactly," Megan agreed. "Axle has all the strengths of a vampire and none of the weaknesses. The vaccine didn't just suppress the virus—it enhanced him."

Haley frowned, her mind spinning. "How?" She still couldn't wrap her head around it.

Megan shrugged, her tone clinical. "We can't exactly run trials or double-blind studies, so we may never know. But I think he reacted differently because he was created differently. He wasn't bitten—he was injected. He was never drained and given vampire blood. The virus mutated, and the vaccine worked better."

Haley wasn't a scientist, but she was a nurse. She knew how to assess trauma, read the signs a body gave when something was wrong. Megan's logic made sense—if vampires were real. If this wasn't some vivid, stress-induced hallucination. But Haley was awake. Her pulse was steady. No fever. No disorientation. No textbook signs of psychosis. Just reality, raw and unrelenting.

"Vampires are real. Like—really real," she said, each word dragging across her throat like sandpaper. The truth had already begun to metabolize, souring in her gut, burning through her chest like acid reflux with no physical cause. Axle and Surratt had told her. She'd seen it— fangs and all. But hearing it again, from new mouths, new angles, made it harder to compartmentalize. Harder to pretend this was anything but a rupture in the natural order.

Her training screamed for a differential diagnosis. Her instincts begged for a way out. But the evidence was mounting, and denial was no longer therapeutic.

She drained her glass, the burn a poor substitute for clarity.

"You might want to slow down," Megan said gently. "It's not the best time to dull your senses."

Haley's guilt flared, then curdled into defiance. "Maybe it is. I need a refill."

"No, you don't," Amber said, snatching the bottle—then poured herself another glass.

Haley's eyes narrowed. "Seriously? Aren't you supposed to be protecting me? Aren't you a cop?"

Amber's smile was razor-thin. "Not anymore. I'm a dhampir. Born to hunt vampires. It's in my blood. So imagine my surprise when I found out I wasn't just a vampire hunter—I was in love with a vampire. So don't drag me into your pity party. Get over it already, and deal with it."

"Amber," Megan said, her voice low, measured. "She's just finding out. Give her a minute."

"She's had a couple of hours," Amber muttered, but the bite had dulled. "Time to put on her big girl panties."

"I will," Haley said. "Just give me a damn minute. And maybe one more glass of wine."

"No," Amber said, finishing the bottle with a smirk.

Haley glared. "But it's fine for you to get wasted?"

Amber's grin turned wicked. "Funny thing—I don't get drunk. Not like mortals. Back in Afghanistan, I could drink any soldier under the table and still walk a straight line. Turns out, it's a dhampir thing."

"It's a vampire thing too," Megan added. "Even taking the vaccine, Vincent can drink as much as he wants and not get drunk."

Haley blinked. "What about cirrhosis?"

"The liver cures itself during the regenerative sleep, even now when it only lasts a couple of hours," Megan said.

"So, you on board with the facts?" Amber asked. "Or do you need another two hour minute?"

Haley exhaled. "No. I'm on board the crazy train with you. Vampires are real. Dhampirs too."

"And Axle is something more than any of us," Megan said.

Haley nodded, but her thoughts were spiraling. Axle wasn't the boy she'd known in high school. He was something else now—something darker. But she trusted him. More than she should. And that terrified her.

"How did Axle know Josh wasn't a vampire until the night he broke into my house?" she asked suddenly, the question clawing its way out.

"You'd have to ask Axle," Megan said.

Amber answered instead. "He smelled different. Before, Josh didn't carry the scent. After Sonia turned him, Axle could tell."

"But Axle never met Josh," Haley said. "It had been weeks since Josh was in my house. His scent wouldn't have lingered. So how did Axle know Josh hadn't always been a vampire?"

"Because I visited him in jail," said a voice from the doorway.

Haley's breath caught. Axle stepped into the kitchen, and the air shifted—denser, charged.

"I went to see him after the arrest," Axle said, moving closer. "Got into his cell undetected. I couldn't erase his memories of you. He doesn't feel emotion like normal mortals. His emotions and memories aren't interconnected. So I made it uncomfortable for him to think about you."

Haley's pulse spiked. "But that didn't stop him."

"No," Axle said, sitting across from her. "After he was released, he went to a bar. That's where Sonia found him. She sensed vampire manipulation. She didn't know it was me, but she knew he'd been exposed, and they hooked up. Things took a turn at some point during the night, and she turned him."

"Does she turn every guy she sleeps with?" Haley snapped. Sonia wasn't just seductive—she was predatory.

Axle's jaw tightened. "No. She thought Josh was vulnerable. She read his thoughts but missed the signs. She didn't know he was a sociopath. She thought he was heartbroken. Thought they might be kindred spirits. So she offered him immortality, and he accepted."

"So she's done it before?" Haley asked, voice sharp. Was he defending her?

"Three or four times. Over centuries," Axle said, his tone clipped. "That's a good track record, considering."

Haley's chest ached. "I don't know how to respond to that."

Megan touched her hand. "I get it. Sonia turned Vincent. They share a bond I'll never fully understand. But Vincent chose me. He's proven it. Give Axle a chance to prove it to you."

"Prove what?" Haley asked, voice barely above a whisper.

"That I love you," Axle said.

Haley froze. Her heart thundered. "What?"

Axle reached for her hands and pulled her to her feet. Amber and Megan rose from their seats and quietly left the room. He leaned in.

"I know I shouldn't," he said. "But I do. I think I've loved you since your brother's graduation."

"But..."

"I know. It doesn't make sense. I barely knew you then. I barely know you now. But I know your heart. And I know mine. Back then, I didn't think I was good enough. Now, I don't think it's safe. But I love you."

Haley swallowed. Hard. She'd dreamed of hearing those words fifteen years ago. Now, they felt like a curse. Axle lived in a world of shadows and blood. A world she wanted no part of. But thanks to Josh, she was already in it.

"You won't erase my memories too, will you?" she whispered.

"Only if you ask me to."

"I don't want to know about vampires," she said. "But I don't want to forget you."

"I don't know how to separate the two," he said, pain flickering in his eyes. "Erasing vampires would mean erasing me. It would be as if you hadn't seen me since high school."

She pulled her hands free and wrapped her arms around his neck. Raising her face to his, she whispered, "Then I don't want to forget a thing. If loving you means accepting the monsters, I'll deal with it. As long as you're here to protect me."

"I'll protect you with my life," he said, and lowered his head to hers.

The kiss was brief—but it burned. With love. With promise. With the kind of truth that rewrites everything.

Chapter 25

Plans were being made—battle lines drawn. But they were still the underdogs.

The "war room" had migrated to the bonus room above the garage—larger, better equipped to hold the biggest crowd Axle had ever gathered. It could've passed for a party, if not for the weight pressing down on every breath.

Megan and Haley sat on the sectional sofa, sorting medical supplies—bandages, tourniquets, suture kits, syringes filled with the vampire sedative Megan had engineered. The same sedative Dr. Weldon had used on Axle during his experiments. All the usual gear for a battle with the undead.

Axle, the vampires, and Reid clustered around the pool table, its felt buried beneath maps of the Bat Cave Preserve Nature Conservatory. Amber stood among them, a quiet force. She'd reminded the group she wasn't just a former Asheville PD detective—she was a combat veteran and a dhampir. Surratt had slipped out not long after Axle disappeared into the kitchen to retrieve Haley, Amber, and Megan.

"From dusk till dawn, we're at our peak," Gerard said, gesturing to himself, Vincent and Nicolas. "So are the unvaccinated vampires. But we have the edge—they drop into the regenerative sleep at sunrise. We don't."

But the vaccine had dulled their strengths. Maybe not mentally, but physically, it had taken a toll—though Gerard refused to admit it.

Axle locked eyes with Sonia, the weight of unspoken truths passing between them. She nodded, confirming what he already knew but hadn't said aloud. They were outmatched. And he was supposed to lead them anyway. Sonia, like the Ekimmu, hadn't taken the vaccine, giving her a physical edge. But she shared their vulnerability. Unlike Gerard, Vincent, and Nicolas, she couldn't stay awake past sunrise. Without protection from even a sliver of sunlight, her body would blister and burn—literally. Nothing would remain but ash.

That ash was convenient. Dead vampires didn't leave bodies to rot. Even fledglings turned to ash upon death—no need to bury, hide, or explain. The catch? Unless sunlight did the job, the head or heart had to be destroyed. A stake through the heart had to stay lodged until the body disintegrated, or the vampire would heal and survive.

Bullets? Unless they were silver—vampires had a fatal allergy to the metal—a clean shot wouldn't kill them. A regular round had to lodge in the heart or brain to do any real damage. A through-and-through only slowed them down.

Decapitation or ripping out the heart worked. Reid had done the former, but he lacked the strength—or the stomach—for the latter.

"They likely outnumber us," Sonia said. "And none of them are vaccinated. Whether you admit it or not, Gerard, the vaccine weakens you."

Gerard scowled. "I was strong when I was mortal, and just because the vaccine let me age a bit doesn't mean I've gone soft. I can still bench-press a Volkswagen."

Sonia rolled her eyes. Unimpressed. She could probably bench two.

Axle? He wasn't about to lift a car to prove anything.

"And you share the same disadvantage as the Ekimmu," Reid reminded her. "At sunrise, you'll drop into the regenerative sleep. Vincent and Gerard will only have a few hours after that."

"What about tonight?" Haley asked, crossing the room to stand beside Axle. He pulled her under his arm.

"Josh could be hunting her now," Megan added, sliding up beside Vincent. He wrapped an arm around her and kissed the top of her head.

Axle's grip on Haley tightened—protective, unyielding. His gaze locked with hers. "We stay together until sunrise. No one touches you. Not while I'm breathing."

"So we wait until dawn," Gerard muttered. "Meanwhile, Ashmada could be prowling Asheville with his horde while we hunch over a damn map, trying to figure out if we can get in and out before noon." He sighed, catching Vincent's eye. "Feels like hiding in French bars again, plotting against the Jacobins."

"Or planning attacks on the British with Lafayette," Vincent added, a nostalgic smile tugging at his lips.

Haley gasped. "The Marquis de Lafayette? The one who helped George Washington?"

"*Oui*," Gerard said. "Gilbert du Motier, Marquis de Lafayette. Vincent and I both knew him."

Axle pulled Haley into a full embrace. "Don't pass out on me, baby. It's wild, I know. But that's how they met—fighting in the American Revolution and then the French. Vincent was a strategist during the war."

Haley turned in Axle's arms, trembling against his chest. He held her tighter. "Of course he was," she muttered.

"Gerard was killed in France during the Revolution. That's when Vincent... well, you know the rest."

Haley shook her head, stunned. "I can't. I just can't."

"Yes, we're that old. Yes, we're vampires," Vincent snapped. "Now, can we get back to these damn maps?" He swept his hand over them. "The Ekimmu know every inch of the caves. They've adapted to total darkness. Time of day won't matter. All they need are rotating sentries—two or three-hour shifts—to guard the nest while the rest sleep in regenerative bliss. We'll never get in undetected."

"Too much of the cave system is still uncharted," Amber said, urgency sharpening her voice. "We don't know what Helene's flooding did to the structure. Sonia detected Josh—and maybe others—in one of the blind zones." She pointed to an unmarked area on the map. "Even if we think we've found them all, some could slip through. The hurricane might've carved out new passages."

"I sensed at least three vampires, including an ancient," Sonia said. "But I had to leave before they sensed me. Amber's right. There could be more. I don't know. But I do know they've mapped every tunnel and escape route. We'll be going in blind."

"It's a cave," Haley said. "You'll all be blind a few hundred feet in unless you bring cellphones and flashlights."

Sonia rolled her eyes. "We won't need them. Vampires have night vision."

"Of course they do," Haley said, dripping sarcasm.

Vincent shot Amber an exasperated look and tapped the map. "Even before the caves were closed to the public, visitors were only allowed in the 300-foot entrance hall—Little Bat Cave. They won't be there. It's too exposed. Too much sunlight. Too high a risk of park rangers noticing. They'll be deep."

"Why does a cave need park rangers? It's a damn bat preserve," Nicolas muttered. "I hate bats."

Axle caught Amber's expression before Nicolas did—her disbelief, her amusement.

"Really, Nicolas? You're scared of bats?"

"Call it PTSD if you want, but yeah," he said. "Back in Germany during the Cold War, I was part of a recon unit near East Germany. One night, I was sent ahead to check out a derelict bunker rumored to hold Soviet gear. There were bats. Lots of them. One hit my helmet. Another clawed my cheek. It was chaos—flapping, shrieking, wings everywhere."

"Who was shrieking?" Gerard asked with a chuckle. "You or the bats?"

"Both," Nicolas replied with a grin.

The laughter rolled through the room, but Axle felt it thinning, losing substance. His instincts were already pulling tight, coiling. The air tasted wrong—metallic, heavy. Something was coming.

He let the laughter die.

"Comic relief's over," he said, voice low, steady. "Josh could be at my door any second. And if he is, I won't wait. I'm not going vampire hunting—I'll take him out here and now. So let's fortify a plan before it's too late."

Sonia stiffened. Axle saw it instantly—her nostrils flaring, pupils narrowing to predatory points. His stomach dropped.

"It's already too late," she said. "Josh is outside."

She vanished before the last syllable left her tongue.

Haley's breath hitched behind him. "Axle?"

Then the sound hit him—Princess Paw Paw barking downstairs, the pitch sharp with terror. A growl. A yelp that sliced straight through him.

Axle locked eyes with Vincent. No words. Just the vow that lived in his bones: *Haley stays safe. No matter what.*

He moved before Haley could reach for him, the world blurring as he streaked downstairs.

Princess had hidden in the laundry room when everyone arrived. Bootsie had bolted upstairs and disappeared—safe, for now. Princess wasn't. Axle felt it in his marrow—cold settling into his chest like a warning he couldn't ignore.

The house had gone still. Too still. Josh hadn't breached the door yet, but Axle felt him—felt the wrongness—circling the property like a predator testing a fence. And there were others with him. Shadows pressing at the edges of his senses.

He scooped up Princess and raced back upstairs, forcing himself to move at mortal speed so he didn't crush her tiny bones.

"Stay," he murmured, setting her down in his bedroom. She bolted under the bed without looking back.

Axle stepped into the hall, closed the door, and returned to the bonus room.

Every head snapped toward him. Fear. Determination. The air thick with the sense of impact coming.

The vampires had instinctively wedged the mortals into a corner, forming a protective barrier between them and whatever waited outside. Reid bristled, trying to slip past Gerard, but the big vampire didn't budge. Reid ended up wedged between Vincent and Nicolas instead.

"I don't need to hide behind vampires," Reid snapped, drawing his weapon as he pushed out of the protective circle.

Axle arched a brow. "That gun's not going to stop a vampire."

"This one will," Reid said with a smirk. "Silver bullets. Courtesy of the BBTF."

Vincent grumbled, "My tax dollars at work. Gold-plated toilet seats in the White House and silver bullets for a secret agency no one even knows exists."

Amber stood beside her husband, one hand on her sidearm, the other gripping Gerard's hand like she needed the grounding.

Gerard glanced over her head at Nicolas. "Well, I guess you don't have to worry about bats. Looks like they brought the fight to us."

"A fight we're not ready for," Amber murmured, her eyes glassy with fear.

"Something's off," Nicolas said. "They wouldn't risk an all-out war in a suburban neighborhood. Too risky."

"Which means this is either a distraction or a trap," Vincent added. "Either way, it's not their endgame."

"It's a trap," Haley said, pushing past Vincent to reach Axle. Her voice trembled, but her resolve didn't. "Josh wants to lure Axle outside—away from me."

Nicolas met Axle's gaze. "He doesn't know what you are. He thinks you're mortal. That gives us an advantage."

"A fatal mistake," Axle said. And he meant it. He'd do anything to protect Haley. But when he met her terrified eyes, the truth hit him hard. She was right. Josh thought he could lure the vampires away, swoop in, and take her—believing Axle couldn't stop him.

Axle could get to Josh and kill him before he ever made it inside. But not without leaving Haley exposed.

"Don't go out there," Haley whispered. "Not without a plan. That's what Josh wants."

Axle pulled her into his arms, feeling the tremor she tried to hide. Josh had gotten away with murder twice as a mortal. Most newly infected vampires clung to some shred of humanity—guilt, restraint, fear. Josh had never possessed any of those things. As a mortal, he'd taken what he wanted without remorse. As a vampire, he wouldn't worry about consequences. He might even savor the chaos.

The narcissistic bastard thought he was unstoppable.

Chapter 26

"I can't let you all risk your lives for me," Haley whispered, her voice barely audible past the knot of dread in her throat. Her chest tightened, breath shallow. Fear clawed at her insides, raw and relentless. She'd never felt so small, so exposed.

"It's not just for you," Megan said. "Josh and the others have to be stopped. Reid's already here—if he clashes with vampires, it'll draw Carl and the BBT's attention. That puts Vincent, Gerard, and even Axle at risk. They'd destroy Vincent and Gerard. No telling what they'd do to Axle."

"More experiments, no doubt," Axle said, his voice strained enough to nearly break Haley's heart.

Dr. Weldon had altered Axle's DNA, turning him into a vampire hybrid. The doctor had run brutal experiments to test Axle's healing, endurance, and pain thresholds. The government would do worse. They'd want to control him—he was the perfect soldier–the ultimate weapon.

"We can't just stand here with our thumbs up our asses and no plan," Reid said. "Amber and I may not be immortal or superhuman like Axle, but we're armed—and we've fought vampires before. And won."

"Not alone you didn't," Gerard said. "Vincent, Nicolas, and I were there. So was Surratt. Remember?"

"I remember stopping Weldon and his clone. I remember rescuing Axle," Reid snapped.

Haley's heart thundered against her ribs, each beat a warning. Would loving Axle mean living in constant terror—always glancing over her shoulder, waiting for the next ambush, the next monster in the dark? Her stomach churned. Could she survive that kind of life? Could she endure the weight of it?

"We need to work together," Amber said. "Megan and Haley are the most vulnerable. We protect them above all else."

"Damn right we do," Axle said, pulling Haley back into his arms.

"Using my blood to make the vaccine gave Megan dhampir abilities like Amber," Vincent said. "They can move at vampire speed, so Gerard and I can get them out if things go sideways. But Haley and Reid are mortal. No whisking them away."

"I'll die protecting Haley," Axle said. But it didn't ease her fear. He was strong—but not invincible.

"And I can take care of myself," Reid said, though his voice held a tremor of fear. He held up his gun. "Silver bullets. Remember?"

Megan stepped away from Vincent and crossed the room to the sectional sofa. She picked up the duffle bag she and Haley had packed earlier. "And I have the vampire sedative."

"They're syringes," Vincent growled. Do you know how close you'd have to get to stick a vampire? It won't help. Not this time."

"I don't have to use syringes." Megan grinned, though her bottom lip trembled. "The sedative is loaded into a tranq pistol. I asked Sonia to get it for me when we first moved to Amsterdam." She shrugged. "I didn't feel safe leaving the U.S., but I didn't want you to know I was afraid, and I swore Sonia to secrecy."

Vincent scowled. "Damn it, Megan. How the hell did you convince Sonia to—"

A low thud echoed from the porch. Deliberate. Taunting. Conversation stopped. Megan jumped. Haley gasped. Axle's arm tightened around her. She pressed into his chest, desperate to absorb his strength, to borrow his courage. But her body betrayed her—tears welled, hot and unrelenting, and her throat constricted like a vice. Her legs trembled beneath her. She wanted to scream, to run, to vanish.

"He's not trying to sneak in," Vincent said, locking eyes with Axle. "Josh wants us to know he's here."

Gerard moved toward the window, parting the curtain just enough to glimpse the yard. Amber stood at his shoulder, her side arm at the ready. "There's three of them," Gerard said. "Josh is in front. The others are flanking him, wide. They're not charging. They're waiting."

"For what?" Reid asked, still gripping his weapon.

"For us to panic," Vincent said. "Or split up."

Amber stepped toward the map. "If they breach the house, we'll have seconds before all hell breaks loose, which will draw the attention of neighbors and risk exposing us all. We need to take this to the caves."

"How will Reid and I get out?" Haley asked. They couldn't move at vampire speed. They'd be left behind. Or Axle would be left alone to protect them.

"I won't let anything happen to you," He vowed. And he'd die keeping that vow.

Gerard frowned. "Axle should stay with Haley and Reid. Reid's armed, and Axle's stronger than a normal vampire. They'll have the advantage. The rest of us will get Megan and Amber to safety and then lure them back to the caves. We'll destroy their lair and any vampire in league with Josh."

"No," Haley said, her voice shaking. "We all stay or we all go. I'm not hiding while the rest of you fight for me."

"You're not hiding," Axle said gently. "You're surviving."

"But what if they go to the caves and the vampires outside don't?" Haley's voice cracked. Tears burned. She gestured toward Gerard and Vincent. "If they whisk Amber and Megan away and head for the caves with Nicolas, how will you fight Josh and protect me and Reid? This isn't a plan—it's panic."

"I'm armed," Reid snapped. "Who doesn't get that? And Megan can leave you the tranq gun."

"And I'm not getting whisked away anywhere," Amber said, glaring at Gerard. "Reid can share his silver bullets."

"Amber, please," Nicolas pleaded. "Listen to reason. You're a dhampir–not a vampire. You only have the advantage during the day."

Outside, the wind shifted. Axle stiffened. "Blood," he whispered, though Haley couldn't smell it. "Fresh. Metallic. Drifting in from outside."

"I smell it too," Nicolas agreed. Vincent and Gerard nodded, their gazes searching one another, silently communicating.

Haley's fear surged, sharp and suffocating. Her throat locked, breath wheezing through tight lungs. A vivid, grotesque image flashed in her mind—Axle's neighbors sprawled across the lawn, throats torn, eyes vacant. Her stomach lurched. She tasted bile. She shook her head violently, as if she could fling the horror away.

"What have they done?" she rasped, barely able to speak.

"They've fed—again," Sonia's voice whispered from the shadows. She reappeared near the pool table, eyes glowing faintly. "This time, they went to the central neighborhoods—high crime areas. No deaths. No attention. Their victims are passed out in an alley and won't remember. But they're sated. Charged. Fast. Reckless–believing they're invincible."

"Then let's make them regret coming here," Gerard growled, cracking his knuckles.

Vincent nodded. "We hold the line. No one gets past us. Not to Haley. Not to anyone."

"You can't fight here," Megan insisted.

Amber agreed. "She's right. A few winos might forget they were dinner tonight, but a war on this street? That's unforgettable—like the massacre at Hobo's. And the vampire activity will draw Carl's attention away from that alley to us."

Reid nodded. "Carl's already assembling a team to meet me at Hobo's tomorrow." He held up his phone. "Just got a text on my burner."

"We need to act. Now," Nicolas said, meeting Amber's gaze. "Dangerous or not—we need to split up."

Sonia nodded. "Josh knows I'm here. He knows I'm stronger. But he won't care that I created him. The emotions he lacked as a mortal prevent any loyalty. I can sense him. He can sense me. That's it. Nothing stops him from trying to destroy me along with the rest of you."

"Then Nicolas, Vincent, and I go to the caves and wipe out the nest," Gerard said. He locked eyes with Amber. "Load your gun with Reid's silver bullets. Stay close to Sonia. Reid and Axle will protect Haley and Megan."

"I'm not leaving Megan," Vincent argued.

"I have the tranq gun," Megan said, though Haley could hear the doubt in her voice.

Vincent snarled. "No. Give the gun to Haley. And for once, don't argue. You're staying by my side."

A sudden knock—three slow raps—rang out from the front door. Josh's voice followed, smooth and venomous. "Haley, my love, I've come to take you to your new home."

Fear froze Haley's blood like ice in her veins. Her throat went desert-dry, her body locked in place. She couldn't move, couldn't breathe. The sound of Josh's voice, once smooth and charming, slithered through her like poison.

Axle touched her chin, lifting her gaze to his. His eyes burned with defiance. "Over my dead body," he said. And Haley knew, with terrifying certainty, that he meant it.

Chapter 27

"We can't stay here," Axle said, fear for Haley making his pulse race like it had when he was still human. "Second floor. One door in, one way out. Even if we reach the hall, there's only one staircase. We'd be trapped." Vampires could jump. Mortals couldn't—not without breaking bones or dying.

"Then we go down now," Vincent said. "Take positions. Be ready to flee out the back when they breach the front."

"There's three of them," Gerard reminded him. "They'll have the back door and the side door covered."

"Josh will come through the front," Sonia agreed. "The others will block the exits. They're fledglings, but loyal. They'll protect him—until they realize they're outnumbered. Then they'll run. And when they do, they'll head for the caves. That's where we finish this."

"I'll take out Josh," Axle said. He'd never killed anyone before, but he'd make an exception. Josh wasn't human. Never had been—not in any moral sense. He'd always been a monster. Now, he had the fangs to match.

Once they all agreed on a strategy, they moved. Axle led, Sonia took the rear. He'd never served in the military, but this was war. And the stakes were high.

When they reached the downstairs landing, the front door rattled—not a knock this time, but pressure. A slow, deliberate push. The wood groaned under the strain.

Haley flinched, breath catching. Axle stepped in front of her, shielding her with his body. Muscles tensed. Eyes locked on the door. He could take Josh—he was sure of it. But he couldn't protect Haley if he was locked in combat. And he feared what she'd see if he lost control and ripped Josh's heart from his chest.

"Back away from the door," Vincent growled, grabbing Megan's arm and dragging her toward the utility room where a door led to a fenced in side yard. "Everyone take position."

Reid gripped his gun tighter, sweat beading at his temple. He followed Megan, who fumbled with the tranq pistol, hands trembling as she stumbled after Vincent.

Amber moved toward the kitchen, flanked by Gerard and Nicolas, sidearm raised. They had the back door. Axle and Sonia would hold the front. Josh would sense Sonia's position before entering. If they were lucky, he'd assume she was the main threat—he didn't know what Axle could do. If they were lucky, he'd retreat before the neighbors noticed and called the cops.

Beside him, Haley's breathing hitched and her knees nearly buckled. Axle grabbed her by the waist, holding her upright. "Stay strong. I can't fight Josh if I'm worried about you."

"I don't want to die," she whispered, barely audible.

Axle turned to her, voice low and fierce. "You won't."

He locked eyes with Sonia. No words. Just a nod—a silent vow to protect Haley from what was coming. Axle didn't want her to see what he could do. He wasn't sure himself. But he knew it would be violent.

The front door burst open. Haley screamed. Axle tensed. Josh stood on the threshold, flanked by two vampires with glowing eyes and blood-slicked mouths. His smile was slow, serpentine.

"Haley," he purred. "You look even more beautiful when you're afraid." He noticed Sonia and smiled. "Thank you for my gift, love, but you're no longer needed. Take this mortal and go," he said, nodding to Axle.

Axle's eyes were drawn to the other two vampires–one he'd met before. Shock held him momentarily speechless.

"Hugh? Lou?" Haley whispered. The fledglings Sonia sensed were the twins who worked for Josh. Haley had known them in high school.

The red haze faded from their eyes. For a moment, they looked human.

"Haley?" Lou asked, confused. He turned to Josh. "She's the one who betrayed you?"

"Yes," Josh hissed. "With this asshole."

"We're not hurting Haley," Hugh said.

Lou nodded, agreeing with his brother. "We said we'd help you take her back. Not kill anyone."

"You'll do what I say," Josh snapped. "Lou, take the back. Hugh, the side. The others are escaping."

"We're not killing anyone," Lou repeated. He looked at Haley. "We didn't kill anybody in Asheville. We just..."

"It was the others," Hugh interjected, confirming what Axle suspected. There were more. But how many?

"Stop your whining. I made you. I can destroy you," Josh snarled. "Now stop the others. They're vampires Ashmada says will destroy us if we don't strike first. Go. I'll handle—"

They vanished, and Axle lunged before Josh could finish, slamming into him with a roar. Surprise flickered in Josh's eyes before he snarled, fangs flashing.

#

Haley stumbled back, heart hammering. Axle hurled Josh into the wall hard enough to leave an imprint in the sheetrock. The house shook. Josh barely flinched. In a blur too fast for Haley to follow, Josh pinned Axle against the far wall. Punches and body slams blurred into chaos, tearing the living room apart.

"We have to move!" Sonia shouted as she grabbed Haley's arm and dragged her toward the back door where Lou had gone after Amber, Gerard, and Nicolas. Hugh had gone after Vincent, Megan, and Reid.

Haley twisted, eyes attempting to track the blur that was Axle. He was locked in combat with Josh, their blows shaking the walls.

"But Axle—" she cried. "You have to help him."

"He doesn't need my help. You do," Sonia snarled. "Move or I'll move you. And you won't like it."

"I can't leave him," Haley sobbed.

"You're a distraction," Sonia snapped. "If you don't leave with me now, you're both dead."

Tears streamed down Haley's face as she fled out the back. The sounds of battle echoed behind her. She didn't look back. If she did, she'd never leave.

#

Axle slammed Josh into the wall, his snarl reverberating through the house as drywall cracked and wood splintered. Josh roared—deep, primal—and twisted mid-impact, driving his elbow into Axle's ribs.

Pain flared, but Axle didn't back down. He couldn't. Not with Haley's life hanging in the balance. He rammed his shoulder into Josh's midsection. Air whooshed from Josh's lungs, but he recovered and lunged. Their bodies locked in a brutal parody of a lover's embrace—twisting, grappling, elbows hammering.

They were evenly matched. No—Axle was stronger. Faster. But rage made Josh erratic. His fingers clawed deep, nails like talons raking Axle's flesh to the bone. Axle seized one of Josh's hands, squeezing until bones snapped. But the moment Josh broke free, his shattered bones straightened, mending themselves—stronger than before.

A scream pierced the chaos—Haley's voice, distant now as Sonia dragged her from the room. Axle's focus wavered. Just for a second. Josh saw it.

He lunged, stepping in close, crossing one leg over Axle's thighs as he slammed his hips into Axle's core. With a tight grip on Axle's triceps, Josh wrapped his other arm around Axle's head, forcing his face into the crook of his bicep, exposing his neck. Fangs bared, he lowered his teeth. Before they could pierce flesh, Axle twisted free, ducked, pivoted, and drove his fist into Josh's gut.

The impact sent Josh skidding across the floor, but he rolled to his feet like liquid shadow, eyes glowing with fury.

"You're one of us?" Josh asked, confused. "You smell mortal." He sniffed. "But not mortal."

Axle didn't answer. He charged.

They collided again—bone against bone, fury against fury. Furniture shattered. The coffee table exploded into splinters. A lamp burst, showering sparks. The room dimmed, lit only by the flickering hallway light and the glow in Josh's eyes.

Axle's strength surged—unnatural, raw. He felt it in his bones, in the hot blood flowing like lava through his veins. He wasn't just fighting. He was transforming. The part of himself he feared was clawing its way to the surface.

Josh noticed. His grin faltered. "You don't even know what you are," he said, voice low, almost fearful. "But you still bleed. And I'm going to gut you."

Axle lifted him off the ground and slammed him into the ceiling. Plaster rained down. Josh kicked free, landed hard, and swept Axle's legs out from under him. Axle hit the floor, breath knocked from his lungs, but he rolled, dodged the next strike, and came up swinging.

Josh hissed, fingers curling like claws aimed for Axle's throat. Axle caught his wrist mid-air, twisted, and drove Josh backward into the fireplace. Stone cracked. Josh roared, fangs flashing.

"You won't touch her," Axle growled. "Not now. Not ever."

Josh lunged again—and this time, Axle didn't hold back. He slammed his fist into Josh's sternum, cracked it open, and ripped out his still-beating heart.

Josh's eyes bulged. His mouth opened in a silent scream. His skin flared red, smoke curling as his body turned to ash. The heart in Axle's hand stopped beating. Blood dripped from his fingers, turning to ash as the charred organ disintegrated in his clenched fist.

Chapter 28

Haley's lungs burned. Her pulse thundered, roaring in her ears like a freight train as they stopped beneath the trees flanking the neighborhood playground. Sonia finally released her arm, and blood surged back into Haley's fingers. She rubbed her bicep, already feeling the bruise blooming beneath her skin—proof she was still alive, still vulnerable.

"Ouch," she whispered, more to herself than Sonia.

Sonia shot her a glare. "A bruised arm's better than a torn-out throat. Quit whining."

"Who's whining?" Haley snapped, voice raw. She wasn't immortal, but she was tired of being treated like a burden. "Sorry I can't match your speed—I'm still mortal. Cut me some slack and tell me what we're doing next."

"We?" Sonia scoffed. "I'm heading to the cave before Ashmada vanishes. With Josh dead, he's our next target."

Haley's stomach dropped. Relief tangled with dread, twisting into something jagged. If Josh was dead... was Axle safe?

"How do you know he's dead? And what about Axle?"

"I heard the end," Sonia said, brows lifting. "The fight was over before we cleared the backyard. Axle's fine. Shaken—he's not used to that kind of violence—but fine."

Haley didn't want to picture it. Didn't want to imagine Axle's hands slick with blood, his eyes wide with horror. Her heart stumbled. Her throat tightened.

"I'm sorry," she whispered.

Sonia blinked. "For what? Not killing the bastard yourself?"

"No. For dragging all of you—Gerard, Vincent, Nicholas...you—into a fight between mortals and..." She hesitated.

"Vampires?" Sonia offered.

Haley nodded. "If I'd handled Josh's obsession myself, I wouldn't have needed to hire Axle, and none of you would've been pulled into this."

Sonia sighed, her posture softening. A shadow crossed her face. "If I hadn't turned Josh, Axle wouldn't have had to kill him. He could've just played detective until the cops had enough to arrest him. This isn't your fault, Haley." Her voice dropped. "It's mine. And I've got a lot to make up for."

Haley nodded, feeling an unexpected kinship with the dangerous woman. Sonia carried centuries of betrayal and grief, but she hadn't surrendered her humanity—not completely. She'd made a promise to Axle—and kept it. Because of her, Haley and Axle were still breathing.

"So... what about me?" Haley asked. "Where do I go while the vampires head to the caves to take out the... nest?"

"If I give you Axle's keys, will you go to the hotel, tell his parents he's safe, and stay there until he comes for you?"

Haley nodded. She didn't know where Britt and LaDonna were staying, but assumed Sonia would give her directions. Still, it felt wrong to hide while others—Megan, Amber, Reid—mortals like her, or mostly mortal—risked everything. She wanted to help. She just didn't know how.

"Go straight to the hotel," Sonia said. "If the officers ask questions, tell them Axle and Reid are coordinating with the BBTF."

"But... Axle's SUV is parked outside his house," Haley said, voice trembling. "Josh, Hugh, and Lou broke down the front door. It sounded like a hurricane. You don't think the neighbors noticed? The place is probably crawling with cops by now."

"Don't move," Sonia said, vanishing into the darkness.

In less than a minute, she reappeared, startling Haley. She yelped, and heart leapt.

"Hold out your hand," Sonia said, dropping the keys into her palm. "I moved the SUV. It's parked over there." She pointed beyond the playground, next to the curb, deep in the shadows.

"The cops?" Haley asked, breath shortening.

"Axle's handling it," Sonia said, offering no details—and Haley didn't ask. She wasn't sure she wanted to know.

Sonia gave her the hotel address and disappeared again into the night.

Haley took a deep breath and crossed the playground, her pulse hammering with every step.

How could she leave Axle to face this alone? He'd killed a man—because of her. Would he have to justify it? Would they arrest him? Would he let them?

Refusing to abandon him, Haley climbed into the SUV and drove back to his house. She parked two doors down and got out.

Neighbors crowded the sidewalk, phones raised, snapping pictures and filming officers ducking under crime scene tape. Axle wasn't in sight, but she spotted Noya Kanati by his patrol car, speaking into a radio. He'd played football with Axle and her cousin, Geoff. She barely knew him, but he recognized her.

"Haley?" he said, releasing the radio button. "What are you doing here? Axle said you were at the hotel with his parents under protective custody."

Her heart sank. She had no idea what Axle had told him. "That's where I'm supposed to be," she said, improvising. "But I was worried about Axle—and my cat, Bootsie. He's here, with Axle's little dog."

"The animals are safe," Noya said. "Animal control just left. You can pick them up in the morning."

"And Axle?" she asked, throat tight.

Noya frowned. "He's coordinating with Reid and Reid's supervisor at the BBTF. DHS is still looking at Josh for murdering Rita Milan Zozaya—the diplomat's daughter."

Haley glanced at the crime scene tape draped across the splintered front door. "Is he okay? What happened?"

"Josh came looking for you," Noya said with a sigh. "Apparently, he had an axe and attacked Axle. They fought. Tore up the room. Splintered some furniture. Axle's got a few gashes but refused medical attention. Josh fled. There was already an APB out on him, but we've escalated it. He's now considered armed and dangerous. You're not safe out here alone."

Josh fled? Haley's mind reeled.

Sonia said Josh was dead. But Noya said he escaped. Where was the body? And an axe? What kind of stalker used an axe? The story was shaky, but Noya seemed convinced. Had the evidence backed it up—or had Axle manipulated the scene?

"Thank God, he's okay," she said, nodding. "I'll just head back to the hotel and wait to hear from him."

Noya grabbed her arm. "Not by yourself, you won't. I'll get an officer to take you. Wait here."

Haley nodded, but as soon as Noya turned away, she bolted for the SUV, jumped behind the wheel, and sped out of the neighborhood.

The vampires had a head start, but she still had time. Her dad's house was on the way. If she could grab the shotgun from the barn, maybe—just maybe—she could reach the caves in time to help.

#

It was after midnight when Haley reached her father's house. Floodlights bathed the front and side yards in harsh white, but the windows were dark. She switched off her headlights and eased down the side drive toward the barn, silently praying her dad was asleep and wouldn't hear the engine.

At the barn, she parked close to the door and flicked on the headlights to illuminate the interior. Her father kept a rifle and pistol inside the house, but the shotgun was stored outside—in a locked cabinet bolted to the barn wall. Haley found the hidden key, retrieved the shotgun and a box of shells, then climbed back into the SUV and headed for Bat Cave, just two miles from Lake Lure.

Bat Cave lay west of Chimney Rock Village. Nestled in the heart of Hickory Nut Gorge along the Rocky Broad River, the area had been ravaged by Hurricane Helene. The swollen river and cascading mudslides had hurled trees and boulders at fifty miles per hour, obliterating roads, bridges, homes—and lives.

Nearly two years later, the town still bore scars. Debris-lined roads and makeshift fixes—like an orange cable strung across the river to provide internet—marked a slow recovery. Progress lagged behind other parts of western North Carolina, like Asheville, where life had mostly returned to normal.

Some roads remained one-lane and guardrail-free, treacherous in daylight and deadly after dark. Haley took the curves slowly, high beams cutting through the gloom, her heart pounding, hands clenched on the wheel. She didn't know what she'd find when she got there, but she was armed—or as armed as any mortal could be to face vampires.

The cave was co-owned by The Nature Conservancy and a private landowner, its entrance restricted. Hikers could still explore the preserve, but the cave itself was off-limits. By the time Haley arrived—just after one a.m.—the trails had long since closed. A standard car would've stalled at the yellow bar guarding the lot, but the SUV rolled over the grass and around it without hesitation. She parked near the first trailhead and climbed the locked gate barring the bridge over the Rocky Broad River.

With the flashlight she'd found in her father's barn—its beam flickering at the edges—Haley hiked through the hardwood forest toward the cave. The air grew colder as she walked. Near the entrance, a damp draft spilled from vents along the cave's flanks, curling around her legs and arms, chilling skin already raw from the night.

Inside the 186-acre Bat Cave Preserve, the main chamber loomed like a dark cathedral—over 300 feet long and nearly 85 feet high. The air was frigid. The night, silent.

Until a shrill scream pierced the stillness, curdling her blood and freezing her heart.

Chapter 29

Axle reached the cave's entrance just ahead of Sonia, the night pressing in around him like a held breath. Inside, the cathedral-like chamber rose around him in vast, echoing silence. Deeper in, he found six empty cots, abandoned in haste. But it was the full-sized, opulent bed that stopped him cold. Ashmada's bed.

The Ekimmu leader had claimed this place like a king. The sight of it radiated arrogance. Permanence. A promise of violence.

Sonia appeared at the mouth of a side cavern, her voice low and urgent. "Haley's safe. She's at the hotel with your parents."

Relief struck Axle like a blow—sharp, dizzying. Haley was safe. Out of reach, but not out of danger. The distinction mattered. It anchored him. It kept him from unraveling.

Ashmada and the other vampires were gone—likely hunting. Megan, Vincent, and Reid had gone after Hugh. Gerard, Amber, and Nicolas were tracking Lou. Axle followed the scent trails threading through the stone—Hugh and Lou's the strongest, thick with the metallic tang of recently consumed blood.

He didn't want them dead. He wanted Megan to sedate them. He still believed they could be saved. But first, he had to keep the others alive long enough for that hope to mean anything.

Through Sonia's link to Vincent, they found him and Megan first. Reid had fallen behind. Vincent had Hugh cornered, demanding names and locations. Megan raised her tranquilizer gun, steady despite the tension vibrating through the air. Their presence inside the cave sent a ripple of awareness through the tunnels—like a stone dropped into still water.

Moments later, the others arrived—drawn by the disturbance. And with them came Ashmada. Ancient. Powerful. Faster than any of them.

His two followers vanished into the dark as Ashmada flung Vincent aside like a ragdoll and tore Hugh's heart from his chest. Hugh disintegrated into ash before he hit the ground. Ashmada turned on Megan. She screamed—but before he could strike, Axle slammed into him. The impact startled the ancient vampire, driving him back into the shadows. Sonia darted after him, fearless and furious.

Megan screamed again, her flashlight shattered in the scuffle. Enhanced senses or not, she couldn't find Vincent in the dark. She crawled blindly, calling his name, her voice cracking with terror. Axle found her and guided her to him. Vincent was unconscious but breathing, the gash on his brow already knitting closed.

Reid stumbled into the cavern, gun raised, his phone's weak flashlight slicing a narrow path through the darkness. Axle ordered him to stay with Megan, then vanished deeper into the tunnels, following Sonia's trail. He had never seen Ashmada, but he smelled ancient—and matched Surratt's description: tan, deeply lined skin, a dishdasha and ghutra draped over his head like a relic from another age.

Axle pushed farther in and was intercepted by another vampire—older than Vincent, younger than Ashmada. They collided in a blur. Axle overpowered him, and the vampire fled. Axle gave chase—until a commotion in a nearby chamber yanked his attention sideways.

He rounded the corner, eyes adjusting to the deeper dark and the thin beam of Amber's flashlight. Gerard and Nicolas were locked in brutal combat with two others. Amber had Lou cornered, gun raised, flashlight trembling.

"Silver bullets," she warned. "Don't test me."

Lou lunged. Amber fired. The bullet struck granite, ricocheted—and hit Sonia as she entered from the far side. The echo was deafening, nearly drowning Lou's scream as he fled—straight into Ashmada's arms.

Axle moved to intercept, but Ashmada killed Lou and vanished again. Lou's body collapsed into ash, settling at Axle's feet like the remnants of a burned photograph. Sonia cried out, clutching her arm. The wound was already festering—her body reacting violently to the silver.

Fever hit fast. Gerard and Nicolas dispatched the two young vampires with ruthless efficiency, twisting their heads until bone and blood dissolved into ash. Amber rushed to Sonia just as Vincent—now conscious—entered with Megan and Reid close behind.

Megan dropped to her knees, unzipping her duffle with shaking hands. She cleaned the wound, injected Toradol and Benadryl. Slowly, Sonia's temperature eased. Her skin cooled. The wound began to heal.

Axle stood nearby, watching as the chaos thinned into a fragile silence. His thoughts flicked to Haley—safe, but unaware of how close the night had come to swallowing them all.

Ashmada was still out there.

But so were they. And they weren't finished yet

#

Ashmada emerged from the cave like a shadow peeled from stone, his tattered dishdasha trailing behind him, blood crusted along the hem. Surratt stood waiting—rigid, silent—the tension between them crackling like static before a storm.

"This must stop," Surratt said, voice firm but pleading. "Your arrogant refusal to stay hidden puts us all in danger. I won't allow it anymore."

"You can't stop me," Ashmada replied, voice low and threatening, his accent thick. "You forget, brother. I made you. Loyalty binds you. You can't destroy me."

Surratt's jaw clenched, but he didn't move. Something in his stance faltered—uncertainty, hesitation. From behind a boulder, Haley watched, shotgun trembling in her grip. Ashmada's eyes flared, glowing with a predator's hunger. Surratt froze mid-step, locked in place by something unseen.

Ashmada slowly advanced–like a lion stalking wounded prey. Surratt never moved.

Haley didn't think. She stood, aimed, and fired. Both barrels. The recoil slammed into her shoulder, but she stayed upright, watching Ashmada stagger sideways. Smoke curled from his side. Blood soaked through the robe, but the wounds were already healing underneath. If not for the torn cloth and the stink of gunpowder, it would've been as if the buckshot never touched him.

Ashmada turned toward her. His eyes met hers, and her breath froze. It wasn't just fear—it was something deeper, colder. Ancient. His gaze pierced her skull, locking her in place. She couldn't move. Couldn't scream. Couldn't even blink.

Then Axle burst from the cave, shouting her name.

Surratt snapped out of the trance like a spell had broken. Ashmada hissed and vanished into the trees, his robe trailing like smoke. Surratt chased after him, disappearing into the dark.

Axle reached Haley, grabbing her arms. "What the hell are you doing here? You were supposed to be at the hotel!"

"I couldn't leave you and the others to fight my battles for me. I had to do something."

"And you thought shooting an ancient vampire was a good idea? My God, Haley—had I not come out when I did, he would've ripped out your throat and drained you dry."

She whimpered. Her voice shook. "I thought he was going to kill Surratt. I had to do something."

He looked furious, but his hands were gentle. "You could've died."

"I know, but I was so worried about you and the others." Her gaze drifted toward the cave. "Where are they? Are they okay?"

Axle's expression darkened. "Hugh and Lou are dead. Ashmada killed them. The others are okay, but one of the Ekimmu escaped before Ashmada came out."

Vincent and Gerard emerged from the cave, supporting Sonia between them. Nicolas and Reid followed, Amber and Megan at their sides. Sonia pulled free, cradling her arm as if it were broken, and approached Haley. Axle's arm tightened around Haley's shoulder.

Sonia shot him a side-eye, then glared at Haley. "I told you to go to the hotel. What the hell are you doing here?"

Haley offered a sheepish grin and half-raised her shotgun. "Protecting Axle?" she said, more question than answer.

Sonia rolled her eyes. "You stupid, mortal. Love is going to get you killed."

"Are you okay?" Haley asked, nodding toward Sonia's arm.

Sonia rolled her shoulder like she was warming up to pitch. Then she shrugged. "I am now."

"What happened?" If she kept Sonia talking, maybe she'd avoid a full-blown lecture. She already felt foolish for thinking she could be of any help to vampires.

"Amber shot me—with a silver bullet," Sonia said, throwing a hard glare over her shoulder at Amber, who cringed. "And vampires have a fatal allergy to silver. The wound wouldn't heal without help."

"I was shooting at Ashmada," Amber snapped. "I don't see as well in the dark as a vampire, and Ashmada's fast—damned fast. The bullet hit the cave wall and ricocheted. You just happened to be standing there."

"Yeah. Whatever," Sonia muttered, turning her back on Haley and meeting Megan's worried gaze. "I guess I owe you my life. Thanks, Megs."

"Don't mention it," Megan said.

"Well, Amber may have missed, but Haley's bullet made contact," Axle said in her defense. "She shot Ashmada."

Amber harrumphed. "She used a shotgun. Even a crappy shooter can hit something with buckshot. It didn't stop him."

"But she saved my life," Surratt said, stepping from the shadows. "Had she not distracted him, my brother would've killed me before Axle exited the cave." He turned to Haley, his gaze soul-deep. "Leave here with the others. My brother's after me now. He won't come for you, and I'll make sure the only evidence of vampires in those caves points to Ashmada and the others."

He handed Reid a new burner phone. "When you get back to Asheville, call Carl. Tell him you found evidence of vampires in the caves. Say you killed four, but two escaped. Have him send a BBFT team to sweep the caves in the morning before they go to the nightclub in Asheville. I'll make sure nothing points back to Axle or the rest of you," he added, nodding to Vincent, Gerard, and Nicolas.

"Now go home. Sonia and I will create evidence to match our version of events."

The vampires agreed to meet at Haley's apartment. Axle gave them the address. They vanished like mist.

The mortals—Axle, Reid, Amber, Megan, and Haley—rode back in Axle's SUV. No one spoke much until they reached Haley's apartment.

Once inside, Reid called Carl as instructed. Carl, thrilled to have new vampires on his radar, agreed to meet Reid with a BBFT team at daybreak.

Surratt had assured him they'd find nothing but beds and piles of ash.

Chapter 30

Before dawn, Reid drove alone to meet Carl and the BBTF team at the airport. Megan, Vincent, Amber, Nicolas, and Gerard took separate Ubers. Megan and Vincent flew back to Amsterdam. Gerard, Amber, and Nicolas returned to Austria. Their planes were lifting off just as Carl's boots hit the tarmac.

Axle and Haley headed to the hotel, slipping into the adjoining room next to his parents and Maybelline—the room Haley should've gone to earlier when she'd fled Axle's house with adrenaline still burning in her veins.

Haley sat stiffly on the edge of the bed, fingers curled around a paper cup of lukewarm coffee she couldn't bring herself to drink. Her shoulders ached from tension, her skin prickling with residual fear. Axle paced near the window, phone pressed to his ear, voice low and clipped. The silence between them felt brittle.

She watched him from the corner of her eye—his steady movements, the way his jaw flexed when he was trying not to feel too much. He'd been her anchor through chaos, but now, in the quiet, she felt adrift. The adrenaline had drained, leaving her hollow and raw. She wanted to reach for him, to ask if he was okay, but the words stuck. What if he wasn't? What if neither of them were?

When the knock came, Haley flinched hard, her heart kicking against her ribs.

Axle ended his call and checked the peephole before opening the door to Gordon Sikes and a BBTF agent under Reid's command. Agent Neil Hargrove nodded once, then took position outside as the family entered. LaDonna swept in first, her tiny frame taut with tension, eyes wide and glistening.

"Haley," she breathed, arms outstretched. "You're safe. Thank God."

Haley slowly stood, legs trembling. She set the coffee on the dresser and stepped into LaDonna's embrace. The scent of lavender detergent and fabric softener hit her like a memory—safe homes, folded laundry, a world untouched by monsters. Her throat tightened. She clung harder than she meant to, afraid that if she let go, she'd fall apart.

Britt followed, towering and composed, his voice low and deliberate. "We've been worried sick," he said, clasping Axle's shoulder. "Everybody okay?"

Haley's gaze flicked to Axle. He looked exhausted but steady when he nodded. She didn't feel steady at all. Every nerve in her body felt frayed. And yet, looking at him calmed her—grounded her as nothing else could. He'd seen her at her worst—bloodied, terrified, broken—and hadn't flinched. He'd fought for her. Killed for her. She didn't know what that meant yet, but it meant something.

Then Maybelline shuffled in, her dentures clicking as she tried to smile. "You're the one," she said when she saw Haley. "The one who came to see Axle. I knew you were more than a client. I knew it."

Haley blinked back tears, her voice barely a whisper. "Hi, Miss Maybelline."

"She's been asking about you," LaDonna murmured, smoothing Maybelline's sleeve. "Ever since we got here yesterday and she found out you were being stalked by a serial killer wanted by Homeland Security."

Haley's stomach dropped. The words felt surreal, like someone else's nightmare. And yet, her whole world was surreal. Josh hadn't actually killed a diplomat's daughter. That was a cover story—crafted by a secret government organization that hunted bad vampires: the Ekimmu. But Josh was a killer. He'd killed Sharon and Ashland. He'd slaughtered those people in Asheville. And he would've kept killing if Axle and...good vampires...hadn't stopped him.

"Agent Hargrove said they've got a location on Josh," Britt said, drawing Haley's attention. "And...he's no longer a threat?"

A knowing look passed between father and son. Britt knew the truth. He knew what his son was. He knew what Josh had been. And he understood exactly what "no longer a threat" meant.

Haley nodded, but her stomach twisted violently. One more mortal who knew vampires existed. One more person pulled into the shadows. Another ally for Axle and the Utukku. Another possible target for the Ekimmu.

"No longer an immediate threat," Axle clarified—though Josh was no threat at all. He was dead, but the sheriff's department believed he'd fled Axle's house and was on the run.

Gordon frowned. "Who found him? And where?"

"Reid called just now. He and a couple of his men tracked him to the preserve in Bat Cave. Unless he finds another way out of the caves, Josh won't get away this time. I'm sure the BBTF can fill you in once they know more, but for now, I just want to get Haley home so she can rest."

Haley barely heard the words. Her mind was fixed on Josh—on his death—on the fact that it had happened at Axle's hands. A brutal end she didn't want to picture, didn't want to understand. She should've felt relief. Instead, she felt hollow, as if something essential had been carved out of her and left open to bleed.

"You two are coming back to the house," Britt insisted. "I'm sure Gordon and some of the other agents will have more questions, and as your father and your attorney, I want to keep you close."

Gordon arched a brow. "You think Axle's going to need an attorney?"

"A man came after him with an axe—a man who's now the subject of a manhunt," Britt said. "I'm not taking any chances with my son's life or his reputation. If Josh comes after him again, it'll be the last time, but it will be self-defense, and I'll be there to make damn sure Axle's not charged."

Agent Hargrove knocked once and stepped inside. "I need the room," he said, effectively dismissing Gordon.

Gordon didn't like it, but he left without arguing. After Axle relayed the details Surratt had instructed him to share, Agent Hargrove nodded.

"I'll debrief Deputy Sikes, but I'm sure he'll want to stop by your father's house to collect everyone's statements for the sheriff's department," he said to Axle. Then he had them all sign paperwork and released them from protective custody.

Before heading to Britt's house, Axle and Haley detoured to the animal shelter to pick up Bootsie and Princess Paw Paw. The dog curled on Axle's lap while he drove. Haley held Bootsie close, despite the cat's half-hearted attempts to break free. She buried her face in his fur, trying to anchor herself to something warm and alive.

Once inside, Bootsie wiggled free and jumped down like he couldn't wait to get away from her. He gave her an indignant look and sauntered off like he owned the place. Princess Paw Paw, more subdued, stuck to Axle's side as they settled on the sofa. Haley curled on her side, head in Axle's lap, her body aching with exhaustion. But sleep wouldn't come.

She felt his hand settle on her shoulder, grounding her. She didn't speak. Didn't need to. Her mind kept replaying the caves, Ashmada's soulless eyes, the kick of her father's rifle, the smell of gunpowder, and the moment she realized Josh was truly gone. But beneath all that, another truth pulsed: Axle had chosen her. Protected her. Stood between her and the dark.

She didn't know what that made them. But she knew what it made her feel—safe, seen, wanted. And terrified of losing it.

LaDonna wrung her hands and sighed. "I don't know about the rest of you, but I'm starving. I'm going to make breakfast. Mama?"

Maybelline smiled and followed her into the kitchen. Britt looked at Haley, who yawned, barely able to keep her eyes open.

"Why don't you stay right there and rest. I'll go help LaDonna and her mother with breakfast. Coffee?" he asked Axle.

"As black and strong as possible," Axle said, dropping his head against the back of the sofa.

Haley didn't move. She just lay there, listening to the quiet hum of the house, the distant clatter of pans, the soft rhythm of Axle's breathing. Her world had shifted again. And she wasn't sure where the pieces would land. But for now, she was here. And he was here. And that was enough.

#

Haley had just started to dream—if it could be called that. The images were jagged, disjointed, a nightmare stitched together from memory and fear. She jolted awake at the sound of Britt's booming voice calling them to breakfast, her heart still racing, her skin clammy with dread.

They ate in silence, the food heavy in her stomach, her nerves too frayed to taste anything. Just as she pushed her plate away, a knock thundered against the front door, sharp and insistent. Her shoulders tensed. Britt, apron tied around his waist, was helping LaDonna with the dishes.

"I got it," Axle said, already moving. Haley followed, her bare feet whispering across the floor as she hovered in the shadows of the hallway. Her pulse quickened as Axle opened the door.

Gordon stormed past him, eyes blazing. "What the hell, Travers? I got the watered-down version at the hotel, but Reid told Noya everything, and I had to hear it secondhand."

Haley flinched at the sharpness of his voice, her body recoiling on instinct. Axle shut the door and followed Gordon into the living room, where Gordon planted himself—an oak rooted to the floor, immovable and imposing.

"Gordon? What are you doing here?" Haley asked as she stepped into the room, rubbing the sleep from her eyes. "If Noya briefed you, then you know everything we do."

"He briefed me, alright," Gordon snapped. "But Axle owed me the courtesy of telling me himself. Instead, I had to hear it secondhand. Do you know how that made me feel?"

Haley's face burned. She didn't care about Gordon's bruised ego. What mattered was surviving the last forty-eight hours without splintering—and keeping Axle from carrying more than he already had. She stepped closer to him, her body angled in quiet defiance, a shield without words.

"I'm sorry you were left out of the loop," Axle said, his tone calm but clipped. "Everything happened fast, and my first priority was protecting Haley—not keeping you updated."

Haley's throat tightened. His words cracked something open inside her—gratitude, guilt, and a fierce, rising instinct to defend him. She reached for his hand, grounding herself in the warmth of his skin.

"Are you accusing my son of something?" Britt asked, stepping into the room with quiet authority. LaDonna and Maybelline slipped past him and settled on the sofa. Maybelline glanced at Haley and patted the cushion beside her.

"Come sit, sweetie," she said gently.

Haley's fingers slid from Axle's, their touch lingering for a heartbeat. She moved toward Maybelline but didn't sit. Her stance was taut, coiled. She needed to stay close to Axle—needed to be ready to step between him and Gordon if things escalated.

"No," Gordon said, voice edged with disbelief, "but I've been thinking about Axle's story, and it doesn't add up. Why would a man who did everything he could to avoid getting caught stalking Haley suddenly show up at your son's house with an axe? And why are you so worried about him needing an attorney? Noya didn't have an answer either, so I'm hoping Axle can explain."

Haley's breath caught. Gordon wasn't wrong. The pieces didn't fit because they'd been forced into place to match the BBTF's cover story.

"Josh was running drugs out of his body shop," Axle said, repeating the lie they'd agreed on. "Dewey didn't know anything about it, but Hugh and Lou did. Josh paid for their silence and used it to blackmail them into helping him grab Haley."

Haley's chest constricted. She hated this part—hated blaming the twins for more than they'd actually done. Even if they'd chosen their path, it didn't make the lie easier to speak aloud.

"Where are you getting your intel?" Gordon demanded.

"Agent Reid Sheridan," Axle said.

Haley's heart sank. She felt the weight of every lie, every half-truth. She wanted to scream, to shake Gordon and make him understand—but her voice felt buried beneath exhaustion and fear.

She stared at the floor, her thoughts spiraling. According to Axle, fledglings had free will. They could refuse their creator's commands. Hugh and Lou hadn't. They'd attacked people. They'd come after her. That had been a choice.

"There's no evidence Josh was selling drugs. No rumors. Not even a whisper," Gordon said, his voice sharp as a blade. "Where's Reid getting his information?"

"The Department of Homeland Security," Axle said with a sigh. "The BBTF has been watching the body shop for months."

Haley's stomach churned. Vincent, Megan, Gerard, Amber, Nicolas—none of them mentioned. Yet she owed them her life. And at least Dewey's name would be cleared. That mattered.

"So why would a man running drugs and stalking your girlfriend take time out of his busy day to come after you—and with an axe?" Gordon asked, incredulous. "Wouldn't a drug dealer have access to guns?"

Haley's skin prickled. Her mind replayed the moment Josh shattered the door. The sound. The fury in his eyes. The way he'd looked at her—like she already belonged to him. Forever.

Axle spoke, but his words barely registered. Her body trembled, caught in the memory. The adrenaline. The fear. Her voice shaking as she'd tried to reason with Hugh and Lou. The horror of Josh's eyes turning red, his fangs descending. He hadn't needed an axe to make her afraid.

She stepped forward, voice low and raw. "Josh had lost it. He was no longer rational—or even lucent. He said I was going with him—no matter who he had to take out to make it happen." Her voice cracked. She swallowed hard, blinking back the sting in her eyes.

"Then why didn't you go to the hotel when Noya told you to?" Gordon asked, sharp.

Haley's breath hitched. "I was afraid Axle would go after Josh alone. I couldn't let that happen."

"And where do you think Axle could've gone if you had his car?"

"I don't know," she whispered. The lie tasted bitter. She hated this—being cornered, being doubted. Her truth felt like glass, fragile and ready to shatter under Gordon's scrutiny.

"That's enough," Britt said, voice booming. "You want to interrogate them like suspects? Fine. Take them in. But unless you've got grounds for an arrest, get the hell out of my house."

Haley flinched, nerves frayed. Axle stepped beside her, pulling her under his arm. She leaned into him, needing the contact, the anchor.

"Gordon, seriously?" Axle said. "Can't this wait? Haley's barely slept in the last two days. She needs rest."

Haley didn't argue. She couldn't. Her body was shutting down, her thoughts unraveling.

Gordon looked at her, then flushed. "Fine," he muttered, tone softening. "I'll meet with Sheridan and ask him directly. Maybe he can make this all make sense. Where is he?"

"He left for the airport at dawn to meet his supervisor, Carl Matheson," Axle said. "Like I told you at the hotel, the BBTF located Josh and the twins in the caves at the Bat Cave Nature Preserve."

Gordon nodded. "I know about the manhunt. Captain Stratford said Asheville PD was providing backup, but I want to talk to Reid personally, and he's not answering his phone. Is he still at the caves?"

Axle's eyes darkened. Haley felt it—that shift. Wherever Reid was, he wouldn't want Gordon showing up until the evidence matched the story.

"I'd try Hobo's first," Axle said. "They think the massacre there had something to do with a drug deal gone wrong. Carl and his team are trying to connect Josh or his supplier to the murders. It'll take time to process the scene and gather evidence, but if Stratford's providing backup, why not talk to him?"

Haley's gut tightened. Gordon didn't know Axle well enough to read him, but she did. And Axle didn't want Gordon anywhere near those caves.

"Are you telling me how to run my investigation?" Gordon snapped.

Axle exhaled. "Just try Reid again. If he doesn't answer, leave a message. I'm sure he'll call you back as soon as he can."

"I'm not wasting time with Agent Sheridan," Gordon said. "I'm calling his boss, Carl Matheson."

He turned sharply, letting Britt show him to the door.

Axle took Haley's hand and led her upstairs. They stripped down to their underwear and crawled beneath the covers, the silence between them thick with exhaustion and dread.

Four hours later, Britt knocked on the bedroom door. "Son, I think you and Haley need to come downstairs. Deputy Kanati's here."

Haley jolted upright, heart slamming against her ribs like it was trying to break free. Her breath hitched—thin, panicked. "Axle?"

"It'll be okay, sweetheart. Get dressed. I'll meet you downstairs."

"No," she whispered, her voice splintering. "Wait for me. I don't want to be alone."

Axle nodded. She dragged on the same dirty clothes she'd worn for two days, her fingers numb and clumsy. The fabric felt stiff, wrong, like it belonged to someone else. Everything inside her felt scraped out, hollowed to the bone.

They descended the stairs together. Haley clung to Axle's side, her grip white-knuckled, as if letting go might send her spinning into the void. The living room was too bright. Too quiet. Noya stood when they entered, his face carved from stone.

"Gordon never made it to Hobo's," he said. "We were supposed to meet there. I went to his house, then back to the Sheriff's office. Nothing. So I called Detective Sheridan. He told me to wait there for him and his boss, Carl Matheson. Said they didn't want me showing up at the caves while they wrapped up their investigation—or that's what he claimed."

Axle's jaw tightened. He looked at Haley, then back to Noya. "What happened?" His voice was low, strained to the breaking point.

Haley's stomach twisted. Her vision tunneled. "Where's Gordon?" she asked, barely recognizing her own voice.

Noya hesitated. His eyes flicked to hers, then back to Axle. "Reid found his body in the caves. Throat torn—an axe in his chest. He didn't wait for me or for BBTF clearance. Even though they didn't need a warrant to search the caves, Detective Matheson didn't want to ruffle any feathers, so he was waiting for permission from The Nature Conservancy before entering." He exhaled shakily. "Gordon didn't wait. He went after Josh alone."

Haley's knees buckled. Axle caught her before she hit the floor, guiding her to the couch. She clutched his arm like a lifeline, her breath coming in ragged, uneven bursts. The room tilted, the edges of her vision pulsing black.

"No," she whispered. "No, no, no—"

Josh couldn't have killed Gordon. Axle had killed Josh last night. And the sun was still out—so a vampire couldn't have done it...unless he'd been deep enough inside the caves to hide from daylight. The thought sliced through her, cold and impossible.

LaDonna gasped, her hand flying to her mouth. Maybelline began to hum, low and tremulous, a gospel tune that sounded like it was trying to hold the world together by sheer will.

"They're saying Josh did it," Noya continued, his voice flat. "That he was high—PCP, meth, something that gave him inhuman strength. Once Gordon went in, the agents didn't wait for permission. They went in after him. Found Josh. It was go deeper or surrender. He didn't do either. He had Gordon's gun, so he fired. They shot back. Hugh and Lou were unarmed but got caught in the crossfire. All three are dead."

Haley's mind reeled. Her mouth opened, but nothing came out. Her body shook—not from cold, but from the sheer force of grief ripping through her. Gordon was dead.

"We'll never know the full story," Noya said quietly.

Haley folded in on herself, pressing her forehead to her knees. The room blurred. Her breath hitched, sharp and broken. She wanted to scream, to claw at the air, to rewind time with her bare hands. But all she could do was sit there, shattered, while the world kept moving forward without her.

Epilogue

The BBTF had done their job. Too well.

The story they fed the public was airtight: Josh ran drugs out of his garage and dragged Hugh and Lou into it. He murdered Rita Milan Zozaya. Killed Sharon Davis and Ashland Clark. He stalked Haley. After attacking Axle with an axe and trying to abduct Haley, he escaped to the caves with Hugh and Lou. The BBTF tracked them down. Gordon went in alone without waiting for a warrant or back up, and Josh killed him. Hugh and Lou were killed in the crossfire.

No mention of vampires. No trace of the truth. Surratt informed them that Ashmada had killed Gordon. When he'd gone in looking for Josh, not knowing he was already dead, he'd moved past the 300-foot entrance hall and into a deeper chamber. Ashmada had already removed all evidence of his presence in the cave and was waiting for sunset to escape. Gordon had served as his midday meal before moving deeper inside the cave.

Axle read the report twice. The lies were seamless. Carl Matheson let Surratt bend the facts to fit the narrative, unaware of Sonia's deeper machinations. The Utukku were ghosts in the system now. The existence of Ekimmus—erased. Their bodies, nothing more than ash.

According to official reports, Josh, Hugh, and Lou's remains went to Buncombe County for autopsy—but there were no bodies. Just ash. Official records showed the state medical examiner performed the autopsies, but Surratt had implanted the memory of corpses and procedures into the examiner's mind and notes.

Afterward, the BBTF returned cremated ashes to the families of Josh, Hugh, and Lou citing public health and national security as the reason for not returning the bodies intact. Gordon's body was the only one that actually reached the medical examiner intact, where his body remained until completion of the investigation and his autopsy.

While the public and Gordon's family waited for the official report, Axle did something he'd never done—he threw a party. It felt wrong. But necessary. Haley had been through hell and back. She deserved a night with the people who loved her.

That night, his house filled with laughter, clinking glasses, and the warmth of people who knew how to pretend. Candles flickered in hurricane vases. Music pulsed low, a heartbeat beneath the chatter. Vincent and Megan flew in from Amsterdam. Nicolas, Amber, and Gerard from Austria. They played their roles well, pretending it was their first time back in the States in years. Reid arrived late, fresh from Colorado. Noya Kanati showed up with his girlfriend, and Britt, LaDonna, and Maybelline helped host.

Haley met Jerome, Axle's younger brother, and Sofia Maria—Jerome's girlfriend, a sharp, sweet premed student at Duke. Haley's family arrived in waves: her father, Uncle Roy and Aunt Jean, her cousin, Brenda and her family—even her brother Joe, his wife Amy, and their six-year-old son Joey flew in from Texas. Joey and Brenda's two daughters played with Princess Paw Paw and an indignant Bootsie while the grown-ups socialized.

For the first time in his adult life, Axle felt normal. Despite everything that had happened, he was happy—content, especially after Geoff arrived—his best friend from high school—the friend he'd let slip away because of Dr. Weldon's experiments.

Axle laughed, served drinks, and was having the time of his life—until Joe asked about Bonnie—his daughter—and the darkness came crashing in to drown out the light.

Bonnie wasn't his blood, but she would always be his daughter, and though he watched over her when he could, she didn't know him. She hadn't seen him in years. Not since he'd become what he was. Not since he'd stopped pretending he could be a normal father.

Haley saved him from the moment, sweeping in with warmth and questions and that easy grace that made people feel welcome. Axle watched her laugh with Amy, tease Geoff about his latest arm candy. Cassie, the blonde, was all gloss and no soul. Axle didn't mind. She made Geoff happy—for now. But Geoff wanted more. He deserved more.

Behind the bar in the bonus room, Axle poured drinks like a pro, pretending the darkness wouldn't return—pretending he and Haley could lead normal lives. He chatted with her family, caught up with old friends, and kept one eye on the door, waiting for Sonia. She never came.

Vincent leaned in, voice low. "She's off grid. I told Reid and Surratt to leave her be. She needs time."

Axle nodded. "She's dangerous, yeah. But she's also broken. I'll make sure Reid doesn't push."

Vincent's sigh was heavy. "That might take some time."

Axle hoped they all had the time to recover, but beneath the music and laughter, Axle felt it—that low hum of threat, like static under his skin. The shadows outside the window were too deep. The flicker of candlelight too erratic. He smiled. He drank. He played host. But he didn't relax. He didn't know if he ever would again.

Then his gaze met Haley's. She smiled. And for a moment, the static quieted. All was right with his world as long as she was in it—and safe. And he'd make damn sure to keep her safe.

Two days later, Gordon's body was released. The official autopsy report read:

Cause of Death: Sharp force injury to the chest.

Mechanism of Death: Exsanguination due to penetrating trauma.

Manner of Death: Homicide.

No mention of vampires. No mention that the man who supposedly committed the murders had been reduced to a pile of ash in Axle's living room. No mention that Gordon's body had been completely drained of blood—or that Reid had struck him with an axe after he was already dead. A traumatic necessity Reid wouldn't likely get over anytime soon.

That Sunday, Gordon was laid to rest at Riverside Cemetery in Asheville.

The sky hung low, pewter and bruised. Rain threatened but never fell. The air smelled of wet stone and wilted roses.

Axle stood beside Haley as the pastor spoke. Britt wore black. LaDonna veiled her face. Maybelline clutched Haley's hand and whispered, "He's watching. He's still watching."

Axle's pulse spiked. He met Haley's eyes—wide, pale, afraid.

"It's okay," he murmured. "Maybelline's not always lucid." But this time, he wasn't sure she was wrong.

He felt it too. Eyes watching. Waiting. Maybe it was the BBTF. Maybe Surratt. Or worse—maybe it was Ashmada.

He remembered the fear in Haley's eyes when she'd faced Ashmada. The terror. The courage. She hadn't stood a chance, and she'd known it—but she'd armed herself to protect him—knowing she was putting her life in danger.

Sonia had called her a fool for love. Maybe she was. But Sonia had never known the kind of love Axle felt for Haley. The kind that burned through bone. The kind that would make him die for her.

He took her hand as the pastor asked them to bow their heads.

"I love you," he whispered.

"I love you too," she whispered back.

Axle bowed his head, but he didn't just pray for Gordon. He prayed for Haley. For strength. For the power to protect her—from the Ekimmu, from Ashmada, from whatever darkness came next. And if the day came when he couldn't protect her, he prayed that God would.

She was his. No vows needed. No rings. Just a bond that had already taken them beyond the darkness—into a light filled with love, and the promise of eternity.

But as the pastor's voice faded and the wind stirred the trees, Axle felt it again. That static. That watching.

Something had survived.

Something was waiting.

And the darkness wasn't done with them yet.

Author bio:

Lilly Gayle is a widow, mother, grandmother, and breast cancer survivor. She lives in North Carolina and when not working as an x-ray technologist and mammographer, Lilly writes paranormal and historical romances.

Visit her at https://lillygayle.com/

Other titles by Lilly Gayle:

Out of the Darkness

Embrace the Darkness

Winds of Time

Slightly Tarnished

Slightly Noble

Wholesale Husband

Helpless Hearts

Wilder Hearts

Don't miss out!

Visit the website below and you can sign up to receive emails whenever Lilly Gayle publishes a new book. There's no charge and no obligation.

https://books2read.com/r/B-A-GCGG-TZMYI

Did you love *Beyond the Darkness*? Then you should read *Embrace the Darkness*[1] by Lilly Gayle!

[2]

An experimental vaccine gives vampire Gerard Delaroache hope for the first time in two centuries--until two people are brutally murdered, and he suspects a conspiracy between vampires and mortals. To solve the crime, he must put his trust in a beautiful detective. But is former soldier and MP turned detective, Amber Buckley, a threat to his existence? Or the answer to his prayers?

Amber Buckley and her partner are assigned to do follow up interviews in the Lifeblood of America slayings. Amber believes she and Reid are just new eyes on a cold case. That is until she meets Gerard Delaroache. Something about him teases long-buried memories Amber would rather not chase. However, the two join together, falling into more than resolution of a murder case. It seems Amber has some dark secrets of her own.

To find their way into the light, Amber and Gerard must first

---

1. https://books2read.com/u/4jdElY

2. https://books2read.com/u/4jdElY

EMBRACE THE DARKNESS

Read more at https://www.lillygayle.com.

Also by Lilly Gayle

Darkness Series
Out of the Darkness
Embrace the Darkness
Beyond the Darkness

Standalone
Winds of Time

Watch for more at https://www.lillygayle.com.

About the Author

Lilly Gayle is a widow, mother, grandmother, and breast cancer survivor. She lives in North Carolina and when not working as an x-ray technologist and mammographer, Lilly writes paranormal and historical romances.

Visit her at https://lillygayle.com/

Read more at lillygayle.com.

www.ingramcontent.com/pod-product-compliance
Lightning Source LLC
LaVergne TN
LVHW010611100826
845148LV00014B/2922

* 9 7 8 1 7 3 2 3 9 0 4 7 8 *